OFF THE BEATEN PATH

For Jason

Eloise Tyner

OFF THE BEATEN PATH

A STONE'S THROW MYSTERY

ELOISE CORVO

First published by Level Best Books 2025

Author Photo Credit: Ariel May Photography

First edition

ISBN: 978-1-68512-932-3

Cover art by Evangeline Gallagher

This book was professionally typeset on Reedsy.
Find out more at reedsy.com

This book is dedicated to the three handsome men who hold my entire heart.

Alex: Thank you for not reading into the fact that I've spent countless hours of my free time thinking about murder. Let's not dig too deep into that. I love you more than I ever thought possible.

Martin Short: You're a real gremlin, but your floppy ears and fuzzy butt more than make up for it. I adore the chaotic energy you bring everywhere you go.

Gumbo: Thank you for curling up on my lap through this process—you made the tough parts less so. And in advance, I apologize for blaming any lingering typos on you.

Praise for Off the Beaten Path

"With small town vibes, a likeable cast of characters, and a little bit of murder to liven things up, *Off the Beaten Path* is everything I want a cozy mystery to be. Put on your hiking boots and pay a visit to Stone's Throw. You won't regret it!"—Tamara Berry, Edgar Award-winning author of the *By the Book Mysteries*

"Fans of smart heroines, atmospheric settings, and irresistible whodunits will devour this must-read series debut!"—Cate Conte, bestselling author of the *Cat Cafe Mysteries*

"From scenic Stone's Throw State Park comes a cozy mystery with the kind of pacing and twists that will keep you guessing until the very end. *Off the Beaten Path* will have you rooting for Maudy Lorso (and her sidekick pup named Martin Short) as she navigates a murder investigation that threatens everything she holds dear. If you enjoy cozy mysteries with relatable characters, small-town charm, and unexpected twists, this is your next must-read."—David Gwyn, host of the *Thriller 101 Podcast*

"Full of small-town drama, quirky characters, and immersive settings, *Off the Beaten Path* is a cozy mystery that will hook you from the start!"—Deana Lisenby, psychological thriller author

Chapter One

The usual pastel color palette of downtown, weathered lovingly by sun and sand, is drained to a stark black and white this morning. Covering every flat surface are flyers with MISSING PERSON plastered boldly across the top. Laughter and pleasantries curdle into whispers, making my short walk to breakfast an oddly eerie one. It's like someone gift-wrapped the town in doom and gloom.

"Did you hear about the guy who went missing this morning?" Nellie whispers to me over her mug as I sit down next to her and her two young girls in the cozy dining room of The Nest B&B. This isn't our usual breakfast spot, and I'm sorely missing the sugary and highly caffeinated lattes at Java Jones.

Nellie's so sweet, trying not to alarm the kiddos who are deep in play, pretending to be dragon-slaying princesses after sneaking a peek at a *Game of Thrones* rerun. The news is all over our mere four hundred-person town; the kids will find out eventually. Frankly, I'm surprised they haven't already. I wonder what she told them all the flyers are for. Lydia's surely old enough to read the huge, abrasive font by now.

"Kelly called me early this morning," I say quietly, pouring myself a cup of coffee from the ancient, olive-green carafe in the middle of the table, sitting on top of an ornate, homemade doily.

As the Head Ranger for Stone's Throw State Park, I've struck up a friendship with Kelly Sherwood, the officer stationed in our village. We first bonded over a nostalgic love of 90s alt-rock and *Buffy the Vampire Slayer*.

"She told me to keep an eye out for anything fishy, but I'm going to do a full search of the park today as a precaution. Just in case. Kelly doesn't seem too concerned; the guy probably went home and didn't tell anybody." I shrug.

Nellie is so nice. She's genuinely concerned for the B&B. Nancy and Greg must be flipping out. I can't imagine someone disappearing like that on my watch...

Even though it's not my first choice, I usually don't mind breakfast at The Nest B&B, burnt coffee and all. It can be sort of fun. The kitschy décor, the courageous fabric choices, all of it. But today, hanging on the wall behind my head, the incessant ticking of an enormous cuckoo clock kills me, dragging my focus away. It's been there forever and has never bothered me before. But today, that Edgar Allan Poe story, *The Tell-Tale Heart,* doesn't seem so far-fetched.

Nellie keeps talking, but all I can hear is the *tick, tick, tick,* of the clock as I mull over a game plan for combing through a forty-square-mile dense forest looking for one guy. The 'needle in a haystack' metaphor feels comically understated. More like a 'needle in a haystack in the Bermuda Triangle.' Without consciously realizing it, I start tapping my fingers in time with the seconds, adding *taps* to the *ticks*.

"Maudy? Maudy!" She quietly knocks her spoon against the table, snapping me back to reality.

"Wha-? Oh, sorry, Nellie."

"You okay, Aunt Dee?" Lydia asks, taking a break from poking her little sister with a stick she brought with her this morning. She's wearing a plastic horned hat, a purple t-shirt with a dragon scale print, and a "magic sword" (stick) that's now leaning against the table's fancy lace linens. A girl after my own heart.

"I'm okay, honey. Just distracted." I smile weakly.

I met Nellie, now one of my closest girlfriends, and her kids in the park. She has a love of nature that is kindred to my own, and we became fast friends and hiking partners. Her girls love my dog, and he loves them right back. We've grown to be more like sisters over the last couple of years. Every time I hear 'Aunt Dee' in one of their cute squeaky voices, my ovaries ache a little. I have to remind my insubordinate organs that we're over men. No dating for me anytime soon.

"Such a shame that man has gone missing." Nellie sighs, tearing off a piece of croissant for three-year-old Gemma. "I hope his disappearance doesn't hurt this place too much."

"Can I get you dears anything else?" Nancy, the elderly B&B owner offers after we finish our pastries, topping off the girls' teacups with orange juice. She stares blankly around at the lifeless dining room, not paying us much attention. By her eye glaze, it's clear she is eager for us to leave.

"That's okay, Nancy," Nellie reassures the older woman, also picking up on her tone. "You've got a lot on your mind today; we'll get out of your hair. We wanted to stop by to offer a bit of support to you and Greg. Thanks for everything, breakfast was delicious. Oh, hang on a second. Lydia, didn't you have something you wanted to give Mrs. Finch?"

"Yeah!" She squeals, digging her hand into her pants pocket. She pulls out a crumpled piece of yellow construction paper. "This is for you!" She hands Nancy the piece of paper.

Nancy unfolds it, revealing a cutout of a sun, colored with markers.

"Lydia, it's just beautiful. Thank you. I'm going to put it out on the desk for all our guests to see."

"Mom said you didn't have any guests, that's why I made—"

"Ha, ha, oh Lydia. Such an imagination." Nellie cuts off her daughter, eyeing her.

Nancy smiles sadly, tilting her head. "Well, either way, thanks so much. Oh, before you go," she scurries back to the front desk to exchange Lydia's drawing for a couple pieces of paper, "take one and please keep an eye out." She hands both Nellie and me a copy of the flyer posted all over town, as if we didn't see a thousand of these on our way here, and nervously wrings her hands on her apron.

"Thanks, Nancy, I will." Leaving a larger-than-usual tip on the table, I take a second to peer behind her desk, noticing more than half of the room keys still hanging from their respective hooks. "By the way, do you happen to know if he," I tap the flyer, "was a big hiker? I'm going to look for him in the park today, and was curious if he talked to you about his plans or any trails he wanted to do while in town."

As I ask, my mind drifts into the densely wooded park, over the soft earth and expansive, gray skies swirling with seagulls over the lake. I rack my brain trying to remember if I saw him over the last few days, but come up blank.

"Oh, I wouldn't know, dear. He didn't request any recommendations from me. He barely spoke to me, actually. Seems like he was working mostly, and I'm fairly sure he hasn't stayed with us before this trip. It doesn't hurt to look, though. Thanks for your help, that's sweet of you."

We both give an awkward smile and nod. With a big hug from Lydia and a promise to take her hunting soon for "mini dragons" (salamanders), we all head out the door.

"See you tonight, Maudy! Say, 'bye, Aunt Dee,' girls!" Nellie waves back at me, gently herding her two children like a Border Collie out the front door.

"Bye, Aunt Dee. Love you," the girls sing in rhythmic unison. They are so stinking cute.

"Can't wait! Bye, girlies, love you too." I laugh, thankful to be leaving before the hour strikes, afraid that blasted wooden bird would jump out of his hell hole and peck the back of my head.

Putting on a scarf and closing the B&B's heavy oak door behind me, the crisp spring air rolling off Lake Michigan tickles my exposed skin. I savor the sharpness in my lungs and turn to the piece of paper in my hands.

Now getting a close-up look, the flyer cuts to the chase. It has the missing person's name, *Michael Price,* last seen yesterday morning at The Nest where he was staying (unfortunately for Nancy), his physical description, and a couple of grainy photos. The man is middle-aged and visiting from Chicago, which is fairly obvious based on how he's dressed. A full body shot, probably from a social media account, has him in a well-tailored suit, a very flashy watch with the White Sox logo encrusted in diamonds, and mirrored sunglasses. His black hair is slicked back with gel, practically cemented to his head. He's giving off big city sleazeball vibes.

Stuffing it in my jacket pocket, I begin my half-mile walk to work. Making my way through downtown and traversing the wooden bridge over Birch River, I hop onto the small front porch of our park office, an old log cabin that was converted into a ranger station long before I started. As I reach the door, my pocket buzzes.

"Morning, Harper." Trying to put on a professional tone for my boss as I answer the phone. "How are you?" I quietly retreat a few feet, hoping my coworker Zach doesn't hear me from inside.

"Good morning, Maudy. I'm doing well, thanks."

"What can I do for you?" *Harper's calling out of the blue? This can't be good.*

"I'll keep it brief. The Michigan Parks & Recreation budget is working through the governor's office right now, and a little birdie tells me it's not looking good for us."

"Merda," I mutter. My Italian side comes out with my temper.

"What was that?" Harper asks earnestly.

"Sorry, nothing. All good, Harper." She and I have had this conversation each budget season since I took this job about two and a half years ago. "Are we on the chopping block for real, or is this just a political stunt like last time?"

"I'm thinking it's very real, unfortunately. I wanted to give you a heads-up in case things go south. I will say, with the leadership as they are, parks that bring in money on their own will be the ones that stay open, so make sure this Memorial Day weekend kicks off with a strong start. We need every single campsite reserved. If we're not booked at full capacity this year, the state will close the park, and you will be out of a job. We can't afford any hiccups. Literally."

"You got it, boss. No mistakes here." I sigh, kicking a small rock as I aimlessly meander the parking lot. The missing man, potentially lost deep in these woods, could, in fact, be a 'hiccup.' I'm itching to get out there to look for him. "There is something you should be aware of...I doubt it's relevant to us, but a tourist did go missing in town early yesterday morning. Nothing indicates he was in the park; however, I am coordinating with local law enforcement to confirm that."

"You're kidding? Maudy, what did I just say? If I wasn't crystal clear, let me be now." Her tongue sharpens. I bet small beads of spit are spraying on her phone right now. "You, Zach, and the rest of your staff will be out of a job if Stone's Throw State Park doesn't bring in its maximum revenue this season. And as you well know, your big, well, only source of revenue is the campsite reservations. Do you know what's supposed to start one week from today? Your campsite reservations."

This condescending tone isn't her usual vibe; she's stressing out big time. Her job is probably on the line too.

"Yeesh, I get it. Loud and clear. No campsites, no job." Fortified by the confrontation, I curtly say goodbye and hang up the phone.

I mean, she's not wrong. In exactly one week, our forty-site campground is set to open for the year. A missing person lost in the wilderness would definitely mess that up. And by 'mess that up,' I mean that this could lead to the permanent closure of my favorite place in the world, leave me unemployed, and force me to move out of this perfect, quiet town. The state would probably sell the parkland and turn it into cookie-cutter condos or something. *Ugh, how horrible would that be?* I need to rule this out as a possibility ASAP. No time to waste.

I decide to keep Harper's little *update* to myself for now. No need to worry Zach until we know more.

Feeling my anxiety rising, I take a few deep breaths and amble around the parking lot. Deep breath in for four seconds, deep breath out for four seconds. Compulsively clenching my fists, I fight off the oncoming panic attack.

Did I really throw away my long-term relationship with Nate just to be laid off, not even three years in? How embarrassing. Yeah, he turned out to be a scumbag. But did I push him there? Should I have not taken this job? Shut up, Maudy, we don't need this right now. Focus up. The clock is ticking.

Chapter Two

My aimless parking lot pacing turns into a full-blown walk, trying my best to save face in front of Zach. I loop back home to grab my dog, figuring a little company would help lighten the mood, and his keen nose could assist in today's search for Michael Price. Win-win.

"Alright, Martin Short, it's time to go." I shut my heavy wooden door behind us after refilling my coffee cup and grabbing the black and white, shaggy dog. Beelining straight to my flower bed, the mutt scrambles to grab one of his buried treasures (a squeaky ball), almost taking me down with him.

"I swear you will be the death of me, dog. You're lucky you're cute," mumbling more as I lead him down the driveway, eager to get moving.

Heading across town once again, my pup leading the way, I take yet another deep breath. The anxiety slowly melts into gratitude. Even when this place is plastered with missing persons flyers, I'm continually amazed that I get to actually live here.

Downtown is incredibly cute with wooden signs, local businesses, a vibrant arts community, and a wonderful indoor-outdoor lifestyle. People here embrace harsh winters and hard work. They grow lush gardens to fill their tables, enjoy outdoor patios in full snowsuits, and acknowledge how special Lake Michigan really is. The culture revolves around the close-knit community, which I am all about. It's safe. It's predictable. It's perfect.

Crossing over into park property for the second time this morning, we walk down the narrow dirt road passing by the entrance gate. I stop and wipe off some grime from our wayfinding map with my jacket sleeve, making sure it's legible for our visitors.

The map shows the entire property. Up ahead a ways is our ranger station at the southern end of the expansive plot of land. Nearby is our outdoor classroom, pollinator garden, and vernal pond just beyond the building. To the west is our main trailhead, which branches off in a complex web of winding trails and loops. There are over twenty miles of trails that stem from that one point, many of which lead to steep, sweeping sand dunes that stretch almost five hundred feet high overlooking Lake Michigan to the west. Staying on this road as it winds to the east leads to our campground, which has forty rustic campsites and another main trailhead to the north. Even with the network of well-marked trails, there are still a few miles of dense forest at the very north end of the park that are basically inaccessible to the public.

"Morning, Zach," I huff, admittedly distracted by today's daunting task. Harper's news makes this so much worse. I set my pack down on my desk chair and unhook Marty. I'm over thirty minutes late.

Inside our office is a couch and coffee table that have both seen better days, two desks, one of which is mine, and shelves that house a fun collection of rocks, educational taxidermy, and historical maps. A fireplace on the northern wall provides most of the heat for the small building, with the old radiator largely useless. A small closet keeps our ancient vacuum, cleaning supplies, a defibrillator, and other safety measures, while a shed outside has our maintenance equipment, snowmobile, four-wheeler, and gardening tools for the pollinator garden adjacent to the cabin.

"Morning, Maudy, ready for today?" My coworker looks up from his laptop for a moment and offers a warm, earnest smile. Zach, our park naturalist and environmental education instructor, is the best employee I've ever had, no contest. He's always on time, completely independent, and somehow wide awake and prepared every morning. He's also become a great friend. I'm completely gutted by the thought of letting him go if our budget gets cut.

This morning, his curly, sandy blonde hair is covered up with a knit beanie from a nearby brewery, and he's bundled up in a winter jacket. Between the hat and the puffy coat, his toothy grin barely pokes through the layers of dark fabric. The young man is so lean that I'm amazed he has enough body fat to make it through northern Michigan winters.

"I am doing…fine, I guess. A little frazzled, but the epic sunrise makes it worth it." I smile back, heading for our full coffee pot (thank you, Zach) to fill up my thermos that I already emptied on the walk over.

"Tell me about it. It's so crazy! A guy just disappears? Here? Seems fishy to me." He waggles his bushy eyebrows like a blonde caterpillar inching across his face. "You know me, though; I'm probably making a mountain out of a molehill again." He has a flair for the dramatic, but at least he's self-aware. "What do you think happened?"

"The dude is crazy rich and from Chicago. He probably chartered a private plane or boat to take him who knows where." I shrug. "Don't get me wrong, we absolutely need to confirm he's not lost in the woods. But it seems far-fetched that something nefarious happened, if you ask me. I may be judging a book by its cover, but he doesn't seem like much of a hiker. I don't remember ever seeing him out here, and I think he's been in town for over a week. Have you run into him?"

"Yeah, that's true. I don't think I've seen him either, but that's far less interesting." He gives me a wide grin from under the fluff of his navy parka. I stir the small fire burning in the stone fireplace to try to warm up the place a little more.

"It looks like he was last seen yesterday morning at The Nest. I mean, it's possible that he went out for a hike and got lost or hurt or something. Nothing indicates he's actually in the park, but I need to be sure." As we quickly pack up our gear, I top off our coffees for the long day ahead.

"Let's stick to the most-used trails today. It's only you and me searching, so we should cover the main routes." We pore over a copy of our park map, choosing which paths to take.

"Sure. I'll go this way." He points down a main vein heading up the center of the narrow park. "It's a fun one to mountain bike. You taking the four-wheeler?"

"I think so. I can cover more ground that way. I'll go up west, towards the challenging parts. If he got stuck, that's probably where he'd be." I point towards a hilly route with a few steep drop-offs. Drop-offs as tall as a forty-five-story skyscraper.

"Good deal. Kelly dropped off some flyers earlier." He points to a crate on the coffee table. "I'll grab some, and you can take the rest."

Without evidence or a real reason to believe Michael is out here, I keep the park open to the public, and I'm glad I have. Seeing folks out this early in the morning makes my heart sing. In the winter, the park is quiet with not very many visitors. We groom a few trails for cross-country skiers and fat tire bikers, but generally our visitor numbers tank. Seeing folks enjoying the sunny, albeit chilly, morning is a sign that the season is changing, and I am here for it. I don't love interrupting their peaceful hikes to probe about the missing tourist (*bearer of bad news, much?*), but I'm thrilled to be out here, nonetheless.

"Good morning." I wave to a hiker who passes me on the trail, someone I don't recognize.

The dotted pattern of the birch tree bark looks like hundreds of eyes lovingly watching over us as Marty and I stop for a quick, mid-morning snack break. With both my, and the dog's, mouths sticky with peanut butter—he's munching on a flavored chewy bone and I a sandwich with some of my friend Eli's strawberry jam—we wave to the passer-by.

"Good morning, beautiful day we're having," the man says, continuing on past us. He looks a few years younger than me, probably in his late twenties. He's wearing a bright orange ski cap, sunglasses, and a legit backpacking pack.

"Yeah, the amount of rain we've gotten in the last two months is practically biblical. I can't remember the last day it's been this sunny and dry." I wave him over, encouraging him to stop and talk to me for a minute.

"Totally. Too bad more storms are rolling in. I'd bet we have maybe an hour or two before the rain comes back." He sighs, looking anxious to get out ahead of the turning sky. I don't blame him. He must've been planning on being out all day based on his gear. *That's a bummer.*

"Well, if you're staying in town for a while, I'd be happy to show you around or give a couple trail recommendations. Believe it or not, some routes are even better when wet. There's a fun family of beavers that dam up a small creek when the water levels get high. They've been having a very productive spring," I laugh. "We also put in a boardwalk last year over there." I point northeast of us. "That area floods often, but those trails are still usable."

"Aw, that sounds fun. For sure, I'll take you up on that. Thanks." He begins to walk off again.

"Oh, before you go," I call after him. "Did you happen to see anything odd or out of the ordinary today?" I hand him a flyer. "A man recently went missing in town, and we're out looking for him."

He takes the flyer and scans it thoroughly before responding, "No, sorry. Beautiful views and a lot of other hikers, but nothing weird."

He says he'll stop by our office sometime soon for those trail recommendations. We smile at one another, and he continues on his way.

As the morning warms into the afternoon, it's clear everyone wants to enjoy the beautiful weather, even if it's just for a couple more hours. The clouds are still rolling in, but the rain is holding out. I see groups, solo hikers, families, and plenty of four-legged companions out on the trails while searching, making sure to stop and ask if they've seen any sign of Michael along the way. Some folks are doing long loops, outfitted with walking poles to assist with the steep, sandy elevation, others out for a quick stroll with young kiddos. It's a great mix of townies and tourists, including Nellie and the girls. Marty makes sure to personally greet every single dog we see with a propeller tail and a loud "yip!" as we speed by on the four-wheeler.

We diligently search the rest of the day, secretly loving the excuse to spend time outside. Fortunately for me, nobody reports any sign of Michael. After Zach and I return to the office and compare notes, I text Kelly to notify her there is no sign of the missing man in the park.

"Any plans for the weekend?" Zach packs up his things around five p.m.

"Cards tonight, and probably working a bit tomorrow. Jim is coming in, and I want to give him the rundown. I convinced him to get a couple days head start."

"Jim has been campground caretaker for decades; he knows the drill! Don't work too hard. A girl should get a little fun in now and again," he laughs. "See ya Monday, Maudy."

"See ya, Zach. Thanks for your help today."

I am exhausted by the time Marty commences his evening stretch and grumbles, stating politely that if we don't head home soon, he'll gnaw on a chair leg. "Ugh, you're right, dude. Sorry about that." It is almost seven p.m., and I completely lost track of time, buried in administrative tasks that need to get done before campers arrive. "Let's get you home. Today kicked my butt." Standing up from my office chair, I hold my arms high above my head in a long stretch and pack up my things.

After an exhausting, fruitless day, ahead of what's about to be an even more exhausting, (but hopefully fruit*ful*) week, the anxious pit in my stomach begins to fade away after remembering it's Friday, which means euchre night at Pop's. Thank frickin' god.

It's always busy at Pop's, what townies lovingly call the local bar, especially on Fridays. The establishment's official name is *Sunset's*, at least that's what's on the barely legible, crusty sign out front. Nobody calls it that, though. Not quite a dive but not fancy either, Pop's is the only bar in town and also happens to serve excellent food.

As I walk through the door, thinking Michael's disappearance might cause it to be the one night it's dead in here, I'm caught off guard by a festive atmosphere ping-ponging throughout the bar. It's somehow even more packed than usual, everyone wanting to get the latest news and swap theories. The hushed tone of the morning has been eclipsed by nosy Midwestern neighbor curiosity.

"Hey, Kevin." I wave to the older man behind the bar, his wispy, curly white hair peeking out from under his signature Detroit Tigers baseball cap and surprisingly strong physique hidden underneath a baggy blue and green flannel. "Hi, Eli," I shout louder to reach the kitchen.

Kevin Nett, the longtime owner and nearly seventy-year-old gentleman, is warm and kind like an idyllic father figure. Hence the name, Pop's. Right before I moved here, his son Eli bought a piece of the business and really upped the cuisine caliber. Eli graduated from the culinary program at the college a couple of counties over and came back to share his talent. His style is still rustic, home cooking like his dad's, but he puts an elevated spin on it.

"Maudy! Welcome, dear." Kevin grins. "We got you set up as usual. Have fun and don't euchre anyone who doesn't deserve it." He winks and gestures over to our usual corner booth where we play cards. Every week, he puts up a *Reserved for the Lake Michigan (card) Sharks* sign on the front corner booth. No matter how busy, he keeps this booth open for us every single Friday night. He really is the father of Stone's Throw. At least mine anyway.

Pop's is surprisingly large, with maybe one hundred or so people able to fit comfortably. On the back wall is a long bar with a glossy, wooden bar top. Booths line either side of the restaurant, along with a smattering of pinball machines. The bulk of the room is taken up by two long community-style tables, and two pool tables that are in desperate need of refelting. The walls are warm maroon and patchworked with pictures of Stone's Throw through the years. As a tribute to Eli's obsession with word puzzles, the black and white frames are arranged like a crossword puzzle snaking across the long wall. Me and a few of my friends, like Eli, have even made a coveted wall spot. It is worn-in and comfy. I love it here.

"With where my mind has been today, I doubt that'll be a problem. I'll be lucky if I can keep the trump suit straight." I smirk back at him. "So, what's the latest theory, Kevin? On the guy who went missing. I imagine you've heard quite a few today. Any of them good?"

"Oh, you bet. Especially after folks get a drink or two in them. You know the funniest one so far is the idea that the guy was a part of some richie-rich secret society that runs the world and got himself assassinated. The Leguminati? Sounds like nonsense to me." He rolls his eyes and barks out a short laugh. I don't have it in me to correct him. I'm too busy thinking about what a secret society of legumes might look like. "I think the general consensus, though, is that he skipped town without telling anybody. Seems the most logical anyway. He hasn't been in here since Wednesday, I think it was. Who knows." He shrugs and goes to help another customer down the bar. I sit down at our booth and separate the deck of cards, getting it good and shuffled.

Euchre is like the faster and wilder cousin of bridge. It's a trick-taking card game that's a Michigan staple. Every kid that grows up around here has a story of their drunk uncle teaching them at the family cabin or learning from friends at summer camp. It's incredibly fun and perfect for playing at a bar over drinks.

I asked my friends to set up a weekly game after my ex, Nate, and I broke up a little over a year ago. We were living downstate together before I took this job, and since he refused to come with me, we tried to do the whole long-distance thing. We fizzled out in a knock-down-drawn-out, horrendous way. I finally cut ties after I caught him cheating. My friends are the only reason I didn't completely lose it, and we've been playing every Friday since.

"Losers buy next round?" Peyton asks as she settles into our booth, the last of our crew to arrive. My ride-or-die, Peyton Becker, owns the bakery in town. She's got a smudge of flour under her chin and perpetually smells like chocolate chip cookies. She specializes in pastries, and went to culinary school with Eli. She's hyper-competitive and a savvy businesswoman. She's also a cutthroat card player.

"How about the loser has to help me chop firewood for the campground this weekend? I could *really* use the extra help." I grin and shuffle the deck, knowing none of them want to give up an entire weekend to do manual labor.

"Uh…sure! In that case…I'm on Peyton's team," Anna laughs. Anna Shill is the daughter of the owners of the local surf shop. It happens to be the only one on the western shoreline of Lake Michigan. Quintessential surfer girl but with a down-to-earth kindness, she's the youngest of our friend group, clocking in at twenty-seven years old.

"Anna, come on. Have some confidence. We can kick their butts, no problem," Nellie chimes in, sipping her beer.

"You might take this one. I've been a hot mess all day. I had some rough news at work, and my brain has turned to mush," I say, dealing five cards to each of us in between sips of hard cider.

"Euchre!" Peyton and Anna shout in unison after dominating the first hand. We all laugh as they tease and smugly mark the extra points.

After an hour or so, the game coming to a close, I walk over to the bar to grab my bill, saddling up next to an unfamiliar face. Sitting in silence, he nurses his drink and looks hazily ahead at the row of tap handles behind the bar. I have a hard time keeping from staring; his gorgeous Greek god vibe is transfixing. He's older, maybe forty or so. He's wearing a crisp button-down shirt under a tight, *tight,* navy knit sweater. His skin is tan, and his eyes are a mesmerizing light amber. *Holy Hercules.*

"Oh, sorry." He turns to me and scooches his stool over to give me a little more room. Now, with a better vantage point and the initial shock of his beauty wearing off, I see he's visibly upset. His mouth contorts into a scrunched line. *Is that supposed to be a smile?*

"No worries. You okay?" I wave to get Kevin's attention. He rings up my tab.

This guy is deep in his own thoughts and takes a long draw of his whisky, not acknowledging my question. *Got it, not in the mood for company.* He puts down his glass and starts picking at his fingernails incessantly.

"Well, enjoy your night," I say, signing my tab. That seems to shake him out of his funk for a moment, and he turns back to me.

"Thanks, you too. Sorry, I'm not trying to ignore you." He turns towards me. "Hey, um, maybe I'll see you around sometime..." The end of his sentence trails off. *Is he asking for my name?*

"Maudy. Maudy Lorso," I say, surprised, signing my check and handing it back to Kevin.

"Maudy Lorso. Well, enjoy your night, Maudy Lorso. If I wasn't just so rude, I might see if you would join me for a round. Perhaps next time."

Raising his glass, he gives me a nod and a slight smile. *Is he hitting on me? He's hitting on me. Well, he's barking up the wrong tree. I don't need any drama in my life right now, even from a guy this hot. Especially from a guy this hot.*

My heart thumps faster, but not in a good, flirty way. In an anxious, panicky way. I do my best to plaster my own fake smile (probably a worse grimace than he gave me) and take in a deep breath for four seconds, and out for four seconds. I tap each second on my pant leg, forcing to slow myself down.

"Perhaps," I say sarcastically, shuffling back to my friends who make kissy faces at me as I join them, apparently noticing the guy too. Eli has poured himself a drink and taken my seat in our booth while I was up, leaving Kevin to tend bar for the few remaining patrons.

Eli's eyes are this bright, brilliant green that has a playful twinkle even from feet away. His perpetual five o'clock shadow and dad bod give him an air of maturity that makes him look a little beyond his thirty-two years, two years my senior. He's my best friend here, maybe because I can't help but love a man who feeds me all the time.

"What was that guy saying to you? Was he giving you a hard time? You look a little out of sorts." He asks with genuine concern as I slide in next to him.

"I was just making small talk. Why, you know him?" I keep tapping seconds on the vinyl booth seat, measuring my breaths. It's already working, I'm almost back to normal.

"Don't get me started. He," nodding towards the bronze statue, "was in here totally wasted with the missing guy and another buddy a few nights back. Michael was blubbering about 'the good old days,' up here, and the two wouldn't shut up. They were being totally disruptive. They were smack dab in the middle of one of the community tables and were so loud that I had to kick them both out."

"Oh my god." Anna leans forward. "Do you think he had something to do with the guy's disappearance?" Her fingers drum on the side of her pint glass in anticipation. She's listened to one too many true crime podcasts lately.

"Who knows, but it wouldn't surprise me."

Chapter Three

My dreams of a restful and restorative weekend are dashed immediately with a comically chipper *ping!* from my phone at five a.m. It's a simple text from Kelly: *Call me ASAP*.

Blinking away the clouds of sleep from my eyes, I sit up in bed and call her. Marty slept right next to me under the covers like a person, with his head on my pillow. His tongue hangs out of his mouth and has left a huge drool stain on my lavender pillowcase. *Wonderful*.

"What's up?" No use beating around the bush. A text from her this early on a weekend must not be to chat about our favorite Buffy episode. Straightening out my duvet, I pick up my book that is lying open near my feet. I must've fallen asleep reading last night. I grab it, placing a bookmark where I think I dozed off.

"I have reason to believe Michael Price did not leave Stone's Throw. We're doing a town-wide search today."

Before she can ask, I volunteer. "I'll comb the park. This time by foot, and off-trail. But I need you to fill me in on the details here. What's changed in the last day?" There's no way a massive, even dangerous forest can be ignored if law enforcement thinks Michael didn't leave the area. Could Zach and I have missed something yesterday? How embarrassing would it be if a camper found something while staying in the park? Harper would kill me. The stomach knot tightens back up; it never disappeared completely.

"Thank you, that'd be amazing. We spent yesterday going through his known contacts back in Chicago, calling hospitals, police stations, airports, car and boat rentals, literally everywhere. There's been no sign of him. He hasn't flown out of any airport in the state, not even private ones. He hasn't rented a car, booked a train or ferry ticket, he hasn't been arrested or hospitalized, he just walked out of The Nest Thursday morning and went 'poof!'"

"So he hasn't gotten far." There aren't many places someone can disappear to around here. The knot in my stomach grows two sizes, making me thankful this call is before breakfast.

"You get it. He's got to be close. Yesterday you took the four-wheeler, right? Only popular routes? I agree, we need to make sure every inch of that park is clear, off the beaten path." There's desperation in her voice. Probably in mine, too. *Merda*.

As a Park Ranger, I'm technically a quasi-law enforcement officer for the state of Michigan. I have the authority to give tickets and even arrest people who are breaking the law in our parkland. While I don't carry a firearm, I can use pepper spray, batons, and handcuffs. Thankfully, this isn't a job function I use often, but it occasionally does lead me to help Kelly out with an investigation.

She continues, "We didn't think it was a big deal yesterday. He's a grown-ass man and has money coming out of his ears. I assumed he left without checking out of the B&B. You know how much of a worrywart Nancy is, I thought she was overreacting."

"Yeah, same. Let me call Zach, get dressed, and get some coffee. I need you to send me some help. Tell whoever you can find to meet us at the ranger station and to wear good shoes. It's wet out there." The dry day turned to torrential thunderstorms all last night. It was amazing to sleep to, the rain bouncing off my metal roof like small marbles, but will make for a soggy search today. It'll be tough to find any traces of Michael.

"Thanks, Maudy. I'm going to go through the paper trails he's left behind and search his room at The Nest today. Then, we'll round up his known contacts for interviews. Let's sync up later, I want to know what you all find."

"You got it."

"Sounds good, I owe you one. I'll buy your spaghetti this Wednesday." Kelly is a regular at Eli's spaghetti night, like me. Every Wednesday, he makes a giant vat of savory, meaty sauce, homemade noodles, and a couple of sides. That's it. It's the only thing on Pop's menu every Wednesday night. It has become a tradition for many Stone's Throwers.

"Ha," I laugh. "No need. I've got this covered. Focus on other parts of town, and I'll keep you looped in." We cut our conversation short, and I yank myself out of bed. Marty licks the side of my face. I give him a scritch behind the ears, and we quickly get a move on.

It's not unreasonable to think someone could get lost or run out of steam while hiking, especially on the western slopes. They're by far the most dangerous. The elevation is insane, the sand makes it difficult to get a secure footing, and there is a legitimate risk of falling in some places. I'm pretty sure Michael isn't in there based on our assessment from yesterday, and from what I know of him so far, but I agree with Kelly that today's effort certainly can't hurt. I need to be super sure that the park isn't involved in this whole thing, so the campground opening goes off without a hitch.

"Alright, Marty, what do we need?" Hands on my hips, surveying my basement storage shelf, I select my hefty, maroon backpacking pack. "This should do it." I throw in a handful of granola bars, extra base layers, and hats in case someone doesn't dress for the weather, as well as a half dozen water bottles.

"Gray again." I sigh, supplies and trusty dog in tow, as I trudge out the door. A hazy, cloud-filled sky looms low overhead. Thankfully, it's thunderstorm-free. For now.

Approaching Java Jones, our local coffee shop, I'm hit with a wall of loud voices and a swirl of energy from down the block. I shouldn't be surprised, I'm sure Kelly didn't only call me this morning, but it's shocking how packed the place is for six a.m. Lydia and Gemma are out front, presumably waiting for one of their moms inside.

"Hey girls." I wave and walk up to the littles. Marty's tail is already spinning around like a helicopter as he bounds towards Lydia. As the squat, black and white fluffy mutt and I approach the bright purple building, the smell of hazelnut coffee greets me lovingly.

"Hi, Aunt Dee." Bending over to hug the dog, Lydia's messy brown hair falls in her face.

"Would you mind watching him for a minute? I'm going to head inside."

"Sure!" They both squeal, excited to have another friend to play with.

Java Jones is somewhere you can't help but be happy. The shop is set up more like a living room than a business, with an overstuffed couch in front of a large wood-burning fireplace and armchairs perched in the front, bay window.

I hook the dog to a bike rack and leave him with the girls to burn some of their boundless collective energy. I walk inside the bustling coffee shop and find Tracy, my favorite barista, and Eli, Nellie, a few other townsfolk, as well as faces I don't recognize. I wave over to Nellie who is ordering a drip coffee up at the counter, and stand behind Eli in line.

"Hey, stranger." He turns around to look at me. "Long time no see."

"Hey, bud." I smile sleepily. "What's got you up so early on a Saturday?" I glance at my watch.

"Well, actually, I'm one of your volunteers. Kelly assigned me to park duty today. She's been waking up everyone this morning." He grins with a hint of condolence on his face. The bags under my eyes must be darker than I realized.

"Good! After I get my fix." I hold up my empty thermos covered in nature stickers, "I'm headed to the office to get situated before other volunteers show up. Come with?"

"Absolutely."

We order our coffee and grab our steamy, sweet brews a few minutes later. As we go to pay, Eli gestures to Tracy that he'll pay for both of ours.

"Um, excuse me? What do you think you're doing? You paid last time, I got it." I clumsily rifle through my massive backpack, digging for my wallet. He gently grabs my hand.

"No, no. I insist." He hands her his credit card before I have a chance to retort.

"Ugh fine, butthead. It's on the record that I will pay next time." I shove him.

"Uh-huh. Whatever you say." He playfully nudges me back and signs the receipt.

Back outside on the sidewalk, Marty is lying on his back, spread-eagle for all to see his doghood. "Have you no shame, pup?" I laugh as he cocks his head to get a better look at me, his tongue resting on the cement. Crouching down in the doorway, I separate him from his tiny human friends and clip his leash onto my backpack.

Preoccupied and stooped over trying to wrangle the thirty-five-pound dog away from his two besties, I bump into someone trying to get through Java Jones' bright purple door. "Ope, excuse me." I turn to lean out of the way, making room.

"It's not a prob—Oh hi, Maude." I look up to see the blonde woman glaring down at me.

She knows I hate being called Maude. Charlotte Roth is much taller than I am, but that's not saying much at my measly five feet two inches. Her shiny hair is pulled back in a tight bun that's peeking out from under a bright green scarf tightly coiled around her neck like a boa constrictor. I'd be lying if I said that I didn't wish it were a real snake sometimes.

"How are you doing? Is your little park getting ready for a busy summer?" She scowls down at the girls playing with the dog and laughing loudly. Restrained disgust spreads across her face.

I swallow my rising temper at her *little park* comment and clear disdain for adorable children and dogs.

She is the Chair of our Chamber of Commerce and a sitting Stone's Throw Village Council member. While not my favorite person as I find her busybody attitude and nosiness extremely off-putting, she cares deeply for Stone's Throw, perhaps more than anyone else.

"We're certainly gearing up for a busy season. It'll be so great to get all of these campers and parkgoers back into town. Don't you worry, I'm sure it'll contribute to your Chamber's annual economic goals." I can't help but quip back, trying hard not to roll my eyes. If she had her way, Michigan would donate the state parkland to Stone's Throw to expand the downtown business district, chopping down the miles and miles of old-growth forest. Which, if I'm being honest with myself, might become reality. We've been having an ongoing debate on the economic value of parks for years. It is an argument I'm getting tired of making, both with her and with the state. I must get this campground season off the ground without any problems to put all this to bed.

"Good, good, yes, it will. Tourist dollars make Stone's Throw go round after all! Well, I best be off. I need to check in with all of the farmers market vendors today and go over the transition protocol before our grand seasonal opening on Friday. Anyways, talk soon, Maude, don't be a stranger!" She is already turning away from me and gives a half-hearted wave in my general direction as she walks into Java Jones.

"Same to you, *Char*," I loudly call after her as she trots into the building. Eli shakes his head and chortles; he's heard me vent about Charlotte more than once.

By eight a.m. Zach, myself, and Eli are ready to go and have a solid plan of attack.

"Alrighty, gentlemen. Everybody good with this?" The three of us are mapping out our groups' routes, trying to cover as much ground as humanly possible.

"Works for me. Do you guys have another walkie-talkie?" We dubbed Eli the third group leader. He loves camping, practically grew up in these woods, and knows them like the back of his hand.

"Here you go." I give each of them a first aid kit and hand Eli our spare walkie-talkie. Cell service is spotty at best deep in the woods.

"So," I say, returning to the map. "Zach is going to take the western slopes. Eli, you head east off the trailhead on the north end of the campground. I'll go up the middle."

Before rallying the troops and heading into the woods, I jog over to the ranger station and stick a note on the door for Jim in case he arrives for his first day while we're out searching. It has a prioritized campground prep to-do list so he can get started before we touch base.

By half past eight, each group is ready to set off after a brief safety talk.

"Are there any questions before we head out?" I clap my hands, using my 'outdoor voice' to make sure everyone can hear me over the rustling of the trees.

I'm met with a dozen blank stares. The volunteers are nervous, and frankly, I am too. We officially closed the park to outside visitors today, and everyone is freaking out at the severity of the situation. I methodically keep my fingers tapping away the seconds and moderate my breathing. It's easier to stay calm when everyone else is freaking out. *I'm the expert here; I can keep it together. They're all depending on me. Michael could be depending on me.*

One gentleman in Eli's group, after a long pause, raises his hand timidly. "What do we do exactly if we find him? Or something that might be related to him?"

"Please don't touch anything you think is suspicious. Tell your group leader immediately. In the event of an emergency, all three of us are first aid and CPR certified. All you have to do is keep your eyes and ears open. Thank you all for your help today. It's clear those flyers, and Kelly's persuasive recruiting tactics, were effective."

A sea of nods bobble before me as a few pull out a copy of the flyer from their pockets to remind them what Michael looks like, reigniting their curiosity. "Alright, no time like the present. Let's move out."

The three groups depart in different directions, as echoes of "Michael!" ring through the park as we call out, hoping for a response.

The only person in my group that I already know is my friend Anna. The other three are all from out of town. A younger husband and wife pair named Adriane and Christopher, who are both avid hikers, and a forty-ish year-old man from Traverse City named Jeremy, who I recognize as the Herculean guy from Pop's last night.

Zach's group are all locals, and Eli's are all non-experienced tourists, including a family of three with a teenage son, and the guy I met hiking yesterday wearing the orange hat, who I now know is named Lucas.

Marty, with his little working-dog vest on, leads the charge. He can tell this isn't a leisurely walk in the woods. He keeps his nose to the ground as we wind our way through the trees and scrubby underbrush, abandoning the marked paths to make sure we cover every inch of the park. Wincing as we wade through patches of poison ivy, I hope the tourists helping out today took my safety warnings to heart. It may look dumb to tuck your pants into your socks, but it saves a week of itchy welts and is well worth the brief humiliation, in my opinion.

Turning around to look at my group behind me, I see Jeremy slowing down, struggling a bit to get through the tangled, thorny brush.

"So Jeremy, what brings you to Stone's Throw?" I ask, trying to distract him and keep his spirits high. We've got hours to go, and I need to keep us moving.

"Oh, actually, I was here to do some work with Michael, the man we're searching for."

"I'm so sorry, how awful." I offer, along with everyone else in our group.

"It is horrible. It's been a tough couple of days. Michael and I work together, he's from Chicago, and I'm from around here. We thought meeting in person would be a nice way to connect and get a lot of work done. Before this trip, we'd never actually met face to face before. I can't believe he actually disappeared. I can't help but feel responsible for suggesting we meet here."

Not planning on doing much hiking on this trip, Jeremy came dressed in khakis and mesh running shoes. Thankfully, Zach had a spare set of boots to lend him, but he's still struggling.

"I'm so sorry, Jeremy. I know it's been tough, but you don't need to take on that responsibility. He is a grown-up. You aren't his babysitter," Anna chimes in. Words of wisdom.

"Rationally, I know that. But it's hard when you're sitting at dinner with someone one night, then searching for them in the woods just a few days later. I'd be shocked if he's out here to be frank, but I guess you never know."

"So, when did you last see him?" I ask, admittedly curious.

"Dinner on Wednesday. The spaghetti thing. We left separately and were supposed to meet up again on Thursday to do more work. I never saw him after that." He's keeping his head towards his feet, slumped over, steeping like a cup of strong tea in his nerves.

"He'll turn up soon. We've got all of us out here today. If he's in the park, we'll find him." I offer to try to cheer him up, but the fact that we're in the middle of a full-blown manhunt is in direct opposition to that sentiment.

Eli's impression of him seems off, at least from what I'm seeing. The drunken, loud 'tool' persona doesn't match the sullen, nervous man before me. Obviously worried about his colleague, we all try to reassure him that Michael probably left early or had a family emergency or something. Getting to know him a little bit and the difficult situation he's in sheds light on the spaced-out attitude he had the other night at the bar. At least he's too distraught to hit on me again. That's a bit of a silver lining, I guess.

The sun is high in the sky, albeit shrouded in graying clouds by the time we stop to take a water break and rest our legs. This section of the park is dense and wet, dominated by paper birch trees with white, flaky bark and a marshy understory. Thankfully, last year, I had our seasonal trail maintenance crew construct a boardwalk to help make it more accessible year-round, even when it's flooded. Sitting on a few benches atop a small lookout platform on the boardwalk, we have a snack, drink water, and take a moment to catch our breath.

When I sit down, I unhitch Marty's leash from my backpack and loop it around my arm while we take a break. I hand out granola bars and lean back, taking in the complex song of hums, chirps, splashes, and buzzes of the marshy forest.

Woodpeckers peck away in the distance, hunting for grubs. Marty pants heavily, splooting on the wood after taking a dip in the shallow, muddy water to cool himself off. The thousands of leaves dance in the breeze as if applauding our efforts.

After maybe fifteen minutes, we pack up to move again as the wind picks up, whistling through the spindly, knotted trees. Marty's nose twitches wildly, latching on to a new smell.

His doggy brain cogs spin, and the fluffball freezes in place, concentrating hard on something. *I know that face. Merda!* I go to snatch the leash from around my arm, but he bolts away before I get a solid grip.

"Martin Short, get back here this instant!" I chase after the dog, but he is lightning-fast and almost immediately out of sight. Those short legs are deceiving, he's a speedy bugger.

"I'll be right back!" I shout back to my group over my shoulder, "Stay here, he usually doesn't go far!"

He bounds off the boardwalk with the grace of an Olympic diver and splashes into the murky, saturated earth. He cuts north, heading out of the flooded area towards one of the lesser-used trails. Knowing full well there's no hope in catching up to him, I stay on the boardwalk and curve around to the trail he's heading towards, futilely attempting to stay dry.

I hear the faint chorus of "Michael!" from the other two groups as I run. They're both far away. I add to the song ringing through the trees, shouting "Marty!" and a string of Italian expletives that would make Tony Soprano blush, chasing after the hound.

Coming around a bend, I see the familiar, fuzzy butt bent over something just off the trail up ahead, with a long, curved tail wagging emphatically. Whatever he found, it's big, maybe a deer?

"Whatcha got there, dude?" I walk up to him, wiping his mud-caked leash on my pants and securing it around my belt loop before he can dash off again.

Crouching down to get a better look, I gasp, drawing in a sharp breath, utterly stunned. Marty didn't find a dead deer; it's the body of Michael Price.

Chapter Four

Tamping down the knee-jerk wave of nausea, I yank the dog back a dozen or so feet and pull out my phone from my jacket pocket.

"Hi, Kelly." My voice shakes.

"Hi. Got something? Tell me you've got something. We're coming up with zilch over here."

"Uh, yep. I'm looking at Michael's body." My eyes, like from an old cartoon, grow ten times their normal size, and cannot peel away from the crumpled man on the waterlogged ground in front of me.

"Ah, crap. Stay where you are. Can you drop me a pin so we can find you?"

"Yeah, I can do that. You'll need to grab the four-wheeler from the shed; it should be unlocked. There's no way a car can make it back here." I'm rhythmically petting Marty's head, keeping him back from tainting the evidence, but more so to distract myself. I'm hyperventilating.

"Thanks. Give us thirty minutes." I can already hear her shouting orders to other officers as she hangs up.

Turning back to the dog, "Thank god he wasn't very far out. I don't have cell service for too much farther." He locks his sweet, big eyes with me and gives my hand a reassuring lick.

Okay, what do I do, what do I do? Probably call off the search? Yeah. That's a good place to start. I pace, trying to focus, tapping the seconds on my leg as they pass. I should call Anna and tell my group to stay on the boardwalk.

"Hey," I stammer, still unable to stop staring at Michael's body. He's so small and unassuming compared to the pictures on his missing person flyer. His well-tailored suit is saturated and clinging to his form. The flashy and wealthy impression he gave me doesn't fit the man who is lying on his stomach, head turned unnaturally sideways, with a gaping head wound. He looks...exposed.

"You find Marty? We're still at the benches. A couple of crows have been eyeing our lunch."

"Uh, yep. I found him. I'm not coming back right away, but we're both safe. Can you and the others stay put for a while? Or do you think you can find your way back to the office without getting lost?"

"...we can stay put..." She pauses. "You okay, Maudy? Did you find something?"

"I'll fill you in later. Me or Kelly's crew will come by when it's okay to leave. Thanks for holding down the fort. Also, keep an eye on those crows; it's probably Bill and Ted. They have a history of stealing sandwiches and car keys." I cut the call before she can ask any questions that I don't want to answer and unclip my walkie.

All three of us are on the same channel, so I'm able to tell Eli and Zach simultaneously.

"Hey, guys. You there?"

They both respond with, "copy."

"Please take your groups back to the office. Keep them on the property until further notice. We've got something."

"Oh, jeez," Zach responds. "Will do."

"On it," Eli confirms.

"Thanks. There's emergency marshmallows and chocolate bars in my bottom desk drawer if you want to build a bonfire and keep spirits up."

I don't need to tell them what happened, they read between the lines. Eli texts my cell right after we get off the walkies asking if I'm okay. I lie and tell him I'm fine. He says he'll send dinner over tonight anyway.

This is bad. Like a car wreck, I just can't look away. My ranger training is no use here. He is long gone. Like a couple of days gone. I gawk at the decaying, bloated man, pallid skin and sopping-wet navy suit from a safe distance away, not wanting to mess anything up for the police.

My head returns to that blasted cuckoo clock at The Nest, incessantly ticking. As I sit, waiting for the police to haul away the dead man, the *tick, tick, tick,* of the wooden bird reverberates through my skull, mocking my fingertips tapping away the seconds, bringing with it the early stages of a migraine.

Desperately needing a distraction, I talk to Marty while we're waiting for Kelly to come. Knowing this area well, I'm pretty sure it'll take her more than the thirty minutes she estimated, even by four-wheeler. I'm doing my best to keep my mind reigned in, not letting it spiral into dark and horrible thoughts that keep cropping up as the minutes predictably march on.

My mind drifts to my ex, Nate, wishing the *stronzo* was by my side. Credit where credit is due, the man knew how to calm me down. *Tick, tick, tick.* Without him here... *No! Maudy, stop it. You don't need him! He's the reason you get these panic attacks in the first place. You're a strong independent woman, remember? Nate is literally the worst. Get your head out of your own a–*

Interrupted by Marty grumbling a string of "bow row rows," either telling me about his latest quantum physics theory or simply demanding a treat, I turn my attention to him.

"Good job, puppy," I coo, scratching behind both ears. "For once, I'm glad you managed to bolt. You're my little hero. Extra peanut butter for you tonight." He recognizes the word "peanut butter," and his tail gives a half-hearted wag.

Marty has a history of running off. He's never trying to run away for good; he knows how cushy he has it, but he literally can't help chasing after small fuzzy things. No matter how much exercise I give him, or how much training we do together, he hasn't been able to break this habit. I think it's in his hunter DNA or something. If the end of his leash isn't secure and the opportunity presents itself, he'll go after whatever he can get his grubby little paws on.

I float away from the dog, away from Michael, into the black depths of Lake Michigan, aimlessly bobbing from one bleak thought to another. Reaching, trying to swim up to the surface, I tell Marty about Eli's new "everything but the turkey" muffin that he's working on. It is some Thanksgiving-inspired monstrosity that uses potato flour, rosemary, cranberries, and cheddar cheese. I tell the dog that I promised we would both be taste testers for him. He scrunches his face and gives a throaty grunt in response; I'm not sure if that means he's excited or dreading it. Honestly, I'm not sure how I feel about it myself.

Drowning back down into the mental darkness, I yank myself up again and recite the plot in the new book I'm reading, and how it includes some great twists and turns that I didn't see coming for once. He listens, or has the decency to appear to, looking deep into my eyes and resting his head on my knee until we hear the low growl of Kelly's motor.

Eli radios in that his group is back at the office. Zach's is still out but will be back soon. I check in with Anna again, who says they are all fine and enjoying the scenery, still on the boardwalk platform where I left them. They've spotted a Bullfrog the size of a salad plate and a Great Blue Heron, which scared off the crows. They seem happily occupied.

Kelly pulls up maybe an hour after I called her. She's driving our State Park four-wheeler, while another, larger one pulls in behind her carrying two medics and a stretcher. Her dirty blonde hair is pulled into a tight ponytail. She's stocky, wearing an official Sheriff's Department jacket and big, black boots. Even from dozens of feet away, I can see her metallic blue nail polish gripping the wheel; it's the only bit of personal flair that can be seen from under her cop attire.

"Hi, Maudy." Kelly walks right up to me after putting the four-wheeler in park. She pulls out a small, red leather notebook and looks at me without saying anything else, giving me her undivided (and intimidating) attention. The EMTs approach Michael and begin taking pictures and writing down notes, also immediately aware the man is beyond saving.

"Hi," I say as I stand up, wrapping my arms around my midsection, still nauseated. Marty sits at my feet, looking up to reassure me everything would be okay. *Thanks, bud. I'll try my best not to puke on you. No promises, though.*

I launch into retracing my steps, what happened from the point that Marty ran off up until now. She takes diligent notes and probes a few additional clarifying questions along the way. Pulling out a piece of beef jerky from her pocket, she tears off a small chunk and offers it to Marty.

"Good job, Detective." She smiles at him, giving him a pat on the head as he scarfs it down. "Would you mind getting all the park volunteers' contact info before they leave? I need to know who exactly has been in the park today."

"Of course. I'll send you everything once I have it."

"Great, whatever you can collect is helpful. I owe you big time, thanks for leading this effort."

"Absolutely. Just doing my job." I try to crack a smile, but give up halfway through.

"Want a ride back to the front entrance? I'm happy to give you one if you wait here while we do what we have to do."

"That's okay, I can walk. I don't need to see what happens next. And

I've left my group back a ways. I want to make sure they make it out safely. When you're done with that," gesturing to the four-wheeler, "could you put it back in the shed? Here, take my key to lock it up." I remove the key from my keyring and hand it to her.

"Will do. I'll swing by your place later today if any other questions pop up after we take a look here."

"Sounds good. I'll be home." Man, The Den sounds so good right now.

On our hike back, I check in with Harper at the state Department of Natural Resources, commonly referred to as the DNR.

"Hi, Harper, do you have a minute?"

"Hi, Maudy, of course. You're not interrupting anything. Is everything alright?" Her absent-minded tenor says otherwise, but I know I'm not doing a good job hiding the shake from my voice.

"We found that missing tourist. Turns out his body was in the park." I let the statement sink in, unsure what else to say to make the news any less disappointing.

"You're kidding," she exclaims. Now I have her full attention.

"I wish. The Sheriff's Department is out there right now."

"Cooperate fully with them. It's in our best interest that this gets resolved quickly. I'll try to do a bit of damage control here in Lansing. Ugh, this is the last thing we need right now. If campers aren't toasting marshmallows this weekend, we've got to shut down for good." She's back to being distracted, probably drafting memos about this already.

"I'll keep you posted, Harper. And yes, I know how poor this timing is, I'll do my absolute best to keep us on schedule this week."

"Good."

We discuss a few protocol measures and hang up as the nauseous pit in my stomach grows even more, getting close to baseball-size territory.

I hook back up with Anna and the others on the way back to the office.

As we approach the small cabin, I see the other search parties around a roaring bonfire. They seem to be doing fine, all things considered. Marshmallows tend to have that effect on people.

I thank them profusely for their time, stay intentionally vague about what happened, and gather their contact info for Kelly. With that done, I quickly usher everyone out of the park. I know Zach can read the stress in my face; he offers a look of concern and a friendly hug before following our volunteers across the Birch River Bridge and into town.

Jim's truck is in the gravel parking lot, and the note on the ranger station door is gone. I figure he's already in the campground working away. With our four-wheeler still in use, I look down at Marty.

"Up for more walking, Martin? It might do me some good, I don't know about you," I ask, trying to keep the tension and exhaustion out of my voice. He does a full-body shake and prances, saying he is up for anything. "Let's make a pit stop inside to get some water."

Lazily knocking off my mud-caked boots on the side of the front porch, Marty and I walk through the office door. Waiting until he gets right next to our upholstered couch, the small dog shakes violently, spraying forest snot all over the furniture. He heads for his water bowl, and I collapse in my chair.

Without the pressure to save face for others, I break down, the image of Michael's body clunkily tumbling over and over in my mind like a pair of tennis shoes in the dryer. Even though I didn't know the guy, I feel for him. It looked to me like he had fallen and hit his head on a rock. The large wound on the side of his skull was very noticeable; it's now living rent-free in my brain.

Coupling the sympathy, an emotional wave of worry and panic floods me from head to toe with the impending doom of the park closure. This isn't going to be good.

Marty lays his fuzzy head on my lap, sitting quietly. I rhythmically pet his curly white chest fur with one hand and tap the seconds as they pass on the arm of my chair with the other. After exactly two hundred and fourteen seconds, I come back down to Earth.

As I stroke my dog's soft head, his kind eyes reassuring me, I get it together. Using my muddy sleeve, I wipe the tears from my eyes, get up, put the search party contact sheet in my pack, and walk towards the campground.

A half-mile dirt road leads east towards the campground, which lets campers keep their cars with them on site. We follow the road, reaching the small camp store in just over four hundred seconds. The building is almost like a miniature version of my office. It's where Jim registers campers and sells a few staples like firewood, grill charcoal, and marshmallows.

As we approach, I can see the older man clearing out a campsite of woody debris that'd fallen over the harsh winter months.

"Jim! It's so great to see you," I exclaim and jog towards him. He lives in the town adjacent to Stone's Throw, a few miles south. He's been such an asset and knows more about these woods than I do. If I wasn't so confident in his ability to get everything up and running, I would've needed Zach to skip out on the search party today.

"Maudy, what the heck is goin' on over there?" He gestures back in the general direction of where the body was found, giving me a one-armed hug. A dissonant symphony of air horns and megaphone announcements rings through the park. Kelly's team is loudly ordering everyone to leave the premises immediately. We've been closed to the public all day, but she has to be sure nobody is lingering.

"I, well, Marty actually, found the body of a tourist that went missing a couple of days ago. A bunch of us were out searching today, and Marty's nose caught the scent."

"That's horrible, I'm sorry, girl. News of that man's disappearance made its way across town. Sorry to hear." Jim is easily in his seventies, but more physically capable than someone half his age. He is respectful, kind, and wise. He is also one of the only men I'd ever let get away with calling me 'girl.'

We discuss plans for opening weekend, and I'm reassured that he'll get it done. "Jim, I'm going to do all I can to reinstate your access back here quickly, but we're going to all need to evacuate soon. If you don't mind, wrap up the absolute necessities that you've already started, and I'll try to get us back out here in a day or two max."

He promises me it will be fine. I give him one more squeeze and turn back towards the Birch River bridge.

After everyone, including Jim and Zach, leaves, I close the gate to the front entrance and re-hang the rusty "Closed" sign. Until this gets resolved, Kelly orders me to stay closed.

Tick, tick, tick.

Chapter Five

My favorite aspect of small-town life also happens to be my least favorite: I can never go anywhere without bumping into someone I know. It's great when I'm up for it. I hated being a faceless cog in the suburban machine, but right now, I just want to get home as fast as possible. I march directly home with a pair of headphones in my ears in an attempt to avoid questions. The past hour of Kelly's wailing sirens isn't helping my cause. I'm positive that the news is all over town already.

Every time I approach my house, nestled in the middle of a residential block a couple of streets over from the main drag, I'm at peace, even now. It's a modest, dark red A-frame that's quaint and cozy. It has a fenced-in backyard that's perfect for the dog, and a second-story loft that I use as my bedroom. Before I bought it, it was a vacation rental and decorated with a boring beach theme, but I scooped it up and quickly made it my own. Affectionately calling it The Den, the dark color scheme and my 'maximalist' approach suit the place much better than the airy light blue it once was.

Walking through my creaky front door and into the living room, I toss my keys into a bowl on top of a small record cabinet, home to my vinyl collection. The walls are a deep green and adorned with a collage of pictures and artwork. Crossing the living room and into the kitchen, I open the pantry door and bend down to get Marty a scoop of kibble, not hungry myself.

I expect that Kelly will stop by sometime tonight to ask more questions, and in preparation, I try to piece together my shattered thoughts. I am a pretty observant person, years spent outdoors, often alone, have sharpened my senses. Even when I'm on the verge of throwing up.

After putting one of my favorite Nirvana albums on the record player, pondering what exactly teen spirit smells like, I sit down on the couch with a cup of coffee and my favorite purple, polka dot notebook. Leaning back, snuggling next to Marty, I close my eyes, take a deep breath, and focus on what I objectively saw, not about the shock I spiraled into. I tap my fingers to the beat of the music and try to scan the scene, thinking back to details that I was actively trying to ignore at the time.

Stitching the image together like a heinous quilt, I envision Michael lying on the ground not far off the trail, maybe a dozen or so feet. The ground cover is low and sopping wet, with a bunch of fallen tree limbs scattered about, like most of the woods in this area. Not unusual. He's lying face down, head next to a boulder about the size of a small ottoman. The angle of his head is severely twisted. *His neck must've broken.* There's a large wound on the side of his forehead, encroaching on his slightly receding hairline. On the tree next to him, the Nest's cuckoo clock is mounted in the trunk. It's ticking faster and faster, counting down the minutes until I have to cancel everyone's campsite reservations and lose my job.

Think, Maudy. Knock it off. What happened here? Shaking the clock off, I return to the body. Did he fall and hit his head on the boulder? I'm not so sure. The wound looked really bad, but I don't see any blood on the plants nearby, the ground, or the boulder. If he hit his head bad enough to cause this injury, wouldn't it have been more…I don't know, gruesome? Plus, wouldn't Zach have seen him when we did our trail search yesterday? He should have covered this part of the park on the mountain bike. The woods aren't *that* dense, and neither is Zach. Either Zach somehow missed this (doubtful), or Michael's body wasn't there when we searched yesterday (interesting).

It's been such a wet spring, and it stormed all night last night. Maybe it all washed away? I guess Zach could have ridden by without noticing. Something seems off. Zach is literally always on his A-game. He would've noticed an entire dead body. Michael was pretty visible from the trail.

As predicted, Kelly knocks on my front door maybe three hours later. I pour her a cup of coffee, refill my own mug, and we take a seat at my kitchen table. Marty, the unabashed beggar that he is, hasn't forgotten about Kelly's beef jerky gift and shamelessly rests his head on her lap, putting on the biggest puppy dog eyes that he can muster.

She strokes his head absentmindedly, sipping her coffee, and looks at me straight on. Her piercing blue-gray eyes are unwavering. "I think we both know why I'm here," she says flatly.

"It wasn't an accident, was it?"

"It wasn't an accident," she confirms. Hearing that, my stomach flops, and my headache clusters right in the middle of my forehead. She clicks her dark blue painted fingernails against the ceramic mug, *tick, tick, tick*.

"There's no way the coroner is finished yet, how are you so sure?" I question, shakily. Our coroner's office is on the other side of the county, almost an hour's drive from here. There hasn't been enough time to conduct a proper autopsy, even if they started right away.

"Cause of death is still *technically* undetermined." She nods, making air quotes with her fingers. "Although that nasty blow to the head seems pretty likely what did him in."

Her callousness used to strike me as insensitive, but now I think it's more of a coping mechanism. Keeping a little detached is her way of self-preservation. She's in the 'old boys club' of rural police. Holding her own can't be easy. I'm not one to judge.

"So, if the cause of death is still undetermined, how are you sure?" I ask, even though I know the answer already. If I was already suspicious, certainly she must be.

"Before we continue this conversation, we have a couple of things to sort out." She sighs and hands me a piece of paper on the Sheriff's Office's official letterhead. She rests her hands under her chin, leaning forward. "I'd like to bring you on as a consultant for this case. I'm not sure where it'll go, but for now, I think you'll be an asset with your familiarity of the park. I know you've done this for us before, but never in the capacity of a homicide. I totally get it if you want to steer clear of this circus, but I'm really hoping you'll help me. Please?"

This isn't the first time Kelly has brought me in as a consultant on one of her cases, usually when the park is connected to an investigation. It's a big piece of property, and folks sometimes think it's a safe place to do shady things.

"So...you're maintaining jurisdiction, not the state police?" I scan the document, finding it standard. I've read these before, they just state that I'm joining the investigation in an 'official' capacity as a consultant, but have no authority beyond what I already have as a Park Ranger. It essentially says I can legally investigate the crime scene and do some light poking around but is crystal clear that I'm not allowed to confront anyone who is deemed dangerous, or make arrests. Like I'd ever want to do that anyway.

After finishing reading, I continue. "I assumed that since the body was found on state land, the state police would be the lead."

"Yes, this is with us for now, but we're keeping them looped in. I'm hoping it stays that way. Are you able to help us?"

"Kelly, of course I'll help," I say as I sign the agreement and hand it back to her. "I'm not sure how useful I'll be, but I've already checked in with the DNR and they've directed me to be fully cooperative." *Meaning, squash this PR nightmare quickly and quietly before word gets out.* "We've got families coming to camp on Friday. A lot is hinging on a successful camping season this year."

"Oh, that's right. Yeah, there's zero chance the campground is opening if this is still unresolved by then." She sinks into the wooden chair further, taking a long sip of coffee, pleased that I've agreed to help, but is obviously apologetic that this whole thing is turning into a pain in my butt, too. I stay quiet, waiting for her to continue.

"I need you to understand that there are things I cannot share with you. It sucks, but that's how this is going to work. Signing this piece of paper doesn't make you a cop, Maudy. It allows you and me to communicate regularly and for you to do some digging on your own. You are my eyes and ears on the ground, and I expect you to share what you find. But I also need you to understand that I cannot share everything that I find with you, and it's for your own good. Capish?" I nod in response, not thrilled with that arrangement. "This is confidential, but I'm trusting you," she says with trepidation. "It is clear to us that he did not die where he was found."

"Oh, I was honestly thinking the same thing." I hand her the notebook that I've been jotting down notes in over the last few hours. She looks a little surprised and impressed. "The page of contact info for the search party volunteers is shoved in the back if you want it, I didn't email you a copy of it yet."

"Thanks, I'll just take a picture, not a problem." She pauses to take a picture of that page, as well as the one with my notes. "And before I forget, here's your shed key back." She places the small key on the table.

I thank her and take a sip of my coffee, using the mug as a shield to hide my stunned face. This whole thing is overwhelming to say the least. She hands me back my notebook and points to a pen nearby. I put down my coffee and grab the pen to take notes.

"Okay. So, we think the body was dumped in the woods, not killed there." She pauses to take a sip herself. "There is not a single trace of blood on the ground, the rock, the underside of the leaves, nothing. Only on Michael's clothes. His skin appears to be cleaned off as well. It doesn't take a medical examiner to see that he has been dead for a couple of days. That wound would be much different had it not been cleaned up."

"But what about the rai—" I interject.

"Nope, it wasn't the rain. We couldn't find a single trace of blood on that ground. Not seeped into the mud, not anywhere. His skin was manually scrubbed clean."

I wrinkle my nose. What I saw was horrible enough; what would it have looked like if Michael's body had been left in its more *natural* state? *Gross.*

She holds up her hands in front of her as if to say, *'And that's all I can say.'*

"Huh..." Distracted, dwelling on the head wound, I take notes. She hands me a copy of the case file. Most of the information has been redacted, and all of the photos are missing. She asks that I keep it confidential for now. Doing everything in my power to not roll my eyes, as the folder she hands me is essentially useless, I flip through the scant pages. "But this means the park isn't a crime scene, right? We can open back up soon?" I'm unable to keep the excitement at that prospect out of my voice.

She looks at me long and hard, without expressing her thoughts on her face. "As of now, *you* can enter. But I can't let you open it up to other staff yet, and definitely not the public."

Ticked off, reactively slumping my shoulders, I huff. Now busy helping Kelly with this case, I don't have the time to personally outfit the entire campground. What good does it do that I can enter? If Jim or Zach can't get in there, we'll have to give refunds to the campers scheduled for this Friday, if not the whole weekend. No campers equals no more park. *Tick, tick, tick.*

Kelly quickly jumps in, "Look, I'm sorry. I know this sucks for you. How about I prioritize clearing Zach? I can send someone to get his alibi and talk to him soon. If I can rule him out, he's fine to go back in."

"Oh, don't be sorry, I get it. Yeah, that'd be great. Jim, too, if you can manage." I pause and tap my index finger on the rim of my mug. "There's just a ton of pressure to have a successful camping season this year. This is literally the worst possible timing."

"Don't worry, I get it." She pats my hand in support. She scoots back her chair, making a high-pitched scratchy sound on my floor, and gathers her things, needing to get back to work.

"Thanks for stopping by, Kelly. I'll keep you posted with what I find."

"Thanks, Maudy. Talk soon. Goodbye, Mr. Martin." She musses the dog's crinkly ear fur, and walks through the front door.

* * *

The last thing I want to do tonight is cook dinner. The last thing I want to do every night is cook dinner, but tonight especially. I know I need to eat, all I've had is coffee and a granola bar today, but I'm wiped. And, since he offered, I send the bat signal for Eli to come to the culinary rescue. It won't hurt to hear what rumors are flying around town, I'm sure he's getting an earful already from the bar all afternoon.

While I wait for him to respond, fighting off the urge to mentally submerge back into the turbulent water of horrible thoughts, I choose to distract myself with a silly craft project I've been meaning to finish. As I'm grabbing my art box from a shelf in my basement, I hear my phone buzz from the living room, directly above me.

"Hang on, I'm coming, I'm coming!" I scramble up the stairs, hurrying to answer it, and trip over the last step. Reaching the phone just in time, I see that it's from Eli. "Well, hey there." *Please be dinner plans, please be dinner plans.*

"Hey, I got your text! Yes, of course, I'll be over with dinner, but give me a minute, we're slammed tonight." I can hear the whirring noise of Pop's kitchen in the background and the smile in his voice. He has something good up his sleeve, I can tell.

"Jeez, no it's okay! I figured if you weren't busy, it'd be nice to not cook. But obviously, Pop's comes first. Don't sweat it."

"Shut up and let me do something nice for you, okay?" he laughs.

"Ha. Okay, fine. You are an absolute gem of a human, Elliot Nett. Thank you so much."

"For you? Anything. Dad can deal without me. How does some chicken soup and garlic bread sound? I had a leftover carcass and turned it into something pretty tasty if I do say so myself."

"Ah-mazing, yes please. The door is unlocked, come on over whenever. Although let's try to refrain from using words like 'carcass' tonight." I shiver.

"Ha. That's fair. I'll be right there."

I hang up and set my small kitchen table.

Maybe half an hour later, Eli sits across from me as I devour dinner like a wild animal. Marty is starving, too. The brazen dog gives the most sorrowful puppy dog eyes at both of us until we each give him a couple of pieces of cooked carrot and chicken.

"So, how was the rest of your day? Hanging in there?" He chomps on crunchy garlic bread and is giving me equally sorrowful puppy dog eyes. This soup is resurrecting me from the stupor I've been in all afternoon. I'm sure I'm not the prettiest sight right now.

"Oh, you know. Just trying to wipe my brain clean. It wasn't pretty. Any chance you have one of those Men in Black flashy-light memory things?" I deflate a bit, soaking in Eli's comfort. "Kelly came by a little while ago and asked that I consult on the police investigation. What do you think happened? I'm shocked we found him out there. How many guys do you know who hike in expensive suits? He was wearing a fancy navy one when I found him." I want to tell him that Michael wasn't killed there, but I shouldn't spread that around yet. Maybe Eli knows something helpful; he did see the guy in Pop's while he was in town.

"Yeah, agreed. He struck me more as a 'sipping a thirty-dollar cocktail in a swanky club' kind of guy. He was never happy with our drinks at the bar." I roll my eyes with a full mouth.

"So, what do *you* think happened?" I query again, pushing him more, with an exaggerated curiosity. "You know, Zach thinks something fishy went down. And honestly, I'm starting to believe him."

"Of course he does, it's Zach," Eli laughs. "Honestly? I think he got out of his depth in the woods, turned around, and fell. He came into the bar a few times and was always on his phone, working. At least until his vision blurred." His laughter darkens a bit. "Maybe he wasn't paying attention and tripped. The guy and his buddies could drink, that's for sure. Maybe he wandered out there after drinking too much."

"You think that guy Jeremy had something to do with it? Seems like a bit of a leap. He was in my search party and was really torn up over the whole thing."

Eli has a good heart, but he's always been a little insecure around other men. I can't tell if he honestly thinks Jeremy is a bad dude, or if he's just jealous. I trust his taste in soups and sauces wholeheartedly, but his judgment of other guys, less so.

"Nah, I doubt he actually did. He's a tool, but probably harmless. Doesn't mean I like him sitting at my bar though." Taking a moment to finish the last of his soup, he pauses. "What's all that?" He points towards the craft supplies spread all over my coffee table.

"I haven't told them yet," I garble with a mouth full of noodles and cooked carrot, "but I reserved a campsite on Friday so we can have our weekly euchre night around a campfire and tell ghost stories. I made sure everyone's schedules are clear and am going to surprise them with a cute invitation." I smile and rub my hands together as I reveal my master plan, proud of myself. "This way I can keep an eye on the other campers on opening night and won't be too far away if something happens. Win-win. Well, if the police investigation is cleared up by then."

"Dang, that sounds fun. If you need someone to stomp around the campsite and make scary bear noises, I'm your guy. Hell, maybe Michael's ghost will stop by and give you guys some *real* ghost stories to scream at," he laughs.

"Dude, too soon." I reluctantly laugh too, throwing a piece of garlic bread at him.

Knowing this could totally be a moot point if the park is still closed, I write out the three invites fairly quickly and draw fun little card designs around the border. Eli hangs around after dinner, I turn on the first *Scream* movie, one of my favorites, and he falls asleep on the couch almost instantly.

He lives kitty-corner from me, our backyards adjacent to one another, so there's really no reason for him to sleep over. I don't mind, though. Maybe he's a little worried. Hell, maybe I'm a little worried, too. I'm grateful for the company after the day I just had.

"Mind if I crash here tonight?" He mutters as I throw a blanket over him and head up to my loft.

"No problemo. There's another blanket in the basket if you need it."

"Thanks. Sleep tight, Muddy."

"Don't let the bed bugs bite, Coach," I reply with a nickname in kind. "See you in the morning."

Chapter Six

I found Michael about an hour's hike from our park office using the most direct route. My search party took a wonky way yesterday, venturing off trail in the effort to be thorough. Now that I know where I'm going, it doesn't take me and the dog long to reach our destination, just as the pink sunrise crests over the forest canopy. I know Kelly told me she and her team searched the area already, but I'm not sure they'd know exactly what to look for. Maybe I can pick up on something that they missed, now that my initial shock has worn off. It's worth a shot anyway.

"Okay, Marty. Now, what exactly are we looking for?" The scruffy dog, still with a bit of bedhead, sits down in the mud, tail gently wagging. Peering over with the whites of his eyes, I imagine he says, '*Hey, I found the guy. It's your turn to do the work!*'

"What's that magic nose of yours smell? Anything? There might be a new squeaky ball in it for you later." He's not above a good bribe. His ears perk up at the word 'ball,' but he stays seated. Looks like I'll need to do the heavy lifting this morning.

Kelly put a few stakes and crime scene tape around where Michael was found, but otherwise, the area is undisturbed. The ground has been trampled over thoroughly by the police—no use trying to ID any footprints.

Dirt jams its way under my fingernails as I methodically crawl on hands and knees, analyzing the groundcover. "Nothing," I huff at Marty, who still isn't paying me any attention.

We spend hours out in the woods, scouring the ground, analyzing tree bark for scratches or signs of struggle, trying to find anything else that might be helpful. With the case file and my handy dandy notebook spread out on a fallen log nearby, I try to recreate the fall, anticipating where blood might spatter or where depressions in the ground would be. I rule out an animal attack. While pretty clear already based on the condition Michael was found in, I thought it necessary to search for the evidence of bears just in case. They're not unheard of here.

There isn't any debris, no blood, no sign of animals, nothing. As I'm about to give up, twenty concentric crawling circles later, I gently move a sprig of wild ginger out of my way. "Huh." I crouch lower.

Two small, rectangular marks are firmly imprinted in the wet ground twenty or so feet away from where Michael was found. After a few more minutes of investigating, I find a few feet of tire track not far off. The imprints are about four inches long and an inch wide; the identical impressions are about two feet apart.

"That's weird." I roughly measure the tracks using the length of my pen. The tire is much thicker than a normal bike, but not as big as a car. "Did Zach take out a fat tire bike on Friday? I think he said he was going to mountain bike, didn't he, Marty?" Still no response from the dog. I take a few photos for good measure and draw a schematic in my notebook.

"Hey Marty, what's four inches long and rectangular? No, this isn't the set-up of a dumb joke." Moving back to the rectangular imprints, the dog looks over at me, preoccupied with a worm that's squirming underneath one of his front paws. *Think Maudy, think.* There isn't much in nature that would leave such straight lines like that. The rectangles aren't like animal tracks. Not coming up with any eureka moments on the spot, I take more pictures and jot down a few more notes to figure it out later. Covered in brambles and with grumbling stomachs, I pack up and we head out of the park.

Maybe Eli will know what these marks in the mud are.

"Pop's for lunch, Martin? You can't come inside, but I can bring you a doggie bag," I offer. He seems to like the idea well enough, and we cross the Birch River Bridge into town. Maybe I'll bump into some of my card sharks and pass along their camping invitations along the way.

I drop Marty back at home with a frozen rubber toy filled with extra peanut butter as promised, which should occupy him until his lunch order (my leftovers) arrives. He trots over to the couch with the treat in his mouth, jumps up, and curls onto a fuzzy throw.

"Oh, the life of a dog," I muse, dreading that future-me will be washing oily peanut butter stains out of the blanket later.

The rescue shelter cautioned me when I adopted Marty. They told me this dog "loves to play and has high energy," which I took to mean, "needs a ton of exercise or else will destroy your house." With all our hiking, he's a well-behaved couch potato *most* of the time. Every once in a while, though, he activates his tornado mode and zooms through the living room with one of my socks in his mouth. I kiss him on the head and lock the door behind me.

Drinking in the lovely breeze and blue sky, I momentarily forget about the harrowing weekend I had and enjoy a moment of quiet.

It is around noon, and the lunch crowd is in full swing. I find a seat at the bar off to the left, take off my jacket, and settle in. Kevin is off on Sundays, and Darci, a college student who is here for the summer, is tending bar.

"Maudy, hey! How goes it? Good to see you out and about." The young woman brushes her shaggy bangs out of her eyes as she washes a pint glass. She's a great bartender and is turning out to be a beloved resident here, even after only a couple of weeks. Kevin and Eli are already trying to bribe her to come back next summer.

Darci is studying veterinary medicine. She came here from Ann Arbor for an internship with our Veterinarian, Laura, for the summer. The beachy, lakeside destination didn't hurt either. If she's this good with her two-legged patrons, I imagine she's a dream with her four-legged ones.

"I've been meaning to ask you; do you know what breed Marty is? A client at the clinic was asking about different dogs, and Marty's funky frame came to mind."

"Your guess is as good as mine. People come up to me all the time saying he looks like different mixes. The most common ones I hear are Border Collies, Black Labs, Corgis, and Spaniels." To me, he looks most like a short Border Collie with long, wavy Cocker Spaniel fur around his ears.

We make small talk for a few minutes while she pours me a pint of hard cider. She's trying hard not to ask me something, her eyes keep darting away, and her freckled face looks half-sad, half-awkward.

"Just ask what you want to ask, Darci. It's fine." I take a sip and lift my eyebrows as if to say, *'You want to know about Michael, yes?'*

"No, no, I can tell you had a rough couple of days, no offense..." She gives me a once-over. "I won't bother you about it."

Maybe I should've showered before coming. I self-consciously brush the dried mud off my jacket. "Darci," I say plainly, "it's fine, really. What have you heard?"

"Not much to be honest, just that you found his...body." She pauses, wincing as she says it out loud.

"Yep, sure did." I take another big swig. "Is that the talk of this place today?"

"Oh yeah." She nods emphatically. "I mean, I don't blame them. It's not like murder happens all the time around he—"

"Whoa, whoa, whoa. Who said anything about murder?" I cut her off. How'd that get out already?

She leans in, speaking quietly. Her eyes dart around to make sure we aren't overheard. "Kelly's been around asking a lot of questions. If it was a simple hiking accident, there's no reason for her to be doing that, right?"

"I plead the fifth," I say with a slight smirk. I mime locking up my mouth and tossing the key into my pint glass before taking another sizable gulp.

"Is there anything I can do to help?" She leans forward even more, eager to assist.

"Keep your ears open and tell me if anyone says anything interesting? People tend to overshare in a bar." That brings me back to my own college days, bartending at a small brewery in downtown Lansing. It's where Nate and I first met. *Now that your safe little life is upheaved you can't stop thinking about Nate? Cut it out, dummy!*

"Absolutely!" She is excited. I write my cell number on a napkin and hand it to her.

"Call or text anytime." I slide the note over to her and order lunch. Today, it's grilled cheese and tomato soup, the ultimate comfort food.

Dozens of eyes sharply bore into my back as I eat; everyone knows I found Michael's body. I might as well have a scarlet letter tattooed on my forehead. Thankfully, they are giving me a little space, and I'm not getting bombarded with questions. Even though Stone's Throwers are a gossipy bunch, every once in a while, Midwestern manners trump curiosity.

As I sop up the last of the soup with the crust of the sandwich, Jeremy walks in and plops down a few barstools from me. He gives me a small wave in acknowledgment. Ready to leave, I gather my things and go over to say hi on my way out. I didn't get a chance to see him at the end of the search party, given how everything went down, and I'm curious as to how he's handling the news.

"Hi, Maudy, how was your day?" he asks, dripping with sarcasm but with a warm smile. He's drained. It must be hard having all this happen to someone you know. *Do I look this rough? Yikes... Actually, I'm covered in mud and have sticks in my hair. I have to look worse. Awesome.*

"Seems to be about as good as yours." I offer a sympathetic smile and gesture to the mud covering my pants and jacket. "Maybe even worse. I'm sorry we didn't get to talk more after...well, you know. My condolences."

"Thanks. Yeah, it's tough. I was on edge and jetted pretty quickly after we were cleared to leave the park." He's wiping his hands on his pants and avoiding my eyes. I lean against an open stool next to him.

"Is there something you want to tell me, Jeremy? Are you alright?" The silence settles in; I hope he's compelled to fill it unprompted. With my hands in my pockets, I privately tap the time as it passes between us: twenty-one seconds.

Finally, he meets my gaze and says, "Michael was a shrewd businessman with a lot of money. Like *a lot* of money. I can't help but guess that someone wanted it, or was unhappy with how he planned on spending it..." he trails off.

I nod and stay silent, making it a little uncomfortable. This time my trick doesn't work. His whisky arrives, and he turns his attention to sipping it. With him turned away, I run my fingers through my hair in an effort to tame it. They get caught halfway through in mud-caked snarls. I throw it up in an emergency messy bun instead.

"Were you guys planning on working over the weekend? How long were you staying in town?"

Just as I ask the question, Eli comes out from the kitchen and waves hello. The bar is getting busier, and Darci pulls him out to help serve drinks. I wave back, then turn my attention back towards Jeremy. The men clock each other, too.

"I rented Michael a room at The Nest through Memorial Day

weekend; he was planning on staying that long at most. If we wrapped things up early, he would go back to Chicago. On late nights," he holds up his drink and jingles the ice, "I've gotten a room for myself there, too. They seem to have plenty of vacancies, and I never drink and drive. Otherwise, I've commuted from the city."

Tipping his head back towards the highway, he clearly means Traverse City. The biggest city in northern Michigan, Traverse City is about forty-five minutes east of here, and how Stone's Throw got its name. 'Just a stone's throw from Traverse City' was an old marketing slogan used to get other Michiganders to come visit. The name stuck, and the town officially rebranded back in the '60s.

"Gotcha. So, remind me when you last saw him? I know we talked about this while searching, but I can't remember what you said."

"I heard you were involved in solving his case. What are you doing here, Ms. Lorso, pumping a suspect for information?" He chuckles and leans into me in an overtly flirty way. "I've already been speaking with the police." He pauses to take another small sip of what I'm guessing is an old fashioned. The bitters and fruity orange scent wafts from the glass as he swirls it.

Inhale, one, two, three, four. Exhale, one, two, three, four. My palms sweat and my cheeks burn, turning flush. Flashes of Nate and I fighting, *screaming,* at one another cloud my vision and I lean on the bar for support, hopefully appearing very cool and super casual. Not like I'm staving off a panic attack. Tapping away the seconds in my jacket pocket, counting my breaths, the Nest's cuckoo clock emerges from the wall of my old suburban house in my vision, turning my helpful *taps* into mocking *ticks.*

"I saw him Wednesday night. Here, actually." Jeremy talks, but I'm still swirling in that old pain, still rooted deeply in my brain. Trying my best to listen, I shut my eyes for a minute, blinking away the harmful memory. He doesn't seem to notice, or at least has the courtesy to pretend. "We had dinner together; the fun weekly spaghetti thing you guys do. I told him I needed to spend Thursday morning at home back in the city to take care of a couple other clients, and that if he wanted me around later to shoot me a text. I never heard from him."

He continues, "I came back in the afternoon to check in with him, but he wasn't at the B&B. I didn't realize anything was wrong until Kelly called me after he was formally reported missing on Friday morning. My name was on his room reservation."

"Oh, right." I'm mentally seventy-five percent back online, able to process most of what he's saying. He's stoic, like he's holding something back. Something's still bothering him. Or maybe he's totally wigged out and thinks I'm insane. Both are equally plausible right now. "So, uh, what time did you drive back to Traverse City Wednesday night?"

"I actually spent that night here in town. I woke up very early on Thursday and headed back for morning meetings, then returned in the afternoon."

"Huh, okay, thanks." I pause, trying to get a timeline together, now feeling better and more present. "Why did Eli have to kick you guys out of here on Wednesday night?"

Offput by that question, his brow scrunches for a second, before regaining composure. "Nothing that concerns you, or Michael's disappearance. I promise."

Right at that moment, Christopher and Adriane approach, the couple in my search party group, requesting the grisly details of what I found yesterday. Seeing the window of opportunity ever so slightly crack open, Jeremy quickly drains the rest of his whisky, throws a twenty-dollar bill on the bar, and struts off without another word.

Calling after him, "For what it's worth, I'm sorry for your loss. If you think of anything else, please let me know." He turns and gives a subtle, suave nod, regaining his Zeusian swagger.

After a few minutes of agonizing chitchat, I politely excuse myself from the couple and walk out the door to head home. I'm pining for a hot shower and my bed. My back is creaky, and my head is swimming. I catch Eli's eye one more time and wave that I'm leaving. He's already looking in my direction and gives me a little nod back.

Putting on jammies and curling up in bed, skin still red and steaming from the lava-hot shower, I sink deep into the mattress, willing to get completely consumed by my soft, fluffy surroundings. I set an early alarm so I can get a jump on the day, and try picking my book back up, but I can't seem to focus and keep rereading paragraphs.

Something else is bothering me, not only the insane fact that my dog discovered a dead man at my place of work. Not that a possible suspect keeps hitting on me and triggering embarrassing panic attacks. It's something else. I absolutely detested sitting in Pop's with all eyes on me. I'd rather get a mouth full of root canals than sit through another five minutes of small talk with Adriane and Christopher. This place is my home; why does it feel like a monster-filled labyrinth? This weekend, I've been the most insecure and unsettled since I moved here. After hours stewing in this anxious, dark pit, I manage to drift off.

A hellish nightmare jolts me out of bed at three a.m. "Raaah!" I shout, realizing I'm not running through the woods, the hideous, wooden bird from the cuckoo clock chasing after me. Startling Marty with my shriek, I hear the pitter-patter of K-9 claws on the floor as he gallops up the stairs to see what's wrong. I turn on music to help me fall back asleep and pull the dog into bed with me. His favorite stuffed animal, a ratty duck the shelter gave us when I adopted him, is in his mouth. He drops it on my pillow as an offering of comfort, albeit a gross one, and nuzzles in with me.

Drifting for a while, my mind fixates on Michael's death, swelling and crashing like the Lake Michigan waves. I know there is a puzzle piece I haven't put together yet. Well, there are many, but something is sticking out as a piece I've already missed. It taunts me.

"Michael's bling!" I say aloud to an empty loft. *That's why he seemed so unassuming. His gaudy jewelry wasn't on him. That studded White Sox watch!* Michael wasn't wearing his watch, gold chain, or sunglasses. He was wearing them all in literally all his photos.

Was Michael Price robbed?

Chapter Seven

After that revelation, there is little hope for getting rest, regardless of how dark the circles under my eyes get. I rip myself out of bed to make a full pot of coffee. The dog is extremely confused at what possibly could be so urgent that requires us to get out of bed at this hour, but commits with me and gripes his way down the stairs.

The heavily redacted case file, upon another look, still doesn't reveal anything useful. Nothing else clicks into place, so I call Kelly. Is she going to be mad that I'm waking her up in the middle of the night? Probably. Could I wait until morning to call her? Theoretically, yes, but there's no way my mind chatter will shut up between now and then.

After five rings, she picks up. "What," she croaks. Not really a question, but at least she answers.

"He was robbed."

"What are you talking about?"

"Michael. He was robbed. All of his stuff, his watch, sunglasses, rings, everything was missing when I found him."

"Uh, okay. Let's talk in the morning." She hangs up without waiting for a response.

"Jeez, not even a 'thank you, Maudy!' 'What a big help, Maudy!'" I shrug at the dog, a little exasperated. "Well, Marty, looks like we're up for the day. Better make good use of it."

I catch up on neglected work emails, eat breakfast, and am out the door by six a.m., a droopy, grouch of a dog in tow.

It's below freezing, and the sun isn't up yet. I put on a winter jacket, a beanie, and mittens for myself, and outfit the dog with a fleece vest that covers his midsection. Marty has medium-length fur on a strip of his back and long, wavy fur on his ears and tail, but most of his body is pretty exposed to the elements. With how much we're outside, regardless of weather, he has almost as much outdoor gear as I do.

"Alright, Mr. Marty, it's time to go," I mumble under my breath, eyes squinting in the dry, frigid air, trying to get out the door. The adrenaline of last night's revelation has faded, leaving behind what feels like a mild hangover in its wake. Packing up my small, patch-covered backpack with essentials like snacks of both the human and dog variety, I clip the dog leash onto my pack's carabiner, grab my thermos, and head out the door.

Thank the caffeine gods that Java Jones opens at six a.m. When I walk through the door after hitching Marty up to the bike rack, I'm the only person inside besides Tracy, who's wiping down the espresso machine, a stark difference from Saturday morning's chaos.

"Whoa, look at you, lady. Early start today, eh?" I'm a good hour and a half earlier than my normal stop-in time.

"Must. Get. Coffee." I stammer like a zombie, which honestly isn't too far off from reality at this point. She snickers as I hand her my thermos, playing up the desperation in my face. She fills it up with a concoction that smells like peanut brittle and hands it back to me.

"Dang Tracy, this smells a-maze-ing! You're a wizard. Forget law school, you should go study with Merlin or something."

"If law wasn't my calling, maybe I would move to New York and become one of those fancy, professional baristas," she laughs.

"Speaking of law, any news yet?" I ask, like I have been doing most mornings for the past month. Her gap year is ending, and she's been waiting for acceptance letters for a few weeks now.

"Yes, actually!" She squeals, grabbing a large manila envelope off the back counter and waving it wildly in the air with excitement. "I've been accepted to Wayne State's environmental law program! Still holding out for MSU, but at least I know I'm going to school!"

"Tracy!" I lean over the counter and hug the girl. "That's amazing! Wayne is awesome. You know, I grew up not far from Detroit. Lots of my friends from high school went to Wayne and are super successful now."

"That's good to hear, it'd be fun to live in a big city for a change."

"Detroit is so cool. You'd have a blast! But you know how I feel about Michigan State." I grin. I went to Michigan State University for both my undergraduate and master's degrees. Their forestry and natural resource programs are by far the best around. The school's reputation helped me land a great job in the Michigan Department of Natural Resources right after graduation, which eventually led me here.

Saying goodbye, I grab the dog and hustle towards the park, a woman on a mission. Now that it is a somewhat reasonable hour, I pull out my phone and text Kelly, reminding her that we need to talk ASAP. *Kelly-join me for lunch today at the ranger station? I have a theory we should talk thru.*

Was his wallet found in his B&B room? Does she already know his watch and fancy things are missing? This deal, where I tell Kelly everything and she tells me nothing, is already getting frustrating. *How am I supposed to get this park open in time if I don't have access to all the information? Ugh.*

I dedicate these early morning hours to campground preparation before returning back to Michael. I begin unpacking the camp store, organizing registration information, and inventorying what we still need to buy. It feels like solid progress, but with just me able to be in here right now, I'm drowning in work that needs to get done before Friday. Even if I had all week to do work on it, it's more than a one-person job.

I squeeze in a quick check-up with the couple hours left of this gorgeous, chilly morning. I try to walk the entire park trail system over the course of a week, taking it section by section, calling it my daily 'check-up.' I see if trails need clearing, invasive species need removing, etc. Monday is Dune Day, where I buckle up for the toughest climb along the steep, western sand dunes along the Lake Michigan shoreline.

While out there, Kelly texts me back confirming lunch and lets me know that Zach has been cleared. "What a relief!" I tell Marty the encouraging news and expel the breath I didn't know I was holding. The dog, still not recuperated from the crappy night's sleep, gives a non-committal tail wag in agreement. He knows the word "Zach" and associates it with scraps of lunch meat. I try to call him, but I have too weak a signal out this far. I'll call him when I get back to the office.

This portion of our park borders the massive lake and is no joke. Between sudden elevation changes and the erosive nature of the sandy soil, they're advanced hikes not for the faint of heart. But, for those that do venture out, they're breathtakingly scenic.

Along the way, dragging the reluctant dog behind me, I find a fallen tree that needs moving, as well as a patch of poison ivy that's creeping too close to the trail for comfort. Looking in the rotting tree trunk blocking the trail, three rattlesnakes hibernate, cozily nestled in the wet, decaying wood. They'll be waking up from their winter slumber soon.

Our general philosophy is to disturb the forest ecosystem as little as possible. That being said, in order for people to enjoy the park safely, we keep trails clear of potentially dangerous plants and animals. I'm not prepared to do any of these projects on the spot, so I make a note in my small pocket journal to fix them later and continue on my way.

The rest of my hike this morning is absolutely lovely, even though it's cut short due to both Marty's cranky attitude and my lunch meeting with Kelly. Marty, not up for a quick pace today, takes every opportunity to stick his face in sticky mud puddles and dew-covered spiderwebs. Rationally, I know he's not trying to tick me off, but he's doing an excellent job of it regardless.

Traversing back to the office now with a stronger cell signal, I call Zach to give him the good news. He, being the hyper-organized person that he is, is even more excited to check off 'to-do' list items than I am.

"Heck yes!" he exclaims. "I'll come in ASAP. I assume I should be focusing on campsite preparations, yes? Is Jim's list still in the camp store?"

"You got it! Yes, the list still should be there. Thank you so much, Zach. You are the absolute best. I don't know what I'd do without you here! If Jim's cleared, he should be in later today, but as of now, let's operate as if you're a one-man show. Prioritize the essentials."

"On it! I'll call you if I need anything."

"Awesome, thank you! I'll be in the office for a couple more hours, but will be out this afternoon." We may be able to pull this off after all. "Oh, by the way, I came across that patch of poison ivy that we've been keeping an eye on out by the big dune today. It's finally crept close enough to treat."

"I'll add it to the list for the maintenance crew. Most aren't starting for a couple more weeks, but I can take the four-wheeler out soon and do some prep work."

"No no, the crew can handle it later. We have to stay focused on the campground this week. There's also a fallen tree out there that's blocking a trail. It'll take at least two people to move anyway. I saw a few Massasaugas hibernating in it; we should wait until they're up for the season to move it."

"Good deal, see you soon."

Walking through the office door, a few minutes before Kelly is set to arrive, I hop on my computer to learn more about Michael. Who was he? Who were his enemies? Who were his loved ones? All these important questions are current black boxes that need recovering.

Settling into my desk chair, I sigh deeply, bracing myself. I've been on a self-imposed social media boycott for the last year or so. When I was in high school and it was a new thing, I was all for it. Now, though, all that's on there are people feigning happiness and political garbage. I deleted most of my accounts post-Nate to resist the urge to keep tabs on how he's doing.

Zach, however, is a social media guru. He has been trying to convince me to start an Instagram account for the park. I've taken the decrepit old lady stance, that it's a waste of our very precious (extremely limited) time, but am slowly warming up to the idea.

Kelly walks in an hour later than planned, and I have scrolled through all of Michael's public accounts. In almost all his pictures, he's wearing flashy clothes and at least one shiny accessory that screams *'I have money!'* He seems to have been single for as far back as the accounts go, 2014. He has plenty of women in his photos, but none are consistent. My Italian Nonna would call someone like him a 'Casanova.'

Along with gorgeous women, which do not make me *at all* self-conscious, his Instagram is full of development projects. He bought commercial buildings and renovated them throughout Chicago. He looks to have been pretty successful, but also controversial. Many of his photos have dozens of negative comments condemning various projects he spearheaded.

There are pictures of him in a fancy sports car and on lavish vacations, even a few recent posts of him here in Stone's Throw. He was in town for at least a full week before he disappeared, based on the dates of the posts.

"Hi, Kell." I look up from my screen as she walks in the door, a dark purple tote bag with the Led Zeppelin logo in her hand. I get up and walk over to the cupboard to grab utensils and sit down on the couch as she drops the bag on the coffee table.

"Hi, Maudy." She opens it up and takes out a few Tupperware containers filled with a mixed green salad, cooked grains, and veggies. "I brought grain bowl fixings," she says with a smile.

"That sounds perfect, thank you." Marty ambles over, following his nose to the vegetables. I take a small piece of beet and hand it to him. Temporarily satisfied, he sits down at our feet, happy to be a part of the conversation (and not still outside hiking).

"So." I get down to it after emptying my bowl, leaning back into the couch cushion, and tucking my legs underneath me. "Can we talk about my theory?"

"Sure thing, let me grab my notebook. Sorry about last night. I went to bed like an hour before you called." She pulls it out of the tote bag along with a pen. "I was a little salty. But why don't you start from the beginning, and we go from there?"

I launch into what I've found and currently suspect: Michael was robbed. He wasn't wearing any glitzy jewelry that his social media is full of, and he was obviously wealthy. She nods along, jotting a couple of notes down as I speak. I tell her about the funky tire tracks I found near the body and show her the pictures I took of the rectangular imprints under the ground cover. After I finish, she looks up.

"Not bad, Giles," she smiles, referring to the brainy librarian from *Buffy the Vampire Slayer*, Rupert Giles.

She flips through her notebook and continues. "Okay, so what I *can* say is that the medical examiner has confirmed the blow to the head is the cause of death. The object that caused the wound had a skinny edge, was heavy, and blunt. It wasn't round like the boulder. The coroner suggested something like the thin edge of a laptop or even the handle of a shovel or something. If this were a game of Clue, we'd have it narrowed down to the lead pipe or the candlestick." I nod along, taking notes myself.

"He also said that Michael died sometime late Wednesday night or early Thursday morning." That tracks; I thought Michael had been dead a while when I found him. "I like your instincts with the robbery theory. His wallet and phone are still missing. They weren't on his person or in his room at The Nest. I hadn't really considered it myself; it seems drastic to kill someone and haul their body out into the woods days later for a simple mugging."

"Hmmm…" I ponder. That's an interesting point. Marty grumbles, either agreeing with me or wanting more bits of beet. From what I know of the man, I'd bet money that he's not just missing a wallet and phone. He had to have been wearing that flashy Sox watch, sunglasses, or something when he died. I need to follow the money and try to find all this stuff. *Mental note to check the town lost and found at the library.*

"I trust your gut, though, so I'll try to look into it more. While I do that, I could use your help with Nancy and Greg Finch. They let us search Michael's room without a warrant, but were pretty tight-lipped during questioning."

"Sure, I'll talk to them. Nancy likes me enough. I'll keep you posted on what they say."

"Thanks. She's never warmed up to me." She shrugs. "In the meantime, I'll go out there and try to ID those imprints you found in the mud."

Stone's Throw is such a small, tight-knit community. And even though Kelly grew up here, her role in law enforcement keeps her at arm's length from really being a part of the town. People like her okay, but she's not always the first one invited to parties, so to speak. Maybe this is why she brought me on, to try to get real, honest responses from people. So far, my nature expertise hasn't been super useful.

"No problem, I'm happy to talk with them, or anybody really. Just let me know."

"Will do. And while we're on the subject, I need you to steer clear of Jeremy Gray for now. While we're not formally calling anyone a suspect per se, he has the closest ties to Michael that we know of and could be dangerous. Leave him to me. Got it?"

"I will do my best," I diplomatically reply, leaving a little room for interpretation. There isn't a lot to go off of at this point, and like she said, Jeremy is the closest person to Michael that's here. She's already not giving me the full case file. So sue me for leaving this door open. *Maybe it wouldn't be the worst thing in the world to chat with him again... I can try to not have a panic attack next time.*

We wrap up, no big breakthroughs coming to either of us, and Kelly gets up to get back to work. I thank her for exonerating Zach once again, and we part ways.

With my marching orders in place, I decide to pay a visit to Greg and Nancy Finch this afternoon. No time like the present.

On my way out of the park, I swing by the campgrounds to check on Zach. His progress is slower than I had wanted. Only five of the forty sites are ready, and the camp store is where I left it. My hopes of a successful launch are dwindling. I wish I could spend the rest of my day out here with him, but if Michael's killer isn't caught, our campsite will for sure remain closed. This way, there's at least a sliver of a chance we'll be good to go. My time is best spent trying to figure this out. Hopefully, Jim can join Zach soon.

* * *

I know it's silly, but telling Marty that he can't come with me breaks my heart every single time I have to do it. The Nest has a strict 'No Dog' policy, and I drop him off at home. The little guy has gotten so used to coming to work with me every day that he sulks like a stubborn child when he has to stay home alone.

In response to the news, he grabs a plastic squeaky toy shaped like a bone straight out of *The Flintstones* and hops up on the couch, giving me plenty of sassy grumbles, side eye, and spiteful squeaks as I go out the front door. "How about a beach walk tonight? Fair trade for not chewing on any of the table legs?" That seems to shut him up. His head perks up and tilts to the side, which I take as a legally binding contract.

It is around two p.m. by the time I walk into The Nest. Having been there just a few days prior, I see surprise, and concern, slowly spread over Nancy's face as I walk in. I'm in Pop's at least twice a week, but The Nest? Not so much. The grandmotherly woman is wearing a festive spring sweater covered in embroidered tulips, her wiry, silver-gray hair pulled back into a low ponytail. She is standing behind the check-in desk in the main room of the Inn. The dining room, where Nellie, the girls, and I had tea last week, is off to the right. A grand staircase separates the two rooms, leading up to ten or so guest suites.

Greg and Nancy Finch have owned the Stone's Throw staple since 2000 and have done a great job maintaining the historic charm. The building is flamboyant with bright, ostentatious wallpaper and eccentric antique furniture. In the summertime, massive blue hydrangeas line the front porch and adorn the dining room tables in eclectic vases.

In the face of companies like Airbnb, The Nest has gone down a bit of a decline. Trying to get business back, Nancy keeps launching more and more events geared at us locals, like breakfast and tea, hoping we will stop in and make up for their shrinking overnight guest income. Nellie seems to have been right, Michael's disappearance, and now death, has put an even bigger dent in their business. Besides Nancy behind the front desk, the place is a ghost town.

"Well, hey there, dear. How are you today?" She doesn't look up from whatever is on her computer screen.

"Hi, Nancy, I'm doing well, how are you?"

"Just fine, just fine. Greg ran out grocery shopping, so I'm holding down the fort myself." She flexes her arm and squeezes her bicep like Rosie the Riveter. Nancy may be on in years, but she is in fantastic shape. She attends some of the beach yoga classes that Anna teaches in the summertime.

I laugh, "That's great to hear, Nancy. Do you have a moment or two to chat with me by chance? If not, I can come back later."

"Sure thing, hon. Why don't you get situated by the fire, and I'll get us some coffee and meet you in there? I'm wrapping up a couple things," she points to the monitor in front of her and a messy desk full of room keys and papers, "and I'll be right in."

"Sounds great." I was secretly hoping she'd offer a cup of coffee. I'm running on empty.

I have the entire dining room to myself, so I take a seat in a large, upholstered wingback chair next to the fireplace, intentionally on the opposite side of the room from the cuckoo clock. There are a couple of other comfy chairs in the space, but most of the room is filled with four to six-person tables. All in all, maybe fifty people can fit comfortably.

In less than five minutes, Nancy is seated across from me in an identical chair. Both of us with a mug of strong (burnt) coffee in our hands, I begin.

"So." I grip my mug tightly. "I know Michael was staying here before he disappeared. That couldn't have been easy for you..." I trail off, realizing this blunt opening may come off as insensitive. "I'm sorry you all have gotten tied up in this, Nancy." I tap the seconds on the ceramic mug, trying to keep the swell of nerves at bay.

"You're not wrong, it hasn't been easy these last couple of days. Other guests checked out early after they heard the news. Did Kelly and her team rope you in?" She sounds almost sorry for me. Or maybe it's condescension that I'm hearing. "Poor dear."

"Yes, since the bod—Michael was found in the park they thought my perspective might be helpful." *You're an authority, Maudy! Don't let her talk down to you.* I straighten up in my chair, attempting to give off an air of confidence that I don't have.

"Well, that makes good sense. You're a smart young cookie, I hope you all can bring whoever did this to justice." She takes another sip of coffee, the crow's feet around her eyes march towards her temples as she smiles over the rim of her cup.

"Nancy, is there anything you remember about Michael? Something that stood out while he was here, or something odd about his reservation?"

She pauses for a second, staring off into the dancing fire before responding. "No…not really. His business partner, Jeremy, was the one who made the reservation. I didn't have Michael's name until he showed up, and it didn't ring any bells. Michael was staying here for a week or so before he disappeared. Jeremy had rented an additional room for himself a couple of times during Michael's stay, but wasn't staying here regularly."

That confirms what Jeremy told me yesterday.

She continues, "They had lots of meetings here." She points to a cozy, two-person table in the corner of the dining room. "It was always just the two of them over stacks of papers and their computers. They would go out for a while and asked that I keep that table vacant for them. Which I did. Sometimes they left their stuff here while they went for a walk. It's not like we're ever full these days, so it didn't hurt anything." Sorrow underscores her voice.

"Did you overhear any of their conversations? Do you know what business they were in?"

"Not really…" She fidgets in her seat and tightens her ponytail. She's lying. Her cheeks flush, and her eyes slide away as I ask the question. "Just lots of talking about numbers and money. I don't have much of a mind for that stuff. Gregory handles our books here. When I didn't see either man down for breakfast on Friday, I knocked on Michael's suite door, which is general protocol for us innkeepers if we don't see a guest for over twenty-four hours. When I didn't get an answer, I called the police. I last saw Michael come down from his room early Thursday morning."

"Okay, that's helpful." I offer a little smile, but it comes out more like a cringe. "Were you and Greg both here all Wednesday night?"

"Yes, I told Kelly this yesterday. It's just like her to not keep you informed and inconvenience a poor old woman by having to repeat herself." She seems put off, but I can't help but agree with her. If only Kelly would share relevant information with me, I wouldn't have to start from scratch and rile this lady up.

"I picked up a carryout order from Pop's for dinner. Neither Greg nor I felt like cooking, and Eli's spaghetti is so darn tasty," she continues. "Besides that, we stayed here at the Inn. A couple of our guests were also here and can confirm that. I gave their contact information to Kelly." She seems to be working herself up as she goes on, now visibly upset.

"What exact time was that?"

"Was what?"

"When you went to Pop's. What time, exactly, was that?" I press her harder.

"Oh, well. I guess I don't know. We usually eat around six, so I'd guess around then?"

"I don't mean to be accusatory. We all just want to do right by Michael."

"I know, I know, hon. I'm sorry. This is all too much, I'm afraid we're going to lose what little customer base we have and be forced to shut our doors for good."

"Well, I'll do my best to make sure that doesn't happen. Tell me more about the papers they left on the table." I gesture to the table in the front window. "Or about what you heard them talking about? You're a great hostess, Nancy; I imagine you filled up their coffee cups now and then and may have overheard something?"

She is wiping the palms of her hands on her dark-wash jeans. "Look, missy. The only person Michael talked to was Jeremy. You should be pestering him, not me."

She gets up from her chair, huffs, and walks out of the room. I'll come back to talk to her again. She needs time to calm down. I'm not going to get anything else useful out of her right now, and I want to boogie over to the library this afternoon anyway.

I wonder what it was she overheard that struck such a raw nerve with her...

Chapter Eight

"*Merda*!" Swear words in Italian are so much more dignified than their English counterparts. I mutter to myself after I walk back outside, equally defeated and intrigued by my weird interaction with Nancy. Did I press her too hard? She was obviously lying! While simmering over my approach, I look down the street towards Nellie's house and remember that I've forgotten to drop off my friends' camping invitations. I fully acknowledge the chances of us camping this weekend are slim to none, but if I don't hang on to that potential glimmer of fun, I may lose it altogether.

I gently knock on the door of Nellie's warm gray-sided home just a couple of blocks away. Nellie's wife Emma loves to garden. She manages the greenhouse and outdoor department of the local hardware store, and her personal flower beds are reemerging after a long, frozen winter. I can see the almost-blooms of what will soon be bright yellow daffodils lining the paved path to their front door. Walking past them, hopeful beacons of the changing seasons, I scamper up their front steps.

After a couple unanswered knocks and neighborly '*helloooos*,' I drop the invite through the mail slot and text her that a fun surprise is waiting at home.

"Well, no time like the present. It's in the general direction of the library anyway." I'm due (like a few of my books) for a visit to the Stone's Throw Public Library, where our town lost and found box lives.

The library is on the farthest block of the downtown area from the beach. The block isn't quite as cute and touristy as the rest, but has a lot of the services important to people who live here year-round. Our police station, small community center, the library, and a post office built into the side of a small general store are all here.

Unlike the hustle and bustle of the other side of downtown, the library is serene and quiet. It's a lovely space that takes up the entire first level of the large brick building. Our community center occupies the second floor. A few big grants and private donations have gone a long way in making the hundred-year-old building warm and inviting. The space is colorful, easy to navigate, and full of local history.

For most of my life, I had always preferred buying books to checking them out from a library. I liked making notes in the margins and highlighting phrases that I enjoyed. When I moved here, I ended up donating most of my books, knowing my space would be much smaller than Nate's and my three-bedroom house. In that transition, I discovered how lovely this library is and have become a frequent user.

I still have a sizable bookcase where my most treasured stories live, a few of them are early editions and pretty valuable. Overall, though, I'm a full-on library convert and evangelize the benefits of libraries to anyone who'll listen.

Walking through the doors, the familiar, papery vanilla smell of old books and Matthew's cologne seeping into my pores, I survey the smaller rooms that offshoot from the main area searching for the librarian. "Hello? Anybody home?" I quietly ask, peeking my head around tall bookcases and a row of computers.

"Down here!" Matthew pops up from underneath the circulation desk, a half-moon-shaped structure smack dab in the middle of the room. He is in his mid-fifties and used to be an English teacher. He took over as librarian not long before I moved here.

He's holding a screwdriver and has thick glasses on, maybe doing a bit of work on his desk chair or something. I never know with him.

"Hey, Matthew. How are you today?"

"Ms. Lorso, I'm doing well. I imagine better than you are based on the news that has been circulating lately. Here for a bit of escapism? We got a new batch of thriller novels, maybe that'll distract you from the thriller your life has turned into, eh?" He smiles. Matthew is a sweet and kind man who loves books more than people but has a savage sense of humor.

"Ha, maybe later. Keep your favorite one on hold for me, and I'll swing by sometime to grab it. Can I ask you a weird question?"

"Ms. Lorso, I'm a librarian. It's literally in the job description. What can I do for you?" He grins and leans forward, glasses slipping down on his nose.

"Can I look through the lost and found box, please?" I plaster on a smile.

"What exactly are you hoping to find? I can tell you if anything that meets your description has been found, but I can't permit you to rummage through everything. Rules are rules." He makes a little *tsk-tsk* sound with his mouth as if to say, *'You know better than that.'*

"Ugh, fine. I'm looking for a wallet, a watch, and any sort of chunky male jewelry. Like a chain, maybe some fancy sunglasses, rings, anything like that."

"Hmm, let me see. One moment!" He ducks back under the desk, and I can hear him digging around for my requested items. It sounds like there are some children's toys squeaking and spare change clanging. "What color is the wallet?"

"Uh, I actually don't know. It's not my wallet..."

"Dear, you know as well as I do that I can't simply hand over someone else's wallet."

"Ugh, Matthew! If you have a wallet, could you at least tell me if

Michael Price's ID is inside? It's missing, but you didn't hear that from me." I hold my index finger up to my lips. He peers up at me, the angle of his glasses magnifying his eyes to comical proportions.

"Let me check." He bends back over to rummage through the box again.

"No Michael Price ID cards in here. My deepest sympathies, Ms. Lorso."

"Ugh, thanks, Matthew. Keep an eye out for it, will you?"

"You have my word. And don't forget about that thriller. Of course, I'd need you to actually return a book for once before I can lend you a new one, so whenever you get a chance, please give back what you've already borrowed. Oh, and if you see Eli, tell him we got in that new puzzle book he requested. It's ready for him whenever he wants to come get it."

I turn and wave as I walk back out the front doors, choosing to ignore the snarky overdue book comment. Where could this wallet be?

* * *

Anna's surf shop is as close to the beach on Main Street as physically possible without actually being on the sand. A small road separates the two, with a parking lot for beachgoers. A wooden sign shaped and painted like a surfboard hangs above the entranceway and swings in the blustery wind coming off the icy water.

A pleasant bell jingles as I walk through the door. The surf shop is hands down the coolest store in town. They cater to all types of water sports enthusiasts, like SUP boarders, kayakers, surfers, and boogie boards for the kids. You can rent equipment for the day, take lessons, and even buy cool t-shirts and sweatshirts with designs inspired by Lake Michigan.

When I first moved here, I bought my lime green kayak from this store, and have since been a regular customer for clothing, outdoor gear, and nature-themed stickers that cover my thermos.

Anna is unloading a box of life jackets and hanging them up on hooks in the back storage room as I walk through the door. I hear her call out, "Be right with you!" Poking my head back to say hi, she ushers me in.

"Maudy! Hey, hey." She turns down the podcast blaring from her phone. Her hair is in a long, blonde ponytail, and she's wearing a Billabong mesh trucker hat and teal puffy vest. "You know, I've been thinking about holding a water safety course next month, and I was wondering if you could give the Park Ranger safety speech to our participants."

"Sure thing, I'll bring the kayak. We can train them on rescues."

"Sweet! I'll text you a few dates, we can do whatever one works best for you."

"Perfect. Also, I have a surprise for you," I sing, waving the invite in my hands. I can't help it; a toothy smile sprouts across my face as I hand her the decorative letter. She opens it slowly, eyeing me with curiosity. After she reads the note, an equally goofy smile sprouts over hers, too.

"Oh. My. God. This will be so fun!" She pauses for a moment, her smile falling. "Actually, I'm not sure I can make it. I'm supposed to be here super early on Saturday to prep for a few private lessons we have booked. Aw, shoot!"

"No, you don't! I took care of everything. Your cousin is taking the shift for you. You may owe her, though," I say, very pleased with my planning skills.

"No way!?" She squeals. "Okay, I'll get everything packed up. Eeeek, I can't wait!"

"Just keep your fingers crossed that we can solve Michael's case beforehand. If not, the park will still be closed, and we'll have to cancel."

"Yeah, totally. Solving a murder? Piece of cake." She winks. "After how this weekend went, I figured Kelly would pull you in."

"Yep, she thought my nerdy nature knowledge could help."

"Good. Between the two of you, I'm sure you'll crack the case." She smiles, leaning over to hug me. "You talked to that other business guy, right? The one in our search party?"

"Jeremy Gray. Briefly, why do you ask?"

"When you ran after Marty and the rest of us were hanging out, waiting for you, he seemed really put out by the whole thing. He kept complaining. Can you imagine? I was like, 'Dude, your friend could be dead right now and you're complaining about being outside?' It seemed weird."

"I mean, yeah, that is a little strange, but people grieve in different ways. He might've been super anxious and worried to pieces on the inside. Sometimes emotions spill out oddly."

As the queen of oddly spilling emotions, I'm not one to judge on this front. That being said, I do think Jeremy is hiding something, but it wouldn't be professional to tell her that. Plus, I'm not totally sure it's relevant. I decide to keep that nugget of information to myself for now.

"Great point, and yeah, I guess I agree. I remember when my uncle died last year. It was a real rollercoaster and still is sometimes. It's just that after that huge fight they got into, I feel like something's *off* about that guy. I think you need to take a look at him." She keeps unloading life jackets as if she didn't drop an info bomb on me.

"What fight?" Eli told me they were being loud, and he kicked them out, but he didn't say anything about a fight. He made it seem like they were happy drunk, like how old friends can get, reminiscing. Not angry drunk.

"Weren't you there? Michael and Jeremy got into a huge fight outside of Pop's on Wednesday night."

"I skipped out on spaghetti night last week, I was exhausted after work and went to bed early," I say, bewildered. "What the hell happened?"

"The two were talking heatedly to one another outside after Eli kicked them out. They were drinking with one other guy, but Eli let him stay, I guess. Anyway, they didn't like, punch each other or anything, at least not that I saw. But they were majorly pissed off. It sounded really charged, like they had a personal beef. Michael stormed off this way, towards the beach. I walked right past them on my way out. Maybe like nine-thirty or so." *Merda. This isn't looking good for Jeremy.*

"Anna, you are more helpful than you know. If I don't catch you beforehand, I'll see you Friday for our campout." I help her finish unloading the rest of the life vests and power walk towards Peyton's bakery, a block away.

The bakery is packed as per usual, filled with people getting a loaf of bread or rolls for dinner. If I could, I would wear the smell of her bakery as a perfume. It's even better than the woods after a rainstorm. I patiently stand in line, waiting for my turn to snag a sugary pick-me-up and give her the invite.

"Hey, how are ya?" I peruse the glass counter, hoping there are cinnamon rolls left over from this morning.

"Oh, it goes, all right. Quite a busy day! Here." She hands me a warm cinnamon roll from behind the counter, knowing me all too well. Her dark red hair is thrown in a curly bun, the knot of a blue bandana adding to an *I Love Lucy* vibe.

"Thank you, you're amazing. I owe you one." I open the white, waxy bag and savor the cinnamon aroma.

"Just doing my job! Hey, great work on Friday, partner. You and I cleaned house."

"You were the one who killed it. That loner hand? Incredible work."

We both laugh and think back to our last card game.

"I gotta get back to it, but I'll catch you later?"

"Definitely. But first." I hand her the invitation.

"What's this?"

"Open it when you get home and have a second. Call me later." I wink and walk off, cinnamon roll in hand.

Chapter Nine

As if by fate, I bump into Jeremy on the street, literally colliding with him after a few more hours of popping into downtown businesses, asking anyone if they saw Michael around town Wednesday night or Thursday morning. Annoyed and frustrated, with headphones in to drown out the incessant self-pity party raging in my head, I walk right into the man. He is staring at his phone and runs right into me, too.

"Just the man I'm looking for." I can't help but smile, shaking off the jostle. *I told Kelly that I'd 'do my best' to avoid Jeremy. I can't help it if my best happens to be crappy.*

"What? Oh, hi, Maudy." He returns to his screen for a moment before putting it into his back pocket and politely smiles at me. "Sorry about that. A few urgent work emails." He's being short; I think he's still a little sour from our last conversation. Time to butter him up.

"Do you have a sec?" I gesture towards Pop's, which is a couple buildings down from where we're standing. "I imagine you and I could both use a drink right about now, and I owe you one after our last conversation." *Is this too obvious? Will he see right through me? I need to figure out what they were arguing about the night Michael died. Who am I kidding? He's a guy. He's distracted. This could work.*

Looking at his watch, which is not nearly as fancy as Michael's, he hesitantly agrees, and we walk through the door.

Eli is behind the bar. It's a little early to serve dinner, and late enough to have everything prepped and ready to go. There's a smattering of folks sipping drinks, and a group playing pool, but otherwise, the place is empty. As Jeremy and I walk in, I smile and wave at my friend. Eli looks right at us and nods in recognition, before turning abruptly to talk with a man sitting on a nearby stool, minding his own business. It's like he's looking for an excuse not to make eye contact with me. Definitely not the warm welcome he and I usually give one another. *That's weird.*

I shake it off, focusing on the discussion at hand, trying to not work myself up too much. This could be a difficult conversation; I'm glad we are in public. We settle into a booth on the right side of the room and take off our jackets.

"I can grab us drinks; what'll you have?"

"I owe you a drink, remember? Please, let me." I retort.

"No, no. I insist." He's already standing up.

"Well, in that case, I'll have a hard cider, please. If they're out, I'll take the hazy IPA," I reply politely, taking off my jacket.

"Coming right up." He smiles and walks to the bar.

Trying to keep myself calm, I watch him order while tapping my sweaty palms on my jeans. "One, two, three, four," I whisper to myself.

I'm too far away to hear what the men are saying, but their body language and the few snippets I can make out are enough to get the gist. Eli squares his shoulders and crosses his arms over his chest. I hear him loudly say, "You have the nerve!" After that, a bunch of gobbledygook, and then, "And now with her!"

The guy sitting at the bar turns towards Jeremy in recognition, presumably taken a little aback by the display of annoying masculinity. It's Lucas, the man I bumped into on the trails last weekend, enjoying a drink by himself. Even from over here, I clock a massive tattoo on his forearm, his flannel sleeves pushed up past his elbows. I can't make it out, but it looks like a bunch of flowers in black and gray ink. It's quite stunning.

I'm not surprised Eli isn't welcoming Jeremy back with open arms since he had to kick the man out last week, but what do I have to do with it? Presuming I'm the "her" he's referring to. Maybe Eli knows Jeremy from his time in culinary school, which is close to Traverse City? Something is weird here. *Mental note to ask Eli more about Jeremy.*

Sitting back at the table, him with whisky and me with cider, he looks me directly in the eye. "What do you want to know?" He states more than asks, taking a sip without breaking eye contact. It's not threatening or intimidating, more along the lines of curious. As cautious as I am of this man, anyone could drown in those golden eyes and die a blissfully happy death.

"Well." I sigh, taking a sip myself to buy some time and gather my thoughts. I remember from some police training that I sat in on that mirroring body language makes people more comfortable. I try to use that tidbit now. "I know you left out a key bit of info when we last chatted. You made that uh…clear. I need to know what happened." I hope he doesn't notice the shake in my voice or the blush on my face.

Eli is angrily washing pint glasses. I glance over, hoping he'll give me a smile and a little moral support. Instead, he meets my eye but looks sad or confused or something, I can't quite pinpoint it. I return my attention to Jeremy and lean back in the booth. Again, mirroring his body language.

He sets down his drink. "You're right. You're lucky you're cute." He smiles and clinks the rim of his glass against mine. *Ugh, cheesy.* "Michael and I did have a…disagreement Wednesday night." He is searching for something. I don't know if it's my intentions, my trustworthiness, or what. But after a long pause, he continues. "I didn't lie to you. Michael and I work together, just not in the way you probably think. He hired me as his real estate agent for this area. I own an agency based in

Traverse City."

"He was interested in expanding his development business outside of Chicago," I say slowly.

"Yes, well, sort of. He was specifically interested in Stone's Throw, but not any of the surrounding towns. I tried to get him to look in a few other places that have better market value right now, no offense, but he wouldn't listen. He came up here to purchase commercial property."

I can tell Jeremy is feeling a little better, getting that off his chest, the formality in his tone wanes, and his shoulders relax. "We were visiting potential opportunities and putting together a few proposals. He was planning on calling his finance team back in Chicago over the weekend and making formal offers today."

"So, what were you two fighting about the other night?"

"'Fighting' is a strong word." He pauses, and a barely perceptible terseness washes over his face. "Over drinks here on Wednesday, he told me that he'd need to cut my commission percentage on the property transactions. I told him that he legally couldn't do that, we had a deal in writing with standard rates outlined. The conversation escalated, and we both got upset."

"And he stormed off," I prod, tapping my nails against my pint glass absentmindedly.

"Yes, he headed towards the beach. He said he needed to blow off some steam, and he'd be in touch. I drank more than I should've that night, so I rented a room at The Nest. I told you that already. I didn't want to drive the forty minutes back home. That night was the last time I saw him. I checked out early on Thursday to get home for a couple of other client meetings back in town, and that was it.

"Nancy called me early Friday morning to see if I'd seen Michael, and for a relative or close friend's contact information to check in on him. She noticed he hadn't been back in a while. When I said that I hadn't seen him, she called the police and reported him missing." He shifts uncomfortably in his seat and picks at his fingernails like he did the other night. *Is he still lying to me?*

"Got it." I pause for a moment to think this through, not completely buying it. "If you were to venture a guess on what happened…" I fade out the sentence unfinished, raising an eyebrow.

"Have you talked to that absolute witch of a Chamber of Commerce lady yet?" He downs the rest of his drink in one, long swig.

"Who? Charlotte Roth?" I'm not exactly sure where he is going, but agree with his judgment of her character.

"Yes, that's her!" He's getting animated, clapping his hands on the tabletop. Maybe this isn't his first drink of the day. "She was throwing a hissy fit that Michael, an 'out-of-towner,'" the last words he puts in air quotes, "was coming in and 'scooping up businesses' out from under locals. The man hadn't even put in an offer anywhere, I don't know how she knew, but she was *livid*.

"It was a long shot anyway. Michael didn't care whether or not a business was actually for sale; his strategy was to send offers and see if the owners would bite."

"So, did Charlotte confront you guys? What happened? You were looking at properties in secret?"

"Yes, he didn't want to tip anyone off that he might be interested before he sent them a formal offer. I pulled their sales history and tax info, and we would scope them out. Charlotte never said anything directly, but she left a letter with Nancy at the front desk, who passed it along to me. I still have it if you want to see it. It's in my office back in Traverse City, but I can have a copy emailed over."

"That'd be great, thanks. Did you happen to tell Kelly any of this?"

He shakes his head, "No. I, uh, left it out of our conversations so far. If you can keep this between us, I had run-ins with the law when I was a kid. That's all decades in the past, but ever since, I've never been a fan of our legal system." He sighs, "I'm glad the cat's out of the bag, though.

It's not like we were doing anything illegal, I just thought it might hurt my chances of doing future business here if word got out that I was sneaking around with a bigwig developer. Real estate is such a people business. If my name sours, I'm done for."

"I get it." I nod my head, thankful for my fairly solitary profession. The most judgment I get is from the crows on what I bring for lunch. "Does Kelly know about your, uh, previous history?"

"Of course she does. It's all on my record. She came to me immediately after his body was found and pressed me pretty hard." He hangs his head while I metaphorically scratch mine. *Kelly didn't think this was important enough to tell me? I'm wasting so much time finding out things she already knows. This is probably why she told me to avoid him.*

"Are you going to the memorial thing for him tomorrow?" A bit of disdain slips out in his tone. It's not for me but for the event.

"This is the first time I'm hearing of it." I sip. "When and where?"

"Tomorrow at the beach, I think. It's still being organized; Nancy Finch is leading the charge. She's trying to recover from a tarnished image with one of her boarders being murdered and all." The accompanying eye roll says that effort is more of a marketing ploy than a true effort of goodwill.

"Nancy doesn't mean any harm; she feels guilty, I think, and wants to try to keep the Inn up and running. I don't blame her for trying. Keep me posted as details get worked out? I'd like to go," I reply.

"Sure, what's your phone number? I'll text you the info. Nancy wants me to give a speech," again, another eye roll.

I squint, hopefully looking playfully skeptical, and take his phone.

"This is for Michael-related conversation, only," I say, handing his phone back to him.

He laughs and grips my hand ever-so-slightly longer than what's needed, giving me a sheepishly charming grin. *What are male sirens called in Greek mythology? Are they a thing? That must be a thing.*

"Well, thanks for everything, including this drink," I say, anxiously pulling my hand away to raise my nearly empty pint glass. "I'm glad you told me all of this." We say our goodbyes, and he walks through the door into the afternoon while I wander over to the bar, going our separate ways.

Eli awkwardly darts into the kitchen. *Ugh, men. What's his deal?*

"Hi, Lucas, how are you doing?" I ask, taking a seat two stools over. He sips on a half-full pint.

"Park Ranger! Hi, I'm doing well. How bad can a day be with a good beer in your hand?" He smiles and sets the glass down.

"Sorry the park is closed down for a while. Hopefully, we'll be up and running again soon for you to get out on some of those hikes."

"Oh, no worries. I heard what's going on. I was in your co-worker's search party group. You're still wrapped up in that, eh?"

"Yep. I'm helping the police out since Michael's body was found in the park." I crane my neck over the bar, looking for Eli. He's still hiding in the kitchen. "Have you seen or heard anything while you've been in town? Anything that might be useful?"

"Hmmm. I don't think so. I've been hanging out in here a lot, like always. Fishing on the river. You know, the usual." He takes another sip.

"Did you see Michael at all? Do you remember him?"

"One or two nights in here around dinner time. He was causing quite a scene, and the bartender kicked him out. But otherwise, no, I don't think so."

"Okie doke, well, thanks anyways. Enjoy the rest of your time here." I get up to leave and sarcastically shout to Eli in the back, "See you later, Eli! You can't hide back there forever!"

As I'm walking out the door, I get a text. *This is Jeremy- Don't be a stranger. For official use only, of course. ;)*

My eyeballs roll so hard they almost pop out of my head and down the sidewalk, but a small smile ekes out as well.

That's future-Maudy problems. Let's think about what we just learned. Jeremy has a record and was seen arguing with a man who died not long after. He claims it's about money, but does that track? Anna said it seemed personal. Two savvy businessmen surely wouldn't get in a drunken shouting match over money, would they? Don't they fight their fights with lawyers in boardrooms?

On the other hand, it isn't a secret that Charlotte and I have our differences. She's like a bureaucratic mama bear protecting her cub. Do I actually think she would commit murder to preserve the small-town charm of Stone's Throw?

Yeah. I honestly do.

Chapter Ten

Cranking the shower up to molten lava, I undress and take a seat in the tub. I lean forward, letting the hot water splash over my confused, gooey head from above. Marty sits right on my navy shag bathmat, chomping away on a peanut butter-flavored treat.

"Whatcha think, Martin? Did Charlotte do it? Or maybe Jeremy?" Doggie contempt stares me down, not enthused to be interrupted from his very important business.

"I know I'm biased, but Charlotte as the killer makes a lot of sense. She grew up here, and as little as she may use the trails now, I'd bet she is familiar with the layout of the state park. I know she cares more than anything about the economic development of Stone's Throw, and maintaining our quaint small-town charm is her self-inflicted life's mission. When Jeremy told me that she wrote a scathing note, that tracks with what I know about her. What do you think? You hate her, too. Remember that one time she stepped on your tail?"

The dog looks back at me, licking incessantly with a face covered in peanut butter.

"Should we be worried that she'll skip town? Nah, she'd rather die here and get caught than voluntarily leave this place." Marty offers a grumble of agreement. "Will she hurt anyone else? Do you think she'll go after Jeremy?" The dog stares back at me, growing tired of this conversation. "You're right. The threat is gone. She'd have no reason to go after him. Good deducing, puppy."

After a long soak, I reluctantly emerge a wrinkled raisin of a woman.

My mind still races, and Marty has been cooped up longer than he (and my furniture) likes, so we spend the evening scrambling to get a couple more campsites ready for Friday.

Confronting Charlotte can wait until tomorrow. A few hours chopping firewood and cleaning grills is a good way to stop myself from stewing in my own thoughts and Marty's peanut butter breath. Counting seconds isn't cutting it. I need to count campsites.

* * *

The next morning, as I savor my nectar of the gods (coffee), questions bubble up. If Charlotte did it, how did she find out about Michael's intention to buy up businesses? Why would she rob him? Not all the puzzle pieces are in place, but it is the best lead I have.

Putting on one of my favorite sweaters, a slouchy, sky-blue cashmere number, I sit down on the couch for a moment to give Marty some love before leaving for the day. He scans my outfit, immediately realizes that today's not a normal workday, and presents his cutest '*please don't leave me here!*' look.

"How'd you sleep, dude? Have any big plans for the day? Curing cancer? Brokering world peace?" He scruffs, licks my hand, and flops over on his back, pleading for belly scratches. I'm mid-scratch when Kelly's name lights up my phone screen.

"Hey, Kelly, what's up?"

"Maudy, glad I caught you. I have two things to say. One, how dare you talk to Jeremy yesterday, after I deliberately told you to stay away from him? You put yourself in danger. Hell, you put me in danger! My boss would tar and feather me if I had a citizen consultant get hurt under my watch. Knock it off." Before I have a chance to plead my case, she keeps going.

"And two, interestingly, forensics found a partial fingerprint and a few hair strands on Michael's clothes. I just heard from them and wanted to pass that on to you. I'm running it through the system now to see if we get any hits; nothing yet. They didn't find anything else helpful." I can tell she is in a hurry, probably knee-deep in a mountain of paperwork.

She's the one putting me in that position by not divulging key information, making my life harder than it needs to be. She's the one jeopardizing *my* job. She wants me to be worried that I'm jeopardizing hers? Whatever. It's not worth the energy to try to explain this all to her.

"That's great, Kelly, and I'm sorry for talking to him, but we bumped into one another on the street and-"

"Yeah, it's better than nothing. Hopefully, we'll get a match soon. Also, Jim isn't cleared yet. I'm having trouble confirming his alibi."

"You don't think Jim could've done this..." That silly, old man could never murder someone. The idea is more ridiculous than accusing Bigfoot.

"Hey, I go where the evidence takes me. My gut agrees, Jim is a sweetie pie. Between you and me, no, I'm not considering him a real suspect at this point."

"Good. There's no way. But you know who it could've been? Charlotte Roth."

"Explain."

"Well, when I coincidentally bumped into Jeremy on the street, he told me that she wrote Michael a nasty note, telling them to stay away from Stone's Throw. She wants to keep the 'mom and pop' feel of the town and doesn't want a big city developer buying up local businesses."

"Interesting..."

"Yeah. My thoughts exactly. I'm going to go talk to her this mor-"

"No, you will not. Let me look into it. I can't have you accusing people of murder without an actual officer investigating. I have to get back to it. Talk soon, Maudy. And please, for the love of god, be safe!"

"Okay, Kell." I hang up the phone and return to my four-legged friend.

"Well, Marty, we have a print. Maybe we'll get lucky and close this thing soon." He looks at me, head upside down with a skeptical expression on his face, probably mimicking my own. "Hey, you never know." I force a smile as a few tears well in the corners of my eyes, my job security wavering before me, as I continue to scratch the fuzzy pink belly.

"Ready to go confront a murderer?"

* * *

What Kelly doesn't know won't hurt her, right? The sooner I get the intel that pins Charlotte to Michael's death, the sooner I can return my attention to job-saving park duties. Kelly's busy and focused on other aspects of the case (I assume, since she won't tell me anything outright), so I'm taking it upon myself. The clock is ticking, and I have a literal forest-sized workload to attend to.

Nobody can get *too* upset with someone who brings over food, so I settle on using breakfast as an opportunity to talk with (sneakily interrogate) Charlotte. If I have to have an awkward conversation, I might as well do it over a bacon, egg, and cheese and one of Tracy's lattes.

I pick up two bagel sandwiches and amaretto lattes from Java Jones and make the short walk over to Charlotte's art gallery. Her role as Chamber of Commerce Chair is in a voluntary capacity. Her day job is as the manager of a small gallery and artist co-op in town, full of local art for sale. She also serves with Kevin Nett and others on the Stone's Throw Village Council.

I figure that she will be at work early this week in preparation for the holiday weekend, like under other circumstances, I would be in the park. The gallery is situated close to the water, not far from Anna's surf shop.

A low tone beeps as I walk through the gallery's glass door. The lights are on, and the white, clean space is devoid of people except for Charlotte, who is framing a few oil paintings that are leaning against the front counter. She has soft, benign piano music playing in the background.

"Welcome t—" she stops when she sees me. "Oh, hello, Maude. How nice of you to pop in. Was there something I could help you with? A piece to spruce up your *cozy* home, by chance?" By 'cozy,' she means 'small.' I let it slide, not ashamed of my modest house.

"Hi, Charlotte, I know how hard you've been working for the town to get ready for the huge tourist season we're about to have." *Jeez, could I lay it on any thicker? I guess it can't hurt.* "I thought you could use a little sustenance." I place the take-out bag and coffees on the counter, intentionally far away from the paintings. I can't afford a refrigerator magnet from the place, let alone a gigantic oil painting.

She is visibly taken aback by this gesture and clearly suspicious of my intentions. In no universe do we have a relationship where this is normal. "Well, thank you, Maude. It's always nice to have hard work recognized. I'll grab us a couple of plates from the back, one moment."

She turns back into an Employees Only section of the gallery and emerges with ceramic plates and cloth napkins. Intrigue is still plastered all over her face.

"Cut the bull, Maudy. What's this about?" She smirks, speaking more with interest than accusation. We unwrap our sandwiches and dig in. I've never paired a breakfast sandwich with a cloth napkin before.

"What? Can't a girl bring over a bite to eat and just say, 'hi'?"

"A girl? Yes. You? No." Her smile widens, eyeing me carefully. "This isn't poisoned, is it? Some mushroom from the woods, or poison ivy leaves masquerading as greens?" she laughs.

"No, of course it's not poisoned," I laugh along with her and throw my hands up, feigning exasperation. "You caught me. I need your help. I hate admitting it, but I do." If she thinks that I came to her for advice, maybe she'll be more amenable to talking. I want to get through this entire conversation without her realizing she's on my suspect list. The last thing I need is for her to make a big stink about this, riling up media outlets and townies even more.

"Well, why didn't you say so? Of course. How can I be of assistance? Does this have to do with that tourist that was found in the park? The whole thing is absolutely dreadful."

"Yep, sure is," I say, nodding with a mouth full of melty cheese and bacon, counting the number of chews between bites. "You're so involved with the town and seem to know everyone! Any ideas on what happened?" I hate sucking up this much, especially to Charlotte. But my Nonna always said, *Si prendono più mosche con una goccia di miele che con un barile di aceto,* or in English, *you catch more flies with honey than with vinegar.* Charlotte Roth is definitely a fly.

"What have you heard?" Suspicion oozes from her tone like the melted cheese from my sandwich.

She knows I know about the letter. Panic bubbles up from my gut, rising through my body. My face grows hot, and my hands go tingly. I place the plate down and jam my hands in my jean pockets, trying to hide the tapping. *She's not accusing you of anything yet. Just keep it together.* I haven't said anything for an eternity (exactly thirty-one seconds) and can't keep pretending like I'm chewing this same bite forever. I pull myself together and string a coherent sentence.

"I heard that Michael was interested in buying up and renovating commercial real estate. Have you heard anything about that?" *Tap, tap, tap. Tap, tap, tap.*

"Yes! You are spot on." She leans forward. "I have it on very good, *and confidential,* authority that he was trying to run the Finches out of business! I heard he was also interested in Java Jones, the pizza shop, and who knows what else." She points to the latte in front of her when she says 'Java Jones.' "Can you believe this man? Completely unrelated to this place, wanting to buy out businesses from underneath us? Absolutely not. Not on my watch. Ugh, the nerve! We have plenty of business-savvy folks right here, thank you very much. People who won't turn everything into a bank or a Chipotle."

She is getting worked up; she's still very passionate about the issue.

She's not fidgeting, she's maintaining good eye contact, and isn't nearly as flushed as I am. She's telling the truth. One thing doesn't make sense, though. Why would she be telling me all of this if she killed him? Wouldn't she try to throw me off or something? The woman has a motive. It's an incredibly dumb one, but I imagine people have killed for a lot less. Did she have the opportunity?

"Hey, one more thing. You're not a spaghetti dinner regular, right? I don't see you there very often. What were you up to last Wednesday night?" *Is this sneaky enough?* This might shoot up a red flag for her. I can't have this conversation getting back to Kelly.

"What I do every Wednesday night." She says simply, shrugging as she continues to frame the painting. "A few friends of mine play bar trivia in Traverse City. I was there all evening; I don't think I got back home until around one a.m."

My brows raise, surprised that she was out that late on a weekday. I give a little "huh" through a mouth full of everything bagel and nod. With her straightforward answers and relatively chill demeanor, my unease relaxes its hold on me. This is going okay.

"The gallery usually isn't busy in the mornings until mid-summer."

She gestures around to the empty room. "I open later on Thursdays so I can sleep in after a night out."

Maybe I can figure out who these friends are and get them to confirm her story.

It's plausible that Michael was killed after one a.m. She had the opportunity. *Mental note to ask Anna, whose surf shop faces the gallery, if Charlotte usually opens late on Thursdays.*

"Sounds fun. I appreciate it, Charlotte, I'll get out of your hair." I stand up to leave, and she thanks me again for breakfast.

"Don't be a stranger. The offer still stands: give me a ring if you want to spruce up with some artwork. It might do you some good. I can even offer you a discount, we'll say it goes towards charitable giving." With my back turned to her, I bite my tongue to stop myself from saying something I'll regret and retreat through the glass door.

Charlotte Roth is still number one on my list, and it's not because she's a pompous meddler. But that doesn't help her case either.

Chapter Eleven

Now days behind on park work, I scramble back to The Den to grab Marty. I need to keep on track with my regular park check-ups, and Zach needs help until Jim can come back to work.

"Charlotte was being so caddy, Marty. Even for her." He turns back to look at me, tongue lolling out of his mouth, as we trot towards the ranger station. I vent the entire way there, and he happily sponges up the gossip.

The office door is locked, but Zach has already been in for the day. There is half a pot of coffee still on the counter, and his computer's ancient screen saver is ricocheting neon geometric shapes. *Post-2010 machines would be nice. Maybe if we stay open, I'll try to budget for them next year.*

Changing out of my sweater, I put on a long-sleeve t-shirt and an extra DNR jacket that I keep in the closet, just in case.

Just as we're about to walk out the door, my phone pings in my back pocket. It's a text from Jeremy. Kelly would kill me if she knew he had my phone number. I do feel a little guilty for going against her. I open the text anyway, he's letting me know that a sunset memorial will be tonight at the beach, at seven p.m., and says that he emailed me the letter from Charlotte.

Sitting down at my desk, I open my email and look at the attachment.

The typed note is printed on official Stone's Throw Chamber of Commerce letterhead. I didn't even know our Chamber of Commerce had an official letterhead. I bet this is something Charlotte made to try to look official. The note was rumpled at some point but has since been smoothed out. The crease lines twist like dense spiderwebs in the scanned photocopy, making a few words hard to read.

Dear Mr. Price,

We, the Stone's Throw Chamber of Commerce, formally request that you cease your pursuit of the purchase of commercial real estate within our village borders. We pride ourselves on our 'homegrown' feel and find that it is a major reason why people visit our charming town. We are not interested in outside, corporate development at this time, and have a strategic economic growth plan already in place, which includes at least one of the properties you are interested in.

Should you pursue, we shall seek legal action per local ordinance, Article 2 Section 3.1 on commercial zoning with the full support of our Village Council. We are prepared to defend our local businesses and caution you in moving forward.

Please don't make this more difficult for yourself than you already have.

Charlotte Roth

Chair, Stone's Throw Chamber of Commerce

"Well, that sounds like Charlotte," I mutter to the dog, rereading the note one more time. Local businesses for sure contribute to the charm of this place, *but come on*. If someone wants to sell their property, they should be able to. In fact, a quick online search of our village website confirms they can.

The ordinance she cites is about regulating building heights, so huge condos and high-rise hotels can't obscure the lake views. She knows as well as I do, that she has no legal legs to stand on. She's so full of crap. But honestly, this isn't as bad as I was anticipating. The woman showed restraint (for her).

Locking the ranger station door behind us, Marty and I walk towards a stand of mature birch trees, while I do a few lunges and stretches. Yesterday's Dune Day has left my muscles sore and my bones creaky. Even after doing this hike weekly for almost three years, my body still aches after every climb.

We hike for a while, completing the daily check-up, marching up and down sandy forest, enjoying the amazing lake vistas and company from Bill and Ted, our friendly neighborhood corvid rascals. The wind whirls fast, it's loud and invigorating. Up here, it feels like nothing has changed. Just an ordinary workday. I've missed this.

The stress of the murder and the impending doom of losing this job has tensed my shoulders and clouded my attitude. Far into the wilderness, I stop and take stock of my surroundings. Seagulls 'caw!' loudly on the wind, rustling the tall grasses and tree branches. Looking down the massive inland slope, I see a green sea of tree canopy. It truly is beautiful. Life isn't all that bad.

After a peaceful break, Marty and I turn around to walk back. Enjoying the hike out, I take the time on the return to stop and take note of maintenance needs. I come across that large, fallen tree completely blocking the path, limiting accessibility beyond it. The snake family is still curled up inside, safe and sound.

Feeling somehow more rested and emotionally rejuvenated after the long trek, we bypass the office heading straight to the campground.

Zach has been working to prepare campsites. That requires cleaning out and repairing fire pit rings, removing fallen brush and overgrown shrubs, scrubbing grills, putting out picnic tables, chopping firewood, and other chores. It's more than a one-person project, but he's made decent progress.

"Hi, Zach," I shout as we approach, futilely trying to compete with the chainsaw he's using. He's towards the back, working on one of the more secluded campsites.

"Maudy, hi!" He yells back, waving.

"How's it going?" I ask him, now much closer. He's put down the chainsaw.

"Oh, you know. Pretty slow. Bill and Ted have been keeping me company." He points to a nearby sugar maple, the pair of crows now pensively watching us from a high branch.

"That's funny. They were following me and Marty earlier, too. Nosy fellas." I wave up to the birds.

"I've got to get to the school and can't stay out here much longer. A couple of classes were supposed to come here today, but with the park closed, I'm bringing nature to them! Are you thinking you'll have time to work on things out here while I'm gone?" He's been slicing a dead tree in small pieces; we'll sell some as firewood and use larger chunks as campfire seating.

"That's the plan, at least for a little bit. Put me to work, what's next on your list?"

He fills me in on where he's at on our checklist and recommends some next steps before he jogs back to our office to prepare for the lessons.

Marty hunts down a big stick and is gnawing happily while I get to work. After shoveling pounds of ash out of a dozen fire pits, my arms turn to Jello, and I switch to organizing the camp store. Maybe an hour or so in, my phone buzzes in my back pocket. It's Jeremy again.

Putting down a case of fire starters, I answer it.

"Hi, Jeremy," I say absent-mindedly, focusing on not losing count of our supply.

"Hello, dear. It's actually Nancy Finch calling on Jeremy's phone. Did I catch you at a bad time? Sorry, I didn't have your cell phone number, myself."

"Just out working, what can I do for you?" I reply a little surprised, attempting to break down a big packing box.

"Well, I'm so sorry to bother. We need a small favor."

"Sure, what's up?" I walk outside and sit down on a hunk of log that Zach recently cut. Marty looks up from his chewed-up, spit-soaked stick to listen in.

"Well, I presume you've heard about the memorial service we're hosting at the beach for Michael."

"Yep, me and Marty will be there. Tonight, right? Around sunset?"

"Yes, that's right, dear. Well...I asked Jeremy to speak at the event, but he's having a bit of a problem. He asked me to call you."

"Oh. Um, okay. I'm not sure what I can do." What is it she's asking of me?

"Could you come over? To the Inn? That would be helpful."

"Sure, give me about a half hour. I'll be there."

I take the dog and hike back to the office to change into my blue sweater, run my fingers through my hair, and put on deodorant. Why couldn't Jeremy need me *before* I did a bunch of sweaty, manual labor? I looked much better this morning.

Marty and I rush over to Nancy's and are there right about when I said we would be. I clip the dog to a bike rack out front of The Nest, with the same slobber-covered stick he's been working on all afternoon.

In the dining room, Jeremy and Nancy are sitting in the front window, each holding a warm mug that smells of old coffee. Nancy has a big ring of keys on the table in front of her, with a crocheted flower keychain attached to it. I've seen it hooked onto her belt loop before. I come in, meet Nancy's concerned gaze, and turn towards Jeremy, taking a seat in the chair next to him.

"Hi." I take off my jacket and drape it over the back of the chair, staring at the cuckoo clock right behind Nancy's head. It's mocking me, the seconds ticking away, counting down to Friday. Blasted bird. "What's going on?" I silently tap my fingers on the tabletop in time with the clock.

"Here." Jeremy thrusts over a piece of paper that's folded in thirds. There's anger in his voice, a sternness I haven't experienced from him before. He stares out the window at Marty.

Slowly opening the paper, nervous for what I'm about to find, I begin reading. It's a note, presumably meant for Jeremy, although no formal greeting is included.

It simply states, *He was a prick. Speaking highly of him would be a lie. But you are a liar, aren't you? Who are you, Jeremy Gray? How have you been lying for twenty years? What a shame if word were to get out...about then and now. Don't make me expose you for what you truly are...and I promise I will. What a shame it would be to end up like your pal, Michael.*

The few lines of text are written in black ink, in a scrawled mix of print and cursive. It's not signed.

"Where'd this come from?" I ask, looking up at Nancy, sitting across from me.

"It was in the mailbox this morning," she says quietly. "No envelope or stamp or anything."

Turning to Jeremy, "Who knew about you speaking at the memorial today?"

Nancy cut in, "Well, most everybody, I think, dear. I didn't keep it a secret when I got the word out about the event. I thought it'd be helpful to share a little agenda beforehand." She shrugs, gripping her mug tighter, clinking her nails on the ceramic. Her mug clinking and my second tapping aren't in sync, and it's irritating me.

Jeremy's head rests in his hands while he stares out the window.

"Nancy, do you mind if me and Maudy have a moment in private, please?" He hasn't looked at either of us since I sat down.

"Of course." She smiles apologetically, picking up her keys and a few files she has on the table next to her. "I've got some work to do today anyway." She gets up and walks back over to the front desk on the other side of the Inn. "You two make yourselves comfortable. There's coffee in the pot, dear, if you'd like. Help yourself."

Jeremy finally turns to me once Nancy is out of earshot and reaches for my hands that are resting on the wooden table. Confused, I let him take them. He looks me dead in the eyes for the first time since I sat down. *God, that jawline could cut glass.*

"I told you already that I got into trouble as a younger man."

I nod, following so far.

"That is true. However, I may have downplayed the severity of that particular situation…"

He bows his head again. Not saying a word, I wait for him to continue. This is hard for him; he'll spit it out in his own time.

Behind him, outside, I see Eli walk past the window, stopping to crouch down and give Marty a friendly scratch behind the ears. He looks around for me, and I clumsily wiggle out of Jeremy's hands to wave. He waves back, face falling when he sees who I'm with. *Merda. I'll deal with that later.*

After a couple of moments, Jeremy speaks.

"I killed someone, Maudy. Because of me, a woman is dead."

Chapter Twelve

"You *what?*" I lean in and exclaim far louder than appropriate for the small bed and breakfast. My eyes widen, unable to hide my shock.

He nods somberly, a horribly ashamed, almost sick, expression on his face. His normally warm skin tone is shading a little green. "It's true. I was eighteen and stupid. A buddy of mine drove us to a party, but he drank too much to drive home that night. It was the middle of the night, the roads were icy, and it was snowing hard. Instead of spending the night like we should have, I took his keys and got behind the wheel. Which I should not have done. Anyway, we were on a dark county road, and I could barely see. Before I knew it, a car flew out from a crossroad and I T-boned her." He looks down and aggressively rubs his eyes.

"Like I said, it was winter, and the road was icy. I kept sliding after slamming on the brakes, but it was too late. The driver of the other car…she…she didn't survive. We hit a tree straight on but were both somehow okay."

"Wow, uh, this is a lot." The anguish in the man's face is heartbreaking. He's been carrying this with him for two decades. His eyes gloss over with held-back tears. His voice is heavy.

"I know, tell me about it. She was a single mother, too. I think about her every day. I've tried to keep it quiet, to get past it, but Traverse City is a small town. Not as small as this, but word still gets around." He's compulsively picking his fingernails, agitated.

"So, what happened? Did you go to jail? Were you over the limit?"

"Yes, I was arrested for involuntary manslaughter and got a DUI and an MIP. I jumped out of my car and tried to get her out of hers. She was in my arms when the police came… I was sentenced to five years and a ton of fines. I ended up serving only a year, though. Plus, I had to file for bankruptcy after all the fines and legal fees. It was bad, but I deserved worse."

My head spins as if I'm the one who had too much to drink. *What do I say? Why did he call me over here?* Utterly tongue-tied, I pivot back to today's problem. "So, what does this have to do with this note?"

"Whoever wrote it is threatening to dig all of that up again. I'm a murderer! I can't have this getting all over town. I'd be out of a job. I'd need to move. My friends and family are all in Traverse City. My roots are here. I can't just pack up and leave."

"Well, I don't know if I'd say you're a *murderer*," I say, more to convince myself than reassure him, trying to get a handle on all this. So, somebody here knows about this car accident from twenty years ago? And knew Michael, too? "Let's cancel the memorial. It's a dumb idea anyway. Whoever wrote this note seems a little unhinged, and we don't need anyone else getting hurt."

"You think Nancy would agree to that? She's looking at it as a way to get good PR and seems pretty desperate." He says that with a sharp edge to his voice, cutting the anger with a twinge of sadness. "Also, just so you're aware, Kelly already knows about the car accident; she asked me about it when she first interviewed me."

I sneak a picture of the note with my phone while his head is down in his hands. *Of course, Kelly knew about this. Yet another piece of information that would've been helpful. No wonder she ordered me to stay away from him. Maybe he is dangerous…*

"Kelly can order Nancy to cancel it. This basically threatens to kill you, Jeremy."

"Tell me about it." He's still picking at his fingernails, head bowed over the table.

He really killed somebody... I know he didn't do it on purpose, but still. Could he have killed Michael, too? He's made poor decisions in the past. He seems remorseful, though. Is he making this note up to throw me off his scent? He still drinks a lot, based on what Eli said. If your drunk driving killed someone, wouldn't you be careful with alcohol? Has he changed as much as he claims? Or maybe the note is real, and whoever wrote it killed Michael? Someone seems to not like Michael very much.

"Jeremy, I'm going to be honest, here. I have no clue what to make of this." My list of questions continues to grow, as I rattle them off in my head. "I'm going to talk to Kelly and ask her to call off the memorial. Just stay here and stay out of trouble for the next couple of hours, will ya?"

"Hi, Kell, got a minute?" I call her immediately as Marty and I head down the block.

"Hey, Maudy. Sure. What's up?"

"I spoke with Charlotte and Jeremy today. And before you get upset, let me tell you what happened. You need to hear this." I launch into recounting my day before she has a chance to yell at me some more.

"You're right, we for sure have to cancel the memorial. This is huge. Read the note back to me one more time?"

I reread the note, word for word, this time suggesting the possibility that Jeremy wrote it himself.

"Uh-huh." She's taking notes. "Send me that photo. I'll confiscate the original from him soon, but we can start doing handwriting analysis with your picture. I'm going to call Nancy right now. Thank you for telling me this, but please, for Pete's sake, leave him alone! I don't want to arrest you for obstruction of justice." She hangs up.

Now onto my next problem. A quick peek into Pop's shows me that Eli isn't in. Kevin tells me that he's probably at home; he must've stopped to pet Marty while walking that way. I decide to run over to his place and see for myself.

I drop Marty off in my backyard and walk through the gate to Eli's. We had it installed a while back, so we didn't have to walk around the block or hop over to see one another.

Peering through his back door, I knock and sit down on a wooden Adirondack chair perched on his back patio. The skies are blue, but clouds have been rolling in heavier and heavier as the day marches on. I hope the oncoming storm will hold out a little longer. I need the sunshine right now.

Eli opens the back door, a meek smile on his face. He's wearing a dark blue apron and a backward baseball cap. "Hi," I say, basking my face in the fleeting, warm sun.

"Hey, I wasn't expecting you. Want to come in? I've got the stove on." He turns back inside without waiting for a reply, leaving the door open for me to follow.

Walking into Eli's house is like walking into what I imagine his brain looks like. It's disorganized, but full of fun trinkets. Everything is meaningful, down to the photos on the wall, the knick-knacks on the bookshelf, and the antique stand mixer in the kitchen. It's decorated in shades of warm browns and deep blues and has stacks of crossword puzzle books everywhere.

I take a seat at one of the two kitchen bar stools while he stirs something on the stove that smells enchanting. He has *The Kinks* blaring over his speaker and turns down the volume so we can hear each other talk.

"Whatcha cookin' up today? Smells great." I lean over the counter to get a better whiff.

"Yeah? It's an oldie but a goodie. My grandpa's lamb stew. I'm just getting it started. Total comfort food."

"Well, it's clear where you get your talent from," I say, smiling at him and secretly hoping I'll get sent home with some.

"Ha, you're too kind. What brings you over? Not that I don't love the company."

I fidget in my seat, unsure if I should tell him what's happening. I might crawl out of my skin if I don't share all this soon. One-sided chats with Marty aren't cutting it. "Can you promise me you'll keep this between us?" I ask, grimacing at my own unprofessionalism.

"Yes…Muddy, what's up?" He's sweet and sad now, much different than before. Maybe he feels bad for avoiding me.

The first handful of times that Eli and I met, we were playing together in the same summer softball beer league. I was coming straight from the park, usually covered in mud, which earned me the nickname 'Muddy.' He was the team's unofficial coach, helping newer players (me) learn the game. Thus 'Coach.' We still call each other that, especially in texts or written notes.

Not able to hold it in any longer, I launch into the bomb that Jeremy dropped on me, showing him the picture I took of the note.

"This is obviously a scam." He scoffs at the photo and angrily chops a potato.

"A scam?" I ask.

"You're kidding, right? Jeremy killed Michael. It's as plain as day." He drops the vegetable chunks into the big pot of stew and stirs it. "He's trying to throw you off. This is the nail in the proverbial coffin."

I have similar suspicions; the note is for sure weird. It's short, and the handwriting looks rushed. It's possible that Jeremy wrote it himself, especially if Kelly already knew he killed someone.

"That's a possibility. A lot of my trails are leading to Jeremy right now. One thing I can't figure out, though, is why would he come back to town if he killed Michael? He's been pretty forthright with the police, too."

"It's not a possibility, it's a fact." His back is to me, stirring his stew rhythmically to the music.

"Do you have something personal against this guy?" This is unlike him, to be *so* adamant. Between this, the face he made walking by The Nest earlier, and the heated interaction he had with Jeremy at the bar, it's clear there's something going on here.

"He's a bad dude, Maudy. I want you to steer clear of him. He doesn't keep great company."

"Thanks, but I'm perfectly capable of taking care of myself." Not that I'm into Jeremy. *Am I into Jeremy?* Do I like looking at the guy? Of course, I'm human. Do I want to date him? No way. He's a main suspect in a murder investigation. I'm on a self-prescribed dating hiatus, regardless of feelings.

Eli is ticking me off, stirring up sour memories of Nate's jealousy like he's stirring up his stew. Nate was constantly interrogating me about who I was spending time with up here, all the while sleeping around back downstate. He hated that Eli and I were becoming good friends. It's a little ironic how the tables have turned. *Who does Eli think he is? I can decide who to spend time with, thank you very much.*

"I know that. I just think he's bad news and I…I care about you, Muddy." He finally turns to me, shrugging his shoulders.

"I'll see you later," I say tersely, grabbing my keys off the counter and getting up abruptly from the chair.

"You don't have to go—"

"See you later, Eli." I march through the back door, seething. I don't have time for this.

Chapter Thirteen

I'm thrilled Kelly agrees to cancel the memorial. There's really no point, and someone, mainly Jeremy, could get seriously hurt. She's having the note looked at for a handwriting analysis and has ordered all visitors to stay in town until Michael's murder is resolved.

"I haven't forgotten my promise, Marty. Let's go to the beach for a quick walk. You've been great today."

Even though the dog is built with disproportionately large paws and webbed toes, he doesn't like to swim. However, he loves rolling around in the wet sand, chomping at oncoming waves, and carrying around driftwood. The beach is one of his favorite places.

As we amble along the shoreline, we come across Nancy's husband, Greg, and a few volunteers who are taking down folding chairs and packing up everything now that the memorial has been canceled. There are a few stragglers who didn't get the memo, but otherwise, the beach is quiet.

We toss a squeaky ball for a while, Marty burning some of his pent-up energy. I watch as Greg tears down a small podium, while a couple others pick up vases of flowers. A woman drags a wagon through the sand back towards town, filled with wasted decorations and chairs. I offer to help, but Greg assures me they are all set.

We take a seat on the wet sand, the toes of my boots barely touching the water as the waves lazily wander in and out. The breeze subsides, the gulls squawk, and the sun barely kisses the western horizon over expansive Lake Michigan.

Pulling out my phone to sift through pictures I've taken, I ruminate over the dozen or so loose ends I have. Maybe looking these back over will unlock something I've missed.

Staring at the picture of the weird rectangle impressions in the ground and the tire track, the metaphorical lightbulb clicks on. Swiveling around to look back at the quickly deteriorating memorial site, I squint to get a good look at the wagon wheels, then back at my phone. Initially, I thought the track was from a fat tire bike. Lots of people ride them in the wintertime on our park trails. The little rectangles didn't make sense before. Now, it all fits.

"It's from a wheelbarrow!" I give Martin a celebratory ear scratch and kiss his forehead. He wags his tail and drops the rock he has stashed in his mouth at my feet.

"It must've been used to move Michael from where he was killed to where you found him!" More tail wags.

What else is a similar size to this wagon, but with only one tire? It must be a wheelbarrow. The rectangles are the rests it sits on when nobody is using it. I honestly forgot about the tire track, having gotten wrapped up in potential motives. It's a good reminder that means are just as important.

"So, who has access to a wheelbarrow?" I ask the dog, who is glancing at the bright orange sun and covered in wet sand from nose to tail, enjoying himself immensely.

"Well, someone who lives here for one," I continue, quietly. It's not like you can inconspicuously hide a huge piece of garden equipment in a bed and breakfast room. If the killer isn't from Stone's Throw, why would they kill Michael *here*?

I close the image and open my texts, sending one to Nellie. "Emma will know," I say to the dog. Emma, Nellie's wife, is the manager of the outdoor center in our hardware store and is a master gardener. Marty's right ear twists almost imperceptibly in my direction, associating the word "Emma" with his two favorite pint-sized playmates. Just a few minutes pass before I get a ping back.

Reading it quickly, "Emma says they've sold over a dozen in the last couple of weeks at the hardware store. Everyone's gearing up to garden now that the weather is beginning to get nice again." *Okay, while not extremely helpful, that's still good to know.*

Butts sandy and energy sufficiently expelled, Marty and I walk back home. I herd the dog into the bathroom, rinse him off, and then head to Pop's for dinner. If I were a gambler, I would bet serious cash that an impromptu memorial is congregating at the bar instead of the formal plans at the beach. Maybe I can snoop and try to find the author of that threatening note. Not to mention, I'm not in the mood to cook (surprise, surprise).

The dog goes straight to the couch and curls up in a tight little ball of fur, looking like a black hole about to swallow my couch cushion. I turn on a reel of funny animal videos for him and plant a kiss on the top of his head.

Walking into the bar a few minutes later, I confirm my Sherlockian hunch. An unofficial memorial has taken over the bar. It feels like I'm walking into a nightmare where I show up naked to high school exams. The place isn't overly busy, but every single person is here for a bit of town drama. I can feel the intensity in their stares. Memorial flower displays are in the corner, and a posterboard with Michael's picture on it stands proudly on an easel. They take turns whispering to one another and glancing at me, the investigator extraordinaire, well out of her element. Pop's used to be my safe haven. Now, standing here in this nightmare-come-to-life, I couldn't be more out of place if I was literally naked.

Politely nodding and waving to folks as I walked through the bar, I do my best to move quickly. I tap my index finger on my pant leg as I navigate the crowd, trying my best to shrink out of view. Even still, a couple of people manage to pull me into a quick conversation.

"Maudy, is everything alright? I hear you canceled the memorial. Why on Earth would you do that?"

"Maudy, chaos sure is following you around lately, eh?"

"Glad to see you out and about, dear. I hear you've met someone new, how great. A woman of your age, it's about time to settle down."

One, two, three, four. My fingertips go numb, tapping them against the rough denim too hard. I keep counting, trying to tune the mind chatter out.

Jeff, our town pharmacist and the front man of the local rock band, *The Uppers,* is playing acoustic guitar in the corner near the flowers. Nancy must have asked him to play the service, and I guess he figured he might as well play here instead. It's like thirty percent normal Pop's vibe and seventy percent funeral. I wave to Jeff as I pass him and dart towards the bar, catching Jeremy looking much better than he did a few hours ago.

Beelining over to him, hoping to find a little calm in the eye of the swirling anxiety storm that is this bar, I find Lucas and a couple of other people I don't recognize all talking in the same group. I gently step between Lucas and Jeremy, letting them know I'm here without interrupting the conversation. Both of the men turn to me, as well as the other two folks in the circle.

"Sorry to interrupt, I just wanted to see how you're doing." I can tell a big weight has lifted off his shoulders since the last time we spoke.

"Maudy, thank you, that's very kind. I'm doing much better, thanks for um, handling that business for me." He smiles back, and my wave of nausea starts to retreat. With the two much taller men on either side, I'm not as visible to the rest of the room.

"I didn't realize you two know each other." I point at Lucas and

Jeremy.

"We both live in Traverse City," Lucas says. "Jeremy actually sold me my last house." He tips his glass towards Jeremy. "We've become fast friends. Jeremy told me about the discounted rate on the cabin rentals this week, so I jumped at the opportunity to hike and do some fly fishing."

"Fast friends indeed," Jeremy replies. "How's the house working out, by the way? What's it been, a few years now? That back patio holding up?"

"Yep. Loving it. The woods are where I belong," Lucas says.

"Wow, what a small world." I laugh, turning back to Jeremy. "So, how did you first meet Michael? I don't think I ever heard the full story."

"Oh, you know. The development business and the real estate business go hand in hand," Jeremy laughs, reminiscing. "I reached out to him after following one of his bigger projects online and thought he might be interested in doing something together up here."

"Wow, you reached out to him cold, eh? And he agreed to work together right off the bat?" Lucas asks, with a detectable hint of skepticism.

"Yep, that's how it went down. I feel awful that it led to the current state of things." A somber silence settles in the air between the five of us. Jeff's cover of *Wind Beneath My Wings* fills it.

"How rude of me. Maudy, I'd like you to meet my temporary neighbors, Alex and Liz. They're staying at the cabin next to mine." Lucas gestures to the couple in our conversation circle and points in the general direction upriver, where a dozen or so rental cabins sit. Mostly used for fly fishing, they're right on the riverbank across from the park. I pass by them each day; the end of the row isn't far from the Birch River bridge.

He's a little distressed, and perhaps a little awkward, keeping one hand jammed in his pants pocket. As he points towards the cabins with his other hand, I see the flower tattoo again. '2-24-2003' surrounded by black and gray flowers. It's very detailed.

"Alex, Liz, great to meet you both," I say, extending my hand out to shake. "Are you enjoying your stay in Stone's Throw? All things considered, of course."

Liz chimes in first with a thick Minnesotan accent, "Well ya know this is the first time we've been here, and I gotta say I'm surprised by all the nighttime ruckus! I coulda sworn a bear was tryin' to get into another cabin the other night. Plus, all the raccoons rattlin' around in the shed, they broke the lock right off the door." That gets her a bunch of bewildered looks from the group, but nobody asks any follow-up questions. She seems...eccentric. Perhaps it is best to let sleeping dogs lie, or rattled raccoons to their ruckus.

"It is a little strange, but besides a couple of disrupted sleeps and this tragedy, of course, it's been lovely," Alex adds. We continue for a bit, sharing our favorite spots around town and giving recommendations on things to do.

"Are you all planning on sticking around town for a while? Have a nice vacation planned, besides attending a memorial?" I loop Jeremy and Lucas back into the conversation, not wanting to be rude.

"Oh sure, although not on our own accord. The police asked all visitors in town at the time of Michael's disappearance to stay until the case is solved," Alex says.

"Ah, I hope that's not too much of an inconvenience for you both. I have to admit part of that is my fault," I reply. "Doing my best, though."

"It's no problem, really. I work remotely, and Lizzie here is retired, so it's not a huge deal. It's nice here, we don't mind." The older man shrugs and smiles, the rest nodding in agreement. Like it or not, they're all stuck here for a while.

We have a pleasant conversation for a few more minutes before I see Kelly walk in. I go to excuse myself from the group, now feeling much better, when Jeremy makes a show of giving me a full-on two-arm hug, which I politely peel myself out of, feeling the glances pop back my direction. *Great, just what I need, more attention. Thank you, Jeremy.*

As I walk to the other side of the bar, cheeks beet red (from embarrassment or butterflies, I'm not sure), I ponder life with a partner again. Jeremy is the first person to have shown interest in me since Nate. I've been a basket case since.

Not that I want to be with Jeremy, but the attention is flattering. *Maybe it is time to put a little more effort in. Is it time to end the dating hiatus?* These thoughts loyally trail behind me all the way to my barstool like little, frightened ducklings following their neurotic mother.

"Hi, Kevin," I groan with a tired, small smile. It is impossible to keep the exhaustion from my voice, and frankly, I'm not trying that hard. Today is catching up with me, and my patience is fading.

"Evening, Maudy. What the heck is going on with you? You look as tired as the wings of a hummingbird." He takes off his hat as he leans down over the bar, watching me with genuine concern. "The place has been buzzing today. I heard it was you who canceled Nancy's memorial service. What's that about? What have you gotten yourself wrapped up in?"

Without asking what I want, he pours a pint of hard cider and yells at Eli to get me a grilled cheese with apple and a bowl of tomato soup. He's the only one here who seems to care about me, not just trying to get the latest scandal update.

Rumor has it that Kevin is planning on retiring soon, leaving the entire bar to Eli. His term on our Village Council is also about to end, and he's already made it known he isn't running again. He's been spending less and less time at the bar, slowly shifting responsibilities over to Eli.

Even so, I doubt the rumors are completely true; Kevin strikes me as someone who will be working for his entire life. I hope he sticks around, even in a limited capacity. Nobody can cheer me up like he does. Kevin has, more than once, been found in my front yard weeding my flowerbeds without being asked to do so. I've welcomed his help, not much of a gardener myself, and always make sure his lemonade glass is full and remind him to reapply sunscreen. He's incapable of sitting still. I'm not sure what retirement means to him, but I doubt it means not working entirely.

"This case is running me ragged, Kevin. I'm trying, but I'm not sure I'll be able to figure out what happened to Michael soon enough. I'm certainly no detective, and Kelly keeps withholding information from me. It sure as hell is making my life a lot harder. Ope, Kelly's coming up. Better change the subject." Kelly sits down on the stool next to me, equally deflated. She's busy doing something on her phone and gives me a quick smile.

My hope that the campground will open on Friday is gone, eroded like the sand on the banks of the Birch River or the passing ticks of the demonic cuckoo clock. By Thursday afternoon, I'll need to reach out to campers and cancel reservations. I have about forty-eight hours until I need to call Harper with the bad news. "Any chance you need another bartender here? It's looking like the park will be closing its doors soon."

"Now don't go putting that into the universe. I'll always bet on you, kid." He hands me a full pint, with a look of sorrow or pity on his face, and goes to pour one for Kelly.

"When I heard the order, I figured it'd be for you." Eli comes out from behind the kitchen, a sheepish look on his face. He places a melty, gooey sandwich with a small cup of broth in front of me. "I didn't have tomato, but I figured this might make an okay substitute." I bend over the plate, the delicious scent reaching my nose in a warm steam. It's version 2.0 of the chicken soup we ate in my kitchen the other day. "Do you want one too, Kelly?"

Eli's question pulls Kelly out of her phone and back to reality. "How about a cheeseburger and fries?" She turns to me, "Sorry, I know this is so rude. Give me two more minutes, just answering an email."

He abruptly turns to walk back into the kitchen, not meeting my gaze or waiting for a response.

"Eli!" I say, loud enough that it'd be bad-mannered for him to ignore. "When we're done here," I point to Kelly and myself, "would you have a minute? Maybe we could walk home together." The kitchen will be closing soon, and Kevin usually stays late since Eli comes early to do kitchen prep.

"Um…sure thing. I should be closing up shop in a little bit." I know my best friend. After our spat earlier, we need to talk it out. I don't have the emotional bandwidth to stay mad at him, and we both clearly feel bad. The weirdness is worse than whatever the conversation could be. I need to apologize for snapping; he hit a particularly sensitive nerve.

"Perfect." I smile big at him, over-exaggerating. I want him to know that I'm not still mad. It is dark out, and a man has just been murdered. He'd never make me walk home alone.

Kelly and I get into the weeds about the case after a few more minutes of her answering email. Well, I get into the weeds of the case, and she hems and haws as I give her my report, taking notes.

I get into the details of my conversation with Charlotte, who is still my number one suspect, even if it doesn't settle quite right yet. As I'm talking to Kelly, Charlotte's ears must be ringing because she walks into the bar, never one to miss a good gossip opportunity.

She takes my spot over with Jeremy and the others. For how much he was bashing her earlier (*didn't he call her a witch?*), the two seem to be getting along fine, now. Good, even. He's smiling at her and politely laughing, pretending whatever dumb thing she said was funny. Maybe they're both just saving face in front of the others. Or maybe he's flirty with everyone.

"Well, Charlotte's timeline checks out." Kelly tugs my attention back to our conversation instead of simmering in my own *jealousy? intrigue? confusion?* watching Jeremy and Charlotte together.

"She was in Traverse on Wednesday night. The bar has cameras, and we confirmed her attendance. Not saying that clears her, though. Based on when she left, she would've been back here by twelve-thirty or so last night. She entered her house through her side door at one o'clock for the night. She has a fancy security system that allows us to look through the keypad history. The window of opportunity would be tight, borderline impossible." She picks up a french fry, dipping it in ketchup before continuing.

"Look, we both hate the woman. She's an absolute pain in the ass, but at this point, I don't think she's a viable suspect. Try to move on to other options, okay?" She finishes her drink and stands up to leave.

It's now past ten and I need to go to bed. My brain's gas tank is on empty, and I know an all-nighter wouldn't be productive. If anything, it would ruin my chances of a good day tomorrow, which I need if there's any hope of getting campers here on Friday.

Kelly takes off, waving goodbye and promising to talk tomorrow. The bar is almost empty, with a few lingering folks finishing up their drinks. I nurse mine, waiting for Eli to wrap up in the kitchen. He pokes his head out, coat in hand, and ushers me behind the bar and through the kitchen door towards the back exit.

We start walking in silence, his eyes stay straight ahead like he's wearing horse blinders as we pass The Nest towards home. We have only six or seven minutes until we're at my front door.

"Elliot Nett, I have a bone to pick with you." I've spent up my daily allotment of tact, so spitting it out is all I got. "We left things off in a bad place earlier, and I'm sorry that my Napoleon Complex reared its ugly head. I just hate being told what to do. It's something I'm working on. Well, it's something I know I need to start working on."

I stop and turn my whole body towards him, blocking his way forward.

He stops, zips his coat up further, and sighs heavily. He's so much taller than I am; the top of my head is about level with his shoulder. Standing close, I crane my neck to meet his eyes, waiting for him to respond.

"We're fine. I'm sorry. I'm protective, and that guy sucks. You're right, you can do whatever you want. It's not my place." He looks down at me but doesn't hold eye contact for very long. Maybe he's still upset.

"C'mon, Eli. What's going on? I know he ticked you off last week when he was being an idiot and shouting in the bar. That reason doesn't match the weirdly deep hatred you seem to have for the guy. What am I missing?" My hands are on my hips, not buying this 'protective friend' excuse.

He scrunches his face and stares at me, not sure what to say, I guess. He softens momentarily, before hardening back up again. "Seriously, it's nothing. Let's drop it. We're fine. I promise."

"No, I won't drop it! This is ridiculous."

"Fine! You want to know what my deal is with him? He looks at you like you're a piece of meat, Maudy. He talks to you like a forty-year-old frat bro who just wants to sleep with you. I can't stand watching that."

He shrinks and jogs around me, leaving me behind.

"Okay...well, I'm here if you want to, I don't know, talk more, or egg my house maybe." I sarcastically shout after him. What else is there to say?

I make it to my door and walk inside. He must be taking an unnecessarily long way because his kitchen light, which is visible from my back window, doesn't turn on for another ten or so minutes.

I hate this feeling. Before anything else decides to crumble around me, I take another long, hot shower and count backwards from one thousand. With my skin properly scalded after reaching the five hundredth second, I put on my favorite, well-worn sweatshirt and crawl into bed. Hoping tomorrow bodes better than today, I drift off to a restless, tumultuous sleep.

Chapter Fourteen

The uneasy queasiness in my stomach hasn't subsided. As hard as I try, I can't get my mind to calm down and spend almost the entire night tossing and turning, creating fragmented scenarios and inventing clues that don't make any sense. Not any more rested than when I went to bed, I get up around six a.m., taking the loss.

I know Kelly said to forget about Charlotte. My ears did hear those words come out of her mouth. But she has a clear motive, is local, and I'm sure she has access to a wheelbarrow if she doesn't own one herself.

As I sit up in bed, wiping the crusties from the corners of my eyes, I can't help but think that Jeremy seems too remorseful to have killed someone intentionally. Not after what happened when he was younger. He wouldn't risk it. He has been laying it on a little thick, though. Is he *pretending* to be interested in me to throw me off the scent?

I sip on my coffee as I plan out the day, sitting on the couch as the pink morning sun peeks through the front window. Marty is enjoying the beautiful sunrise outside in the yard, lying on his belly on the deck.

As I write out my to-do list, still hyper-fixating on Charlotte, something she said yesterday during my breakfast interrogation rings in a way it didn't initially. 'He was trying to run the Finches out of business! I heard he also wanted Java Jones and the pizza shop… Can you believe this man? Completely unrelated to this place, wanting to buy out businesses from underneath us? Absolutely not. Not on my watch...'

Michael wanted to run the Finches out of business...it couldn't be. Could it? I hastily reason through the new scenario.

The Finches are having major money problems, that isn't a secret. Nancy had the letter that Charlotte wrote to Michael and Jeremy. Jeremy said that Nancy gave it to him, so she had access. Could she have read it before delivering it to Jeremy? Maybe she overheard the two men in the dining room and was the 'confidential source' who told Charlotte what they were doing in the first place...? The Finches were at the B&B when he was murdered. Did Michael come back late, and they saw an opportunity while nobody was around? Did Nancy and Greg kill Michael to stop him from taking their B&B away? Maybe they are in debt and the bank would be forced to take an offer or something?

Even though it is still early, I shoot a text to Zach, asking if he'd meet me for breakfast at The Nest before work. The theory is rough at best, the motive not totally making sense yet, but it's worth sleuthing out. I can kill two birds with one stone. Zach and I can figure out our contingency plan if the park stays closed, and I can press the Finches.

I gather my bag, let Marty back inside, and leave for breakfast. Zach is an early riser, and he responds to my message quickly and enthusiastically. It is no surprise when he is already seated at a large round table in the middle of The Nest's dining room, notepads and binders splayed out in front of him by the time that I arrive.

"Morning, Zach. Thanks so much for meeting me on such short notice," I greet him. Sitting down across the table from the bright-eyed blonde man, I pull out my own notebook and smile at it. Nate gave me a personalized stationery kit when I took this job, filled with nature-themed paper, sticky notes, and greeting cards. This notebook was part of that set and brings back nice memories of us together, before the very same job that this stationery celebrated led to our ultimate downfall.

Nancy is quick to bring coffee and a small basket of pastries from Peyton's bakery to our table. I snag a cinnamon roll and start picking it apart as we launch into our discussion.

"Okay, so here's where we're at." He begins, flipping through his notes. "Our campsites are almost all set. There's a handful that still need to be cleaned out, and a few administrative things in the store that we need to finish up, but otherwise, we are good to go. I'm still waiting on the final shipment of supplies, but nothing is crucial. If that doesn't get here before Friday, it's not the end of the world. I'm feeling pretty good on this front. There's maybe a half a day's work left if we tackle it together. Another full day if it's just me."

"Great!" I nod, letting him continue as I glance around to keep an eye on Nancy and Greg. The cuckoo clock is out of my eyeline, but I still hear the unrelenting ticking. Glancing down at my phone, I see the top of the hour is in just a few minutes. *Merda.*

"Yep! So let's pretend the park has to stay closed this weekend. What will we do?"

I start to answer that question, but he holds up a finger, asking me to keep listening.

"The Village Parks & Rec staff have agreed to allow twenty of our campers to stay on their piece of the beach for the weekend, over by the lighthouse. They don't have designated campsites, and it will require extra waivers to be signed, but because it's an extenuating circumstance, they're amenable to covering for us. I know it's not all forty, but it's better than nothing, right?"

I am reminded, once again, how much I appreciate Zach. While I've been busy with Kelly, he could've easily thrown in the towel and essentially taken free vacation days. Instead, he's really taken charge of the situation.

"Totally. That leaves nineteen additional camper groups unaccounted for if the park must stay closed. Well, twenty, but one is my reservation, which I have no trouble canceling."

"I figured you wouldn't mind." He smiles at me, proud of his work. "Based on registration information, just over half of our campers are from within the state, and only traveling a few hours max. I've found a few more spots open in other parks in the region and have their sites on hold for us in case we need to redirect folks to other towns. Not ideal." He shrugs. "At most, it looks like we'll only need to cancel six or seven camp groups if we can't open on time."

"This is great, Zach. Thanks so much for working all of this out." While he's been explaining this, I'm doing back-of-the-envelope revenue calculations. Even with his plan, the financial loss is not good.

"Cuckoo! Cuckoo!" The bird leaps out of its wooden hole, springing back and forth like an even scarier jack-in-the-box, which I didn't know was possible. I shudder, tingles shooting down my neck.

"You okay?" He eyes me suspiciously.

"Oh, yeah. Sorry about that. The AC just kicked on or something." What a blatant lie. He doesn't buy it but doesn't press me further.

With the hour now passed and the bird back in his hell hole, the clock ticks amplify. It's like someone is holding a microphone up to it. I tap along on the tabletop with my pen.

"One more thing, I really think we need to start an Instagram account. Just hear me out before you say 'no' again." He shows me a few links to other parks' accounts so I can get a sense for what he is envisioning. After looking them over, I have to admit it might just be worth the time. With the added pressure from Harper, maybe an online presence could help get folks into the park.

"Sure. Go ahead." I'm too frazzled to argue, and frankly, he's right. "I'm sorry for being such a crotchety old lady about this. We're just short-staffed as it is and have lots of pressing things to work on. I trust you, though. Go with your gut." *Maybe this can help us do some fundraising, too.*

We wrap up our conversation, and he goes on his way. He has to check in with Stone's Throw Village Parks & Rec again to secure waivers.

After Zach leaves, I stick around the dining room to talk to the Finches. Greg comes by a little later to refill my coffee cup while I'm engrossed in the details of the camping contingency plans that Zach gave me to review and formally approve.

"Good morning, Greg. How are you today?" I put down my pen and look up at the jovial man. He's wearing a bright green striped golf polo under a black cardigan.

"I'm doing okay, Maudy. It's nice to see you." The older man has a surprisingly full head of silvery gray hair and a well-trimmed beard. He doesn't look a day over sixty.

"You too. Do you have a minute to chat? There's something I want to talk to you and Nancy about."

He's confused by the request. I wouldn't say that we are close like me and Kevin. Nancy's much more of the people-person out of the pair. "Well, sure, let me grab Nancy. If I know my wife, she won't want to pass up an opportunity to sit and visit for a while." I smile and nod over the rim of my coffee cup. Just a couple of moments later, the two sit down at the table, each with a colorful mug in front of them as well.

"I need your help," I say with an authority that I don't feel, folding my hands in my lap. *Kind but stern, you can do it, Maudy.* "I need you to tell me exactly what happened here last week. No detail is too small. I know you omitted some things last time we spoke, Nancy. I need you to be honest with me." I look directly at her as I say this. Panic strikes across her face.

"Let's start with Wednesday morning," I say as more of a statement than a suggestion. The two look at each other. Greg appears sincerely bewildered, and Nancy appears shifty, like she's hiding something.

Concern drips down her face, and she twists the frilly, polka dot apron she's wearing in her hands.

"Maudy dear, we already told everything we know to the police. I hope you don't take offense to this, but I'm not sure there's anything else we can say." Greg takes the lead, picking up on Nancy's apprehension.

"It's okay, Greg. She's working with Kelly. I must've forgotten to tell you." She looks at him with a small, reassuring smile and pats his hand.

"I see. Sorry, I didn't know. Is it on account of the park being where he was found?"

I nod in affirmation. "No offense taken. If I can't get Michael's death resolved soon, I won't be able to open the park campground, and we'll get shut down by the state. This is really important to me, so thanks for taking the time to chat." I reassure him. Turning back to Nancy, I say, "So, Wednesday morning."

"Wednesday morning." She pauses. "Wednesday morning, I hosted breakfast service here while Greg worked in the garden. Now that it's warming up, we've been prepping our beds to plant flowers this upcoming week." The two look at each other, Greg nodding along.

"Jeremy and Michael had breakfast here around, oh maybe ten a.m. It was later for sure. They've been getting late starts to the day. I usually saw them closer to lunchtime than for a proper breakfast. They were night owls and stayed out late. Anyway, that morning they stayed for an hour or so, then left."

"It was by foot, though," Greg interjects, holding up a finger. "Jeremy's little Audi stayed parked outside all day. I saw it from the flower beds. We don't have a lot of those nice cars driving around here all the time. I don't think Michael had a car here, or at least he didn't park it with us."

That's odd. Jeremy must've picked him up from the small airport in Traverse City.

Nancy continues, "The rest of the day went like it usually does. I told you we picked up spaghetti dinner takeout from Pop's and were here otherwise."

"Nothing out of the ordinary," Greg confirms.

"Did you notice if Jeremy and Michael came back that night?" I ask, prodding further.

"I was still down here when Jeremy came back, maybe a little before ten p.m. He asked for his own room for the night and said he'd be leaving early in the morning. I gave him one, he paid for it, and that was that. He mentioned that Michael had gone out for a while and may be back late."

"So, you didn't see Michael come back at all on Wednesday?"

"Uh, nope. I went to bed around midnight, I'd guess. He wasn't back by then," she says hesitantly. "All of the room keys also unlock the front door to the building, so he could've come back after we were asleep."

"Okay, how about Thursday? Could you walk me through that day as well? You saw Michael Thursday morning, right? That's what the police report says." I ask, trying to keep her talking. I feel her pulling away from me.

"Thursday was like any other," Nancy continues slowly, glancing towards her husband. Then she stops and looks down at her lap. "I didn't see Jeremy or Michael for breakfast; I assumed they had gotten an early start to the day, like Jeremy said they would. I...I lied to Kelly." Her voice quivers.

"Jeremy came back to see if Michael was in later Thursday afternoon. I told him that I didn't think so and passed on a note that Charlotte Roth had left for Michael. I found it in the mailbox Thursday morning."

Nancy looks like she's going to cry, but I hold strong, the pressure building. *Kind but stern, kind but stern. Don't let a little old lady get to you. She could be a stone-cold killer...*

"Nancy, you knew why Michael was in town, didn't you? Tell the truth." I set down my mug and lean forward.

"Don't be upset, Greg." She pauses and looks at her husband, now taking both of his hands in hers. Turning back to me, "I overheard Jeremy and Michael scheming earlier in the week over all their papers." Her voice stops shaking and develops an edge. "That wretched man wanted to buy the Inn right from under us."

This is clearly news to Greg. I take a sip of my coffee in a weak attempt to hide the surprise from my face, allowing them to keep talking without interruption.

"I heard them saying something about offering us quite a bit of money for the Inn, but it just made my blood boil. This is our home for heaven's sake." She shakes her head in disgust.

"Why didn't you tell me?" Greg leans into her, talking quietly. His face reddens, embarrassed to be having this conversation in front of me. "We should've talked about that together…" The man looks disappointed and frankly, ticked off. His mouth purses into a thin line. I've never seen Greg upset before; it's a little unnerving.

"I knew you'd take the offer, so I hid it from you." Her gaze turns down to her lap again, ashamed of herself. "I told Charlotte instead. I thought she'd be able to put a stop to it before he even made an offer, what with her being in charge of the Chamber of Commerce group. I didn't want you to find out and sell it. I know money is tight, but I could never leave this Inn." She enunciates the last few words, emphasizing her point.

"You knew what the letter said, didn't you? You told Charlotte, and she offered to write a letter on behalf of the Chamber of Commerce." I push farther.

"Yes. That's exactly what happened." She takes a sip of her coffee and steadies herself. "When I didn't see him on Thursday morning, I figured that Charlotte had talked to him and that he'd left town already. I thought the letter was a formality, something in writing in case he got lawyers involved, that they had already spoken and she cleared it all up for me."

"I did see her skulking around out front Wednesday night from our bedroom window," Greg chimes in.

"Oh, she was probably just dropping off the letter, Gregory. It was in the mailbox in the morning."

"Interesting, thanks Greg..." I make note of this revelation. *Perhaps around the same time Michael was murdered?* "Nancy, I still don't understand why you lied to the police about seeing Michael on Thursday. Explain that to me better."

"Oh...well, when he still didn't turn up on Friday, and his business partner Jeremy hadn't heard from him, I felt a little guilty that I didn't call them earlier. When I finally did call on Friday, I didn't want it to seem like I waited too long, so I told them I saw him early Thursday morning. As small inn owners, we are supposed to notify the authorities if we don't hear from a guest for more than twenty-four hours.

"I guess I hoped he left town. It's not like people go missing often, right? When Jeremy came back Thursday afternoon and hadn't seen Michael either, that's when I thought something might be wrong. The man didn't have his own car after all... I swear I'm not hiding anything." She turns to her husband with a pleading look on her face.

"Nancy, why didn't you tell me any of this? We don't keep secrets from one another." He squeezes her hand, but his voice is rigid.

"Oh, Gregory. I knew you'd jump at the opportunity to sell this place with how things have been going lately. The building is technically in *your* name, not both our names. I couldn't bear to think about leaving this place."

I sympathize with Nancy. I get it. I'm the same way about our park. I'd do just about anything to save the park.

"Thank you for your honesty, both of you." I reach over and pat Nancy's shoulder. "One last question, and I promise I'll leave you alone."

"Anything, dear," Nancy says. I see the relief on her face, having come clean.

"Do you own a wheelbarrow?"

Chapter Fifteen

"Of course, we have quite the landscaping to maintain," Greg humbly brags, full of pride. "It's in the shed out back, happy to show you if you'd like. Not sure what good it'll do, it's a regular old wheelbarrow."

We finish our coffee and walk out back. The shed is sizable, maybe eight feet by eight feet, and covered in weathered wood shingles painted to match the main home. There is a small window next to an oversized door, built to accommodate a tractor or four-wheeler. Greg unlocks the door and lets me inside. It's a typical garden shed with tools, a riding mower, a leaf blower, and other usual gear. There is a rack of firewood in the back corner, as well as a fluorescent orange wheelbarrow parked in the corner.

"Have you used it recently?" I ask, pointing to the equipment in question.

"Yup, last week. Like I said earlier, I've been prepping our flower beds. Moving a lot of dirt around to get ready."

I take the few steps needed to get close to the wheelbarrow. It has spots of dirt and mud caked in the tire treads. I take a few photos with my phone. Swiping my finger through the gunk, I smush some of the mud between my fingers, examining it closely.

Topsoil. The dirt in our park is sandier and lighter in color than what's packed into this tire. This is store-bought topsoil for gardening, dark in color, and pumped with added nutrients. It's great for manicured gardens, but definitely doesn't match the park's natural composition.

"Do you have a tape measure by chance?" I ask, and Greg grabs a rake that has inch tic marks notched on the handle. I hold it next to the tire and take a few more photos. I don't see blood or anything else out of the ordinary, so I thank them both. That unsettled feeling in my stomach grows with each step. *Tick, tick, tick.*

"I trust you're going to tell Kelly everything you told me," I shout back. Nancy looks down, ashamed, and nods from the shed, promising to do so.

They may be telling the truth, but this nagging feeling won't let go. The Nest holds secrets that'll unlock this thing; all the relevant people circle around this place. Hell, it might even be where Michael was murdered. No good detective would go without checking it out…*right*? Channeling Veronica Mars, I walk around to the front of the building and make the split decision to dart in the B&B's front door while the two owners are still out back. What Kelly doesn't know won't hurt her.

There are five doors on either side of the upstairs hallway, ten guest rooms in total. Each has a small chalkboard that says "Welcome!" and the guest's name if occupied.

"How the heck am I supposed to know which one was his? Merda!" I whisper to myself, pacing the hallway. None of the doors say Michael on them. Of course, they removed that already. I didn't think this through. At the end of the hall is a window overlooking the back gardens; I can see Nancy and Greg outside by the shed, in a heated discussion by the looks of Greg's waving arms. He is more upset than he let on.

Three of the chalkboards have names on them. Assuming the police wouldn't allow his room to be occupied by someone new immediately after he died, I rule them out. Taking my chances, I jiggle the handle of an unoccupied door, testing my luck, but it's locked. Sneaking back down the stairs, I wake up Nancy's computer. The booking software is already pulled up, and with a couple of clicks, I find that Michael was in room eight. On the nights that Jeremy stayed here, he was in the adjoining room ten. His name is still on room ten's door sign.

Greg's elevated voice is getting louder; they're walking back around to the front of the Inn. I panic and duck behind the front desk right as the door opens. Pressing myself against the wood, attempting to hide among the disorganized books and files, I hold my breath and cross my fingers.

"I'm not sure what else I can say, Gregory! What's done is done! What more do you want from me? I've said I'm sorry a thousand times."

"It's the principle of the thing, Nancy. You lied to me. We don't lie to each other! We've been married for almost fifty years!" It's the loudest I've ever heard the normally gentle man.

Their voices travel into the dining room. I hear the tinkling of a kettle and the stoking of their big fireplace. Peeking out from the side of the desk, I find the coast temporarily clear. I grab Nancy's set of keys, crochet keychain and all, and slink back up the staircase without crossing their line of sight. With a quick prayer to the blonde detective goddesses (Buffy and Veronica), I move quickly up the stairs and unlock room eight, closing the door behind me with a reluctant squeak of the antique hinges.

Letting out the breath that I've been holding for eons, I relax for a second and take in the small room. It's fairly standard, but unkempt. The police have tossed it. There's a queen-sized bed against the far wall, flanked by delicate, pear-shaped glass lamps on top of wooden side tables. The furniture looks handmade, all of natural woods except for an upholstered wingback armchair in one corner, and the cream upholstered headboard. There's a gorgeous quilt crumpled up near the foot of the bed. The overall vibe is yard sale glam, just like the rest of the place.

The closet is empty except for a dozen hangers strewn about and a wide-open safe. It's empty, too. The police have taken all his belongings already. I crouch down and take a closer look at the heavy, metal box. Straining to lift it up to peer behind, I almost throw out my back. It's too heavy to move.

Not finding much else interesting, I unlock the door connected to the adjoining room. If Jeremy is in here, I can play dumb or try to flirt my way out of it, but my gut says he'll be gone at this time of day, out and about. What does Jeremy have to hide?

It feels a little intrusive to rifle through his stuff, but not too intrusive to stop me from doing it. *My job is on the line*. The bones of the room are the same as Michael's. The furniture is largely identical, except for a few fabric choices. The lamps are of clear green instead of blue, but the same fragile glass.

Jeremy is neat and organized. Everything is in a proper place, nothing thrown around or crumpled. The bed is made, and the closet is tidy. The safe is locked. I see that gorgeous sweater he was wearing the first time we met folded neatly on a shelf. On his desk is an open briefcase.

Since I already have a potential B&E charge, not to mention the obstruction of justice charge Kelly threatened me with, I might as well add invasion of privacy to the laundry list. With a shrug and a can-do (screw it) attitude, I carefully sift through the contents of the briefcase.

I'm not fluent in legalese, and some of this is over my head, but the gist is clear. There are offer letters for Michael to buy The Nest, Java Jones, and the pizza place. There are lines crossed out and notes written by hand in the margins, like they're still drafts. There's also a forest green book titled *Trail Blazers* written in gold script that looks delicate and old. There are drafts of other contracts in here too. Reviewing loose pages, I find one that is for a big land parcel. There's always a big new development project happening around Traverse City. People are moving up here in droves.

Looking closer at the business offers, the two had gone back and forth negotiating the terms. They worked it out, though; they both signed off and dated all the language tweaks last Tuesday, coming to a mutual agreement.

There's also a handful of pamphlets for Jeremy's company, Jeremy Gray Realty with the slogan, "Gray skies turn blue with Jeremy Gray Realty," a *super* flattering picture of him (I bite my lip), a picture of a recent multi-million-dollar sale from a neighboring town, and his contact information.

I keep shuffling through layers of paper until I reach a pocket built into the bottom of the case, like where a laptop would go. Peeping in, a cracked cell phone and mud-caked black leather wallet stare back at me threateningly.

That very moment, I hear Nancy's footsteps slowly climb the creaky stairs as she hums a little tune. Pure terror hits me like a ton of bricks, and I now regret this incredibly stupid decision. Without thinking, I shove the phone and wallet into my jacket pocket. Eyes darting wildly for a place to hide, I slide into Jeremy's closet and close the doors.

"Knock, Knock! Housekeeping! Jeremy, are you in?" Nancy gently raps on the door a few times before I hear rustling. "Shoot, I left my keys downstairs." I hear her humming soften as she retreats down to the front desk.

I climb out of the closet, careful not to get any grime on Jeremy's fancy clothes, and look at the keyring that I took. The very key ring Nancy is headed downstairs to grab. The garden shed, where the three of us examined their wheelbarrow, is in clear view of one of the windows in this room. For better or worse, I open the window and hurl the keys; they land not far from the shed door.

From downstairs, I hear Nancy calling to Greg, "Did you have the room keys, Gregory? They're not behind the desk." I crack the room door to hear a little better.

"Nope, I don't think so, Nancy. You had 'em last," he calls back. It sounds like he's still in the dining room.

"Huh. Maybe I dropped 'em outside. Come help me search if you're not too bitter." The two have made up, at least enough to carry on, business as usual.

I hear the front door open and close and frantically dash down the stairs, shutting Jeremy's door behind me. Once safely on the sidewalk a block away, I catch my breath. *Breaking and entering?! Who the hell are you, Lorso?*

The guilt of thievery quickly (too quickly?) easing up, I turn to the burgled phone and wallet that's burning a hole in my pocket. I need to take a closer look, somewhere safe.

Chapter Sixteen

The aftermath of the adrenaline spike leaves me with an emotional hangover. Coupled with the recent stint of sleepless nights, I trudge over to Java Jones, then to my office to think all this through in peace. Not to mention examine the stolen evidence I'm casually harboring in my pocket. I can spread out in my locked office, hopefully connecting some dots without the distractions of being at home (or nosy neighbors peeking through windows).

"I vant a cup of covvee," I cry like a vampire to Tracy behind the counter.

"Ha, ha, hey Maudy! Coming right up." The barista laughs and begins working on her latest creation. I stand in front of the counter, watching her do her magic.

"Guess what?" She asks, a massive grin on her face. A grin much too large to be from my dumb vampire impersonation.

"What?" I ask.

"I got into Michigan State! Victory for MSU!" She sings in excitement. I join in her elation, thankful for this bit of good news. After a not-so-great rendition of the school's fight song, we settle down, and she hands me my coffee.

"Tracy, that is so amazing! I know I'm biased and don't feel pressure, but where do you think you'll end up going? Now that your options are wide open, Ms. Smarty Pants."

"Oh, State for sure. Without a doubt." She nods to herself, sure of her decision. "It's got the best program. And, Lansing isn't too far from here, what, like three hours? That's nothing."

"I'm *so* proud of you." She comes out from around the counter and hugs me.

"Thanks so much for your help on the application, I owe you. Those essays wouldn't have been half as good without your edits."

"You owe me nothing! It was no big deal. I owe *you* a drink to celebrate a fellow Spartan."

"Deal! There's a lot to plan and organize in the next few months, but I'm pumped. Thanks for everything, Maudy."

I leave Java Jones revived, the news (and caffeine) perking me up. I'll be sad to see her go, but she's on to great things. It'll be fun to watch her grow.

As I walk to the park entrance, heading for the ranger station, the sky begins to shift from blue to gray, reminding me of Jeremy's business slogan. A thunderstorm is brewing over the dark, swirling water. Unlocking the door and dumping my bag on my desk, I put on yet another pot of coffee, already draining Tracy's brew on the walk over, build a fire, and lock myself in the building for the rest of the morning.

First things first: the wallet. Michael's wallet has seen better days. The black leather is encrusted in mud. Using a paper napkin to prevent myself from leaving fingerprints (does this actually work? It does on TV, so it's good enough for me), I unfold it, turning my head away from the moldy stink wafting off it.

Inside are a couple of waterlogged hundred-dollar bills, a Jeremy Gray reality flyer, credit cards, and an old Polaroid picture. It's hard to make out the details of the picture, but it looks like a woman and a kid, maybe? Michael's loved ones, perhaps? They're standing in front of a small, wooden cabin.

The phone is dead and cracked, so no new information there. I don't think covering it in rice, or even the jaws of life, would bring this thing back to life.

I can't believe Jeremy had these. It's hard to go against evidence like this. Before calling Kelly, I want to sit down and think through all of the possibilities. She won't let me see these again once I hand them over. I have to take this opportunity while I have it, legal or not.

An hour later, looking outside at the darkening sky with no new revelations, I check my phone and confirm my suspicions about the weather. We're due for a rainstorm rolling in from Lake Michigan this afternoon that looks like a doozy. I've hit a mental wall and need an extra brain to bounce ideas off of, too. With Kelly being stupendously unhelpful, I turn to the next best thing.

I text Eli, using Marty's fear of thunderstorms as an excuse. Eli doesn't usually start work for a couple of hours and responds quickly, saying he'll run the little guy over.

I'm not lying to him about the dog. Marty is terrified of thunder. With Stone's Throw so close to the massive lake, we get some gnarly thunderstorms. When they come in, Marty sticks to me like glue. I can't leave him home alone. Eli is being so weird right now, but he's a sucker for Marty. Everyone is a sucker for Marty.

Not fifteen minutes later, a sweaty Eli and a panting dog arrive at the park entrance, both breathing fast from the exercise. I usher them through the closed-off parking lot. *Kelly won't mind if he stops by for a minute, right? I know we're closed to the public but is he 'the public'?* Marty takes a drink of water and lies down on his bed, belly up and tongue hanging out of his mouth. Eli sits down on the coffee table to avoid getting the couch upholstery sweaty. If only he knew the amount of dog slobber and forest gunk that thing has endured over the years.

"Thanks for running him over. I didn't necessarily mean that literally, though," I joke. "You know how he gets when it's storming."

"Yeah, no problem. I was planning on going for a jog today, anyway.

It was good to get it out of the way before the rain comes. What's up? What's all this?"

On the floor in the middle of the room lies what once was the office bulletin board and is now home to my crazy murder notes. It's covered in colorful stickies with hairbrained clues, evidence, and suspects. Next to it on the ground is a stack of notecards, already with unanswered questions jotted on them in thick, permanent marker.

"Oh, just a bit of brainstorming. I need to straighten out a few things." I keep it vague, but don't prevent him from looking through what I've written so far. I know this man can't resist a puzzle.

"Charlotte was at The Nest Wednesday night?" He asks, seeing my notecard that says, "Did Charlotte go inside the Nest or just drop off a letter?" after taking a moment to snoop.

"You didn't hear it from me, but yes. I'm trying to figure out if she went inside the building or if she just walked past. Nancy said she found a letter from Charlotte in her mailbox the next morning, and Greg noticed her briefly from their window."

"I bet I can find that out for you. We have a security camera on the back door of Pop's. The street in front of the B&B might be in view. We for sure have a direct shot of their backyard at least."

"That'd be great! Can you check today? Can you see if Michael came back sometime that night?"

"Sure, I'll text you what I see, no problem. Well, I'm going to keep trucking. Are you coming for spaghetti tonight?"

"I'm not sure. It'll depend on how far I get with this whole mess." I sweep my hand a la Vanna White across the corkboard.

"Okay, no worries. Well, see ya later." He jogs back out the door, jumping over the chain hanging across the entryway on his way out.

He is quick to leave and still a little awkward, but all in all, we're getting back on track.

"Okie dokie, arti-Marty, so what do we know?" The dog looks up at me briefly, not amused, and grumbles back to sleep.

"Main suspects we got: Charlotte Roth, Jeremy Gray, and Nancy Finch. Right? Am I missing somebody?" No response from the dog, which I take as an iron-clad confirmation.

"Who knew Michael? Jeremy, obviously, Nancy, and Greg for sure, anyone else? Lucas probably? He and Jeremy are buddies from Traverse City.

"Okay, now who has a motive? Jeremy again, oh boy, this isn't looking great for him, Charlotte for sure, Nancy Finch too, for the same reason as Charlotte. Let's go through them all one by one.

"Jeremy was seen yelling with Michael right before he died, although I still don't know what about. Jeremy's being cagey about this. It's probably just business, from what he said, but we don't know for a fact. The notes on the contract drafts made it seem like they were on the same page. Who knows, though. He also had Michael's phone and wallet. I can't ignore that fun, little fact.

"Charlotte was desperate to stop him from purchasing property. She's all for development, but she wants it from folks who live here, who own small, cute businesses. She can't stand big corporate types and chains like the stuff Michael does.

"And last but not least, Nancy Finch, who was terrified Michael would make an offer to buy her B&B that her husband, who does all the bookkeeping, couldn't refuse. You hear that, Marty? An offer he couldn't refuse," I wheeze in my best (horrible) Godfather impression. The dog declines to acknowledge it, embarrassed to be associated with me even in private.

I draw a line that runs along the bottom of the corkboard, noting specific time windows and events, beginning with Wednesday night when Michael was last seen.

Stepping back to look at my work, I'm faced with a tangled web of a lot of questions and not a lot of answers. "Where are the gaps?

What am I missing?" The dog opens one eye, realizes I'm not doing anything that involves peanut butter or squeaky toys, and drifts back to sleep. *Useless dog.* I stand above my bulletin board, fully embodying the infamous Charlie Kelly meme, positive that I'm missing something.

Spinning around in my office chair, staring at the ceiling, hoping an idea will dislodge if I whirl around fast enough, Eli texts me.

It reads, *Hey Mud, I went through the Wed. footage, all the way through Thurs. morning. The street was basically dead past ten. Charlotte did walk by at a quarter to one but didn't go in, at least I doubt it. From the cam's view of the backyard, I see her pass by one side of the house and then the other in just a few seconds. No direct view of the mailbox, she could've dropped something off. She looks like she's walking home. No sign of Michael all night.*

I can't imagine Charlotte killing the man out in the open; she's physically much weaker than I am, and Michael was a pretty big dude. He was killed by a hit to the head. Charlotte is petite, I'm not sure she could pull that off. While it could *technically* still be possible for her to have killed him, the probability dwindles, and I reluctantly run a heavy Sharpie line through her suspect sticky note. Why would she leave a letter if she knew he was dead? Kelly is right. It's time to give up on the Charlotte theory.

* * *

Marty and I order a pizza from the shop down the street, which is kind enough to deliver it to the park entrance. The rain gently falls, with the threatening promise of severe storms to come. Chowing down on a slice of pepperoni and onion, I give a few crust scraps to the dog to keep him awake enough to listen to me talk.

"We know that Michael was last seen on Wednesday night by Jeremy and Anna, heading towards the beach. He and Jeremy had gotten into a fight about who knows what (money maybe?), and Jeremy was furious.

"We know he was killed sometime that night, but nobody seemed to notice. His body was carted by a wheelbarrow into the park and dumped where you," I say, pointing at the fluffy pup with my pizza slice, "found him on Saturday morning.

"Nancy Finch knew he wanted to buy her Inn but kept it from her husband. She told Charlotte, the town's official busybody, who wrote an angry letter ordering him to stop. Did Charlotte talk to him before he disappeared? Nancy thinks so, but neither Charlotte nor Jeremy mentioned that. So that's still an unknown.

"Nancy didn't report him missing or start asking around until Friday morning, she says it's because she had hoped he'd left town. But Greg said he didn't have a car here, and presumably Nancy knew that. That still seems fishy to me."

"Bow row row," the dog chatters, asking for more crust. I hand him a small piece and he lies down again.

"Anyway, I thought it could've been a random mugging at first. His wallet, phone, watch, and jewelry were all missing. That doesn't seem to be the case anymore, though, since we found his wallet, still with a ton of cash inside, and his busted phone in Jeremy's briefcase. Big yikes. Do you think I need to tell Kelly about that right now? She's busy with the hair and fingerprints. This might just have her abandon that effort and arrest Jeremy right away."

The dog's nose follows my hand as I gesture wildly with the slice of pizza as I talk. I know the evidence is incriminating, but I'm not completely convinced (or refuse to believe it). How did he get a wheelbarrow? Why would he keep the wallet and phone? I need more time to keep mulling it over.

"Kelly's got hair strands and a fingerprint she's trying to ID; remind me to ask her about that next time we talk," I order the dog. He licks his lips, asking for another pizza bribe. I oblige.

I frenetically churn on this for the rest of the day, hunkering down in my office, with only my dog to tell me my harebrained ideas are crazy. I need this alone time. My mind wanders through a labyrinth of rabbit holes, even somehow considering that Jim, our campground caretaker, could have done it since Kelly was having a hard time confirming his alibi.

Peering out the office's front window, the small, quietly pattering rain is starting to drop more forcefully, thumping louder and louder on the wooden porch in front of our building. The patter hits the roof rhythmically, mimicking the *tick, tick, tick* of The Nest's cuckoo clock. Compulsively, I tap my finger on my desk, keeping time.

"Marty, you're a great companion, but not much of a conversationalist. If I don't talk with another human soon, I'm a goner." Hoping Peyton isn't too swamped at the bakery, I grab my phone and give her a call. Maybe, just maybe, I can convince her to join me for a slice of this pizza, and maybe, just maybe, she can keep me distracted enough to not spiral too far. After the fourth ring, she picks up. I hear the hum of bakery customers and ovens in the background.

"Hey, Maudy, how you holding up?" She must be busy; she sounds far away and a little garbled with all of the background noise.

"Oh, you know. Just trying to solve a man's murder and save my job. Same old, same old." The rhythmic rain grows louder as the storm marches towards me.

"Ha. Well, would a fresh almond croissant help? I find that when problems get big and I go loopy, the butter in French pastries tends to help straighten things out. I just pulled a batch out of the oven."

"I'll trade you a croissant for a slice of pizza? I ordered one and have a ton left over. Think you'll be ready to take a break soon? Do you have help there today?"

"Oh, pizza sounds great! And yes, I do. Hang on one sec—Uh-huh, that'll be $7.29." She is checking out a customer. "Sorry about that."

"Good! I'm glad you have some help. Selfishly, that means I get company. Do you want to come here, or should I head towards you?"

"If it's not too much trouble, it'd be great if you could come here. I'm not sure I can scoot away for too long. I'll make us a little smorgasbord."

I look over at the sleeping dog in the corner. He'll be fine here alone for a while. "Sure, that sounds great. I'll bring the za. I'm at my office, give me like ten minutes and I'll be there." We hang up.

"Okay, Marty, I'm trusting you, dude. I won't be more than forty-five minutes, tops. Please, *please* don't destroy anything. I'll be back before the storm picks up." One large, brown eye slowly opens. I take a peanut butter-flavored chewy stick out of my desk drawer and drop it near his bed. "Take this as a bribe. Love you, fluff butt."

With my hood up, pizza box in hand, I make it to the bakery without getting too wet. It's still busy inside, but I manage to grab Peyton's attention, so she knows I'm here. She is working hard, trying to shrink the line that snakes throughout the small space, but she waves me around back.

The vast majority of the behind-the-scenes space is taken up by an immaculately tidy kitchen. Behind that is a small break room that has a couple of employee lockers, a coat rack, and a table. In the back, a small staircase leads up to her apartment. She lives right above the bakery.

Peyton has placed an adorable wicker basket filled with pastries in the center of the table, with two plates and cutlery already set up for us.

I set my backpack down on a bench near the lockers, hang up my jacket on a coat rack next to the back door, and set the pizza on the table. She joins me, pulling two mugs of hot apple cider from the microwave and bringing them over to the table.

"Thanks for meeting me, Peyton. I need to get out of my head. It's not pretty in there." I rub my temples with my fingers, trying to stave off the anxious mind chatter.

"Anytime. I know how hard this week has been on you." She reaches out her hand and squeezes mine. The look on her face is past concern and into full-on worry territory.

"I'll be fine, Peyton. Really, I promise." Her trepidation turns into a smirk of doubt. As if to say, *'Yeah yeah okay,'* sarcastically.

While quick, our lunch date is a life preserver thrown to me as I'm mentally drowning. We have more than our fill of sweets and pizza, and after about twenty minutes of benign, non-murdery chit-chat, I stretch out my arms and stand up from my chair, which is the universal Midwestern 'ope, best be on my way' signal.

Grabbing my backpack and throwing on my jacket to return to the office, praying to any god that will listen that Marty hasn't ripped up our office couch, my phone buzzes. "One sec," I say to Peyton, finishing the last of the cider in my mug to pick up the call. It's Kelly.

"Maudy, glad I caught you."

"Hey Kell, what's up?" *Act casual. She has no way of knowing that you're concealing stolen evidence right now.* I rub my forehead with the heel of my hand again, trying to massage away the headache sparking like the lightning off in the distance.

"It's that hair we found. We have a match. Well, not a *match* but helpful intel nonetheless."

"And?" The urgency is not hidden in my voice.

"Some of the hair strands aren't Michael's. They're his son's."

Chapter Seventeen

I stop; Peyton bumps into me as she clears our dishes. "They're *whose?*" My chin hits the floor.

"What's going on?" Peyton asks quietly.

I wave at her to be quiet, concentrating on Kelly.

"You heard correctly." She sighs. "His son. The DNA of some, but *not all* of the hair we found, shows a filial relationship and has a Y chromosome, so..." she trails off.

I'm stunned. Without any unoccupied brain cells to respond to her, I keep listening, mouth hanging open. Peyton's eyes are locked on mine, both utterly confused. After exactly seven seconds of silence, Kelly continues.

"Hair follicle DNA isn't the most reliable technology anymore; it can provide inaccurate results, for sure. That being said, the forensics lab seemed pretty jazzed when they called me with the news. All the hair samples came back as male; only a few are his son's. The rest are Michael's."

"Wow...this is...wow." *What an astute observation, Maudy.*

"Tell me about it. Look, I need to get back to it. I'm spending the day coordinating with Chicago PD; I'm hoping they can help connect some of these dots. Let me know if you find anything."

I give Peyton a hug and power walk back to the park. The rain is coming down hard now, but I couldn't care less. By the time I reach my office door, I'm sopping wet; I might as well have swum over here. Stepping inside, I peel off the clingy, cold layers and drop them on the hearth of the fireplace to dry.

"You would not believe what happened, Marty." The pooch is still curled up on his bed near my desk. He woke up at some point; the peanut butter stick is nibbled down to a pointy nub, about half its original size. I give a quick 'thank you' to the canine gods, appreciating that Marty's tornado mode wasn't activated, and that the thunder held off while I was gone.

"What, were you going to break out of here if I didn't come back soon? Fashion yourself a little doggie shiv, did ya?" I muss his shaggy ear fur and kiss the side of his long snout.

I wring out my frizzy dark hair, tie it back into a top knot, and restart the small fire.

"He has a kid!" I cry to the dog, who opens both eyes this time, perturbed by all the disturbance. "The hair that Kelly found on Michael's body—it's his son's!" Waddling over to me, still half asleep, Marty stretches and sits down at my feet.

I remember searching through Michael's social media and can't remember anyone who could've been a son. Maybe it's the young boy in the old photograph from his wallet? He isn't married and seems to not be dating anyone seriously. It seemed that he had been dating many women casually.

I crack open my laptop, hoping to dig something up with this new information. I bet Michael is in his mid to late forties. Checking the copy of the case file that Kelly lent me, I confirm he was forty-five when he died. *Mental note to ask Jeremy about Michael's personal life. Did he talk about a family at all?*

Kelly didn't tell me how old Michael's son is, can DNA even do that? I don't know, but based on Michael's age, I guess his kid is at most around twenty-five. Maybe a little older if Michael was a teenager when he was born.

Searching "Michael Price court case" and "Michael Price lawsuit" yields too many results to efficiently sift through. I try to find a custody battle or divorce settlement that would be public record, but instead, pages and pages of news articles, public hearings, and interviews about different development ventures flood the search results. Some of his projects had significant community pushback. After reading some of the headlines, I tend to agree with some of the pushback.

On the flip side, "Michael Price family," "Michael Price children," "Michael Price custody" come up with nothing.

Over an hour later, still scrolling, a quiet scratching at the door brings me back down to rainy reality. Our door is solid wood, with the top half housing a small window. The scratching continues, but I can't see anyone out there. The thunderstorm has reared its head, darkening the skies. Marty is lying underneath my desk on top of my feet, waiting for it to pass.

Whatever the scratching is, it grabs Marty's attention too, and his ears pop up. A low rumbly growl ruptures from his throat, and the ridge of long fur spikes along his back, giving a mohawk effect. *Guard dog mode activated.* Peering out of the large window near my desk, with a clear view of our porch, I crane to see if someone's standing at the door. Maybe it's a kid who is shorter than the window?

Still seeing nobody, I open the door with Marty cemented to my side and am greeted by the chaotic splashing of heavy rain in the forest as well as the mews of a very small, sopping-wet, black kitten.

Marty's tail immediately wags in full swing the second he lays his big eyes on the little creature. The teensy cat is pawing at the bottom of the door with even teensier front claws. It meows and clumsily leaps inside, trying to escape the cold rain. Not afraid of Marty in the slightest, the pint-sized furball walks right up to the dog and sniffs his front paw. Marty, tail now rivaling a windmill, bows down on his front legs so his head rests on the floor in front of the kitten, butt still sticking straight up in the air.

The growl stops and is replaced by a short, yippy, high-pitched bark that is his 'play with me!' sound. He makes the same goofy noise to Nellie's girls.

The kitten rubs up onto the side of the dog's face, its entire body the size of Marty's snout. "Marty, be gentle…" I warn, afraid he's going to pick up the poor animal and throw it around like a toy. To my complete surprise, the dog doesn't make a move. Instead, he lies down on his side and the kitten ambles over, kneading biscuits on the dog's pink belly.

My heart melts, loving this adorable, unlikely animal friendship for a moment before pulling myself together. Cautiously bending down towards the cat, I check to see if it's hurt. I can tell that it is, in fact, a 'he', and that he doesn't have any visible wounds. He's small but not a baby, maybe six months to a year old if I have to venture an uneducated guess, and is jet-black from nose to tail. His eyes are an amber-gold color, with the left one mostly fogged over in a milky scar.

Now reassured that Marty isn't going to swallow him whole, I watch the two of them cuddle, hoping the dog's body heat will keep the cat warm. I call Laura's office, our town veterinarian, to see if she could see the cat soon.

"Sticks and Stone's Throw Veterinary, how can I help you?" Darci answers with a rote, sing-song receptionist tone.

"Hi, Darci, it's Maudy."

"Hi, Maudy, is everything alright? Is Marty okay?"

"Marty's fine, thanks. A kitten wandered into the park office today. He is all wet and cold. He's cuddling with Marty now, but he should probably see you guys to make sure everything's okay. He got in a fight or something, one of his eyes is all cloudy."

"Oh, poor guy! Of course. Why don't I come over to grab him? I can bring our van if you can meet me at the entrance."

"That'd be great, thanks so much! I'll keep an eye out for you."

We end our conversation; she promises to be here in the next couple of hours.

"You'll be just fine." I gently pet the kitten's head, who is now fast asleep as Marty's little spoon.

* * *

Now that the rain has hit torrential downpour status, I assume that Zach will make an appearance soon. He's out working on the campground, and I can't imagine he'll stay out there much longer. Right on cue, with a binder held over his head in a futile attempt to stay dry, a soggy Zach frantically jiggles the door handle, asking me to unlock the door.

Darting through the doorway, he quickly sheds layers and unloads his stuff on his desk, jogging right past us. Shaking off the water like a wet dog, his curly blonde hair slapping against his forehead, he rummages through our closet and finds a clean, dry sweatshirt and a pair of socks.

The cuddle puddle wakes up, disbanding with the commotion. Marty scampers over to say hello to his favorite co-worker, while the cat quickly settles back on Marty's warm bed.

I discreetly flip the murder board upside down, wanting to keep my investigation to myself. I trust Zach, but I don't want to get him involved in this. He's got enough going on, and I need his full attention on the campground. He eyes me suspiciously as I turn it over, but doesn't say anything.

"We have a new park employee." I point to Marty's bed, where the black cat lies knotted in a tight ball.

"Aww, who is this delight?" He approaches the cat slowly, pulling on an old DNR sweatshirt.

"He just wandered in. I'm guessing he was looking for someplace to get out of the rain. I called Laura's office; Darci is about to come get him and check him out."

"Poor cutie kitty. Here, little kitty." He crouches down, trying not to startle him. The cat opens one eye, doesn't seem to assess Zach as a threat, and closes it again. "He's so sweet!"

"Oh, I know. He's adorable! Marty was being such a good friend, too. He let the little guy sleep right next to him and warm him up."

"This is so precious." He grabs his phone and snaps pictures of the cat. "Our followers are going to *love* this."

After a few more minutes of cooing at the new officemate, we settle down at our desks and continue to refine the contingency plan.

"One more day." I sink further into my overstuffed desk chair, a fresh mug of coffee in front of my face.

"I'm afraid so…we can handle it though. It'll all be okay." His eyes dart towards the bulletin board. "Not only that, but a little birdie tells me you might have a new love interest." Both of his eyebrows creep up, a grin widening so big it puts the Cheshire Cat to shame.

Who is he talking about? Jeremy? Perplexed, I ask, "What? What did you hear? I'm not seeing anyone."

"Well not yet, but rumor has it that a certain fancy, hunky realtor has taken an interest in you. Why do you think he's stuck around so long?"

"Um, because Kelly *ordered* him to. The police asked everyone in town at the time Michael disappeared to stay until the whole thing is resolved." *Is everyone talking behind my back about this?* This makes my skin crawl, and I nervously tap the seconds to stay grounded. *One, two, three, four.*

"Even if that's true, he seems to be making the most of the extended stay." The smile creeps even larger. "I think he *liiiiiiikes* you," he jabs, poking fun and causing my cheeks to redden. *One, two, three, four.* "He even told Eli to 'back down' the other day at Pop's. You know, when you two were on a *daaaate*," singing again. "Nancy Finch let it slip that he called *you* when he was upset and going through something."

"We were NOT on a date!" I shriek, louder than intended, unable to contain my frustration. His grin curdles into surprise.

"Whoa, whoa, I'm just playing around. I'm sorry." He holds up his hands in a, *'don't shoot'* gesture.

"He's been flirting with me, but I promise you it hasn't been reciprocated." I ball up a sticky note and throw it at him. After six seconds, I calm down. "Don't be sorry, I'm the one who's sorry. I'm on edge. That's all. Didn't mean to take it out on you."

He smiles that same sympathy-borderline-pity smile everyone's been giving me all week.

"It's okay, don't worry about it. But you might want to tell him that you're not into him. News is traveling quickly, and that's the hottest tea that's spilling all across town." He winks at me, sipping from an invisible teacup, pinky out and everything.

After another hour of work, both of us working on campground logistics, Darci stops by and honks the horn of the clinic's van. I hand off the kitten, reassured that he'll be in great hands, and promise to check in on him soon.

With our contingency plan set, I call Harper to give her a heads-up on the case's progress and the unfortunate possibility of needing to relocate campers.

"Is the uh, body problem solved?" She asks flatly, without any greeting.

"Not quite, but we do have a plan in case it stays that way." I offer, hopeful she'll be okay with our new plan.

"Lay it on me."

While not enthused, she's grateful for our effort and emphasizes *yet again* that I need to try to figure this out before having to make those calls tomorrow. *Yeesh, I get it.* I tell her that we're going to have to split the reservation fees with the Village Parks and Rec so their staff can be compensated for their time this weekend. Our revenue would end up at about thirty percent of the original projection. It's not good, but it is a hell of a lot better than nothing.

The uneasy feeling in the pit of my stomach grows like a tumor after hanging up the phone. This won't be enough to save the park. I'm proud of Zach for trying to find the best-case alternative, but I'll have a lot of work to do this summer to make up for the lost reservation fees if given the opportunity.

As the workday trudges on, I keep glancing at the back of the murder board, frustrated with myself. *What the heck am I missing?* I text Kelly and tell her that I didn't find much in the way of who Michael's son might be and apologize.

About thirty minutes later, she responds. It's short and to the point.

Don't worry about the son thing, that doesn't matter. We have a positive match on the fingerprint. We got our guy. It's Jeremy, and he didn't do it alone.

Chapter Eighteen

"C'mon, Kelly. Pick up, pick up." After two rings, the call goes to her voicemail. She screens me.

"Hi, you've reached the voicemail box of Officer Kelly Sherwood, please leave a message." I hang up, frustrated.

Excellent. She's probably in the middle of arresting Jeremy Gray, the only man who's shown a romantic interest in me in the last year. The murderer. *Yikes, let's not look at that too closely.*

Zach is eyeing me like I'm crazy, his hands held out asking, 'what is it?' I hold my index finger up, 'give me a minute.' I need to spin around in my desk chair in a futile attempt to organize my thoughts.

Jeremy is still on my list of suspects, too, and I guess it does make sense... He had the dead man's missing phone and wallet. He was arguing with him right before he died, and he has a bit of a history...

On the other hand, Jeremy's access to a wheelbarrow isn't super clear. He could have stolen it from The Nest's shed, but the door was kept locked. I saw Greg unlock it when he took me to see for myself. Not to mention, the wheel still had topsoil embedded in the treads from when Greg was gardening Wednesday morning before Michael was killed.

Rain peppers the roof of the office, like thousands of pebbles launched from thousands of slingshots. The thunder roars over the lake, turning the sky a menacing greenish charcoal. I'm grateful the black cat found us, shuddering at the idea of the poor guy alone, wet, and scared out of his mind out in this weather. Laura and Darci will take good care of him.

Should I take him in? Marty seems to have latched on pretty quick. I look at the dog. He's quiet now, but he can be a handful and a half. I can't be outnumbered. The Lorso familia is plenty big with its current two members. *Maybe I can convince one of my friends to take him in, so he and Marty can still hang out. That would be nice.*

After all of that talk and teasing about Jeremy's interest in me, I dance around sharing the news with Zach. "Okay, so I need you to promise me this stays between us for now…"

"Absolutely… Is everything alright?" He looks alarmed, and slightly frustrated that I've been sitting here in silence for the last few minutes (two hundred and seventy-one seconds, to be precise), spinning around and around in my chair, lost in thought.

"Kelly solved the case." I almost don't believe the words coming out of my mouth, and shrug. "She's arresting Jeremy as we speak. She'll probably need to tie up a few loose ends, but it seems to have been resolved."

This is anticlimactic. A text telling me everything is buttoned up? That's it? Not that I'm one for fanfare, I just assumed there'd be some real closure. Poirot and Sherlock always have a dramatic reveal at the end.

However it ends, I'm just glad that it's over. We'll probably be able to open the park in time. The weight of a Sisyphean-esque boulder finally lifts off my shoulders.

"Oh my gosh, that's fantastic! Well, for Kelly, anyways. You're dating a murderer, so you may need to do a bit of soul searching." He laughs, obviously kidding. I throw another balled-up sticky note at him in a lighthearted retaliation.

We return to our work, I answer a few emails, and he goes through lesson plans for student group visits next week, presuming that park activities resume as planned by then. Until I hear otherwise, I must keep the camping contingency plan as is, with the park closed tomorrow. Who knows, the police may have more to document out in the woods. I have no idea how that all works, but will hound Kelly to give us the green light to reopen ASAP. If only she'd answer her damn phone.

"Need a ride home?" Zach offers. With the rain coming down in epic proportions, I take him up on it.

Safely in our driveway, I wave goodbye to Zach as Marty and I dash through The Den's front door.

Dancing around the kitchen, I lean into the positive feelings of relief that follow Kelly's news and treat myself to a real, home-cooked (from *this* home, not Eli's or Pop's) dinner. After visiting Eli and smelling his grandpa's recipe, I've had stew on the brain and throw together a recipe I find on Food Network. Feeling extra fancy, I even toss a batch of break-and-bake chocolate chip cookies into the oven. With a big glass of Chianti in hand, swirling around the kitchen, I'm as light (and tipsy) as Ina Garten on *The Barefoot Contessa.*

This is the second Wednesday spaghetti dinner in a row that I've missed. When was the last time that happened? Ever? After my last time in there, and with the rumor mill spinning yarn about me and Jeremy, I opt for skipping out tonight. Alone time sounds good right now.

"Ah, that was good. Wasn't it, Martin?" I grab a box of blank cards and a couple of fun-colored pens from a shelf behind the couch and plop down next to the dog.

"Who should we start with? Zach probably." I have so many people I want to thank for their help this week. Zach, for handling this disruption with such grace, Kelly for her diligence (even though she made my job harder), and Eli, as more of an apology for whatever the heck Jeremy said to him. Cookies and a handwritten note should do the trick. I tie up three small parcels, each with a few cookies, and place them in my backpack so I don't forget them on my way out the door tomorrow.

With that out of the way, I tackle Dish Mountain that's taken over my sink, when an unknown number calls my phone. Letting it go to voicemail, I'm happily preoccupied in campground daydreams and sudsy hands.

Listening to the voicemail about thirty minutes later, an unfamiliar gruff voice bellows in my ear.

"Ms. Lorso, this is Sheriff Mike Landry. Officer Kelly Sherwood has notified me of how helpful you've been, so I'd like to personally extend my gratitude. Thank you for your assistance this week. I'm calling to let you know you are free to open the park up to the public. We're closing this case. Well, take care."

Yes! Thank the park gods. It's too late now, but in the morning, I'll call Zach and let him know that we can call off our contingencies. Hot tears of relief fall down my cheeks in a massive, crashing swell. The queasy knot that has claimed squatters' rights in my stomach is finally starting to pack up and move out. The incessant, rhythmic ticking begins to wane.

"Looks like things will be going back to normal, Marty." I glance over at the dog, who is busy gnawing on a toy. Crunching loudly, he looks up at me with the whites of his eyes. With a loving pat, I leave him to it and mosey back over to the couch.

'Back to normal' is all I've craved. I want my regular euchre nights, my spaghetti dinners without the town's collective eyes boring into my back, my hikes alone with Marty, and my amazing friends. Now that I have it, why does it seem a little like a letdown? Dare I say disappointing even?

Shelving that existential question for a later time, I distract myself from this hellish week with a Buffy rerun. Cuddled on the couch with a second glass of wine, I shoot the other card sharks a text in our group chat, letting them know we're all clear for our camping trip.

After three episodes and with all my friends on board, I start packing for the camping trip, making sure the most precious cargo (ghost stories, decks of cards, marshmallows) makes it into my duffel. With *Good Charlotte* blaring in the background, Marty and I party our way through The Den, packing our way as we go, allowing the stress to melt away.

Once the dance party ends and my eyes droop, I pick a book from the shelf and take it with me up to the loft. Nestling in tight, Marty at my feet, I get about five pages in before drifting off into a much-needed, sound sleep.

Chapter Nineteen

For the first time in over a week, since Harper's budget call, I sleep through the night. I think Marty knows how much I need it. He keeps himself busy looking out of the loft window into the backyard at a few robins perched in my old, gnarled apple tree. I stretch and grab my phone, realizing it's already eight-thirty a.m. Time to call in the big dogs.

"Jim! Great news, we can open back up." I fist bump the air, sitting up in bed.

"Well, that certainly is great news. Lemme feed the chickens and I'll be right in. I'll head straight to the campground, don't you worry."

"Awesome, thank you! I'll be right in; you'll probably beat me, though. I'm going to call Zach and run an errand before coming in."

"Roger that, no problem. I'll get us started." I hang up and dial Zach.

"Morning, Zach!" The excitement oozing from every pore in my body.

"Did we get the all clear?" I hear him sipping coffee. He's probably been up for a few hours already.

"Yes, sir, we did. Are you able to come in this morning? We've got one day until campers arrive. Jim's heading in now."

"I'll be there in twenty! Wow, we were cutting it close there, eh? I'll start calling the other campsites and let them know we won't need their open spots. I'll meet you guys in the campground after that stuff is done."

"What would I do without you?"

"You'd have a much worse haircut and a horrible filing system," he teases.

I get out of bed, put on a pot of coffee, and let Marty outside. The rain has passed, but it left everything soggy and mushy in its wake. The dog is pawing at an earthworm that surfaced during the storm, now stranded on the back patio. Marty's legs, belly, and snout are already covered in mud. He's quite the happy pooch. My couch will not be enthused.

Ready to go, I grab my backpack, filled with stolen murder evidence, and hitch up the dog. Today is going to be a good day, and I step outside into the damp, but sunny morning.

Running through today's checklist, I make a quick pitstop by the police station and talk with Kelly before planting myself in the park for the rest of the day. Not only do I need to give her thank-you cookies, but also sheepishly turn over Michael's phone and wallet and beg for forgiveness before she adds a second homicide to this week's crime record. I'm dying to know what happened since she still hasn't answered my many texts or calls.

The walk to the police station is a nice one. There's a nip in the air, but a cloudless blue sky radiates overhead. Marty's enjoying himself, his wet nose going crazy with all the smells that last night's storm stirred up. We take the long way into town, dropping off the cookies and card in Eli's trout-shaped mailbox on our way.

I completely forgot that tomorrow is the first outdoor farmers market of the year. The street is already bustling with preparations. All of Main Street is blocked off, giving vendors a full day to get set up for tomorrow's festivities. Most of our local businesses have booths at the market, like Peyton's bakery. This time of year, there isn't much fresh produce available yet, but meat and dairy farmers sell their goods, as well as local wineries. Even our bookstore brings a few reading-related knick-knacks and used books to sell.

The first market is always a huge deal, more like a mini festival rather than a simple farmers market. From over a block away, I can hear Charlotte shouting orders, instructing a volunteer crew where to set up the bandstand. There'll be live music, a few carnival games, and tons of great food. It's usually a fun day.

I take Marty's leash off my backpack and clip it to a bike rack in front of the police station. He flops down immediately, back legs splooting to each side like a frog, warming his fur in the sun.

The station is small, proportionate to the amount of crime that (typically) happens in Stone's Throw. Most of it is tourist-related, either getting into a bar fight, stealing something from a store, or illegal bonfires on the beach. Frankly, I've been impressed that the Sheriff's Department has been able to handle a homicide. It is more than our rural county is used to dealing with. Altogether, I would guess there are maybe three regular staff posted in our local branch office, at least one of whom is part-time.

The building is open. Walking through the reinforced glass doors, I'm standing in a cream-colored room that houses three messy desks, a break area in the back corner with a round, plastic table and vending machine, and a small waiting section off to the right. Behind this room is a holding cell used almost exclusively as a drunk tank and a locker room for officers.

Kelly is sitting at one of the desks, a large thermal to-go mug in her hand. Leaning back in her chair, she sees me walk in and waves me over. There's an empty chair next to her desk that I take. "Morning, Maudy." She's beaming. Her smile is toothy, and her icy blue eyes are bright, even with the enormous, puffy, purple bags under them.

"Hi, Kell, congratulations!" I take off my backpack and set it on the floor. "Sorry to pop by like this. I got a call from Sheriff Landry saying the park was good to open today, so I figured I'd come in and hear what happened. I admit, my interest is piqued." I take out my sugary token of appreciation and put it on her desk. *Best to butter her up with cookies first. Confess to evidence tampering after.*

"Thanks!" She pulls out a cookie and starts nibbling. "I figured you might be in sometime today. Sorry about ghosting you, things got crazy, and I needed to focus here." In front of her are four large stacks of papers and a computer screen with a dozen tabs open.

"No worries. So, before we dive into what happened, I figured you'd want these." I wince as I lean forward, pulling the phone and wallet out of my backpack, and place them on her desk. "Sorry." I grin, hoping she won't eviscerate me on the spot.

"Are those what I think they are?" Her eyes pop, mouth full of chocolate.

"Uh-huh. They're Michael's. I found them in Jeremy's briefcase."

She calmly dusts her hands on her pants, wiping away cookie crumbs.

"Jesus Christ, Maudy. I'm guessing I don't want to know how you obtained such evidence, do I?"

"I'm guessing you don't. I'm not sure how helpful this is to you now, but it does support Jeremy as the murderer. So, kudos."

"I'm going to pretend you didn't show me these. I have no idea what to do with this right now." She pulls out a rubber glove from a desk drawer and uses it to put the items off to the side. "So let's just move forward, and I'll try to figure out a way to not get you thrown in jail. Deal?" She's fuming, but thankfully, too jazzed to act on it right now.

"Deal." I smile widely and hand her another cookie.

"Besides this fiasco, you were actually very helpful. So, thanks for that. Oh, and before I forget," she rummages through one of the stacks and pulls out an envelope, "for your assistance."

"Whoa." Inside the envelope is a check. A big check. "You don't need to do this, Kelly. The DNR ordered me to cooperate. I was on the clock all week."

"Just take the money and say, 'thank you,' will ya?"

"Thank you." I smile and put the envelope in my backpack. *Maybe this could get us new computers or keep the lights on a few more weeks if the budget is slashed.*

"So, you got my text, that Jeremy Gray killed Michael Price," she segues.

"Yes, I got your text," I reply, trying to keep the deadpan sarcasm out of my voice. "But I'm stuck on this whole kid thing. Who is his son?"

"Yeah, we don't know yet. That's still an open question for me, too. We found one fingerprint and a bunch of hair follicles on Michael's body. The fingerprint matches Jeremy Gray, who is already in the system for…well, you know. Previous indiscretions. Other hair, that isn't Michael's, came back as his kid's. We can't find a match in the system, though, and Chicago PD isn't helpful. Michael never married and isn't listed as the father on any birth records that I could find." She shrugs.

"Anyway," she continues, "here's what we know. Jeremy and Michael were seen Wednesday night fighting, presumably over business dealings." I think back to the draft business offers I found in Jeremy's briefcase. It's possible.

"The Finches, and a couple of other guests at The Nest, corroborate that Jeremy came back that night *without* Michael and asked for his own room. The next day, Nancy shares the letter that Charlotte Roth wrote to them, which is extremely threatening and impassioned." She rolls her eyes.

"We think Jeremy scoffs or laughs or something when Nancy gave him the letter, which upset Nancy. Nancy originally told Charlotte about Michael's plans to buy The Nest. Thanks for needling that out of her, by the way. She came to talk to me."

"You're welcome." I wave it off like no big deal.

"So when Nancy sees Jeremy laughing at Charlotte's efforts to help her, she snaps. She desperately doesn't want Michael to put in an offer on the Inn, knowing full well Greg would take him up on it."

This must be why the letter was in such bad shape; one of them crumpled it. I know Charlotte, and she would never deliver a crumpled-up letter. Especially if it was on behalf of the Chamber of Commerce.

"Michael comes back late at night or the next morning while everyone's asleep, and continues fighting, probably still about money, with Jeremy, who is in the room adjoining his own. Jeremy hits him over the head with the edge of a lamp base and accidentally kills him in the heat of the argument. Nancy either hears the commotion or Jeremy tells her about it later, because she lets him use their wheelbarrow to move the body into the park. I doubt that she's an active participant in his murder, but it's looking like she was at least complicit.

"I remember you saying that you had breakfast at The Nest last Friday with Nellie. I think that Nancy overheard that you were doing a sweep of the park to look for Michael and instructed Jeremy to wait to dump the body until after your search was done. I haven't figured out yet where they were hiding his body at that point, but she didn't count on you going through the park a second time the next day. With a bunch of volunteers, no less."

Kelly is working herself up while telling me the story, now on her feet and gesturing wildly. "There are still quite a few things we need to confirm, a lot of this is still conjecture at this point, but overall, the County seems pleased with the solution, and we should have enough evidence to go to trial. I am still curious about the kid thing, though. I'm going to keep trying to dig that up.

"I'm hoping we'll get enough to get Nancy, too," Kelly continues. "We've formally arrested Jeremy and are holding him here for the next day until further information comes in." She uses her thumb to point to the room out back, where the holding cell is. "He'll move to County after that. I've got a ton to do to make sure that all happens and am hunkering down at our main office to get it done. You caught me at the right time, I'm headed out in a few minutes and will probably be working there through the night."

Her theory seems plausible, even if it's not totally on track with what I'm thinking. I'm pretty sure the Finches' wheelbarrow wasn't in the park, at least the dirt in the treads didn't match the forest's profile. And would Jeremy really kill someone over money? Granted, it could have been *a ton* of money, but still. He seemed well off already and not a super flashy, materialistic guy. At least not like Michael. But hey, my park can open. I'm a happy camper. I offer my congratulations once again and hug her.

"He's been asking about you, you know. He wants to talk to you. You can go in if you'd like, he's allowed visitors." She smiles an even wider, toothier grin.

I hesitate. Do I want to talk to this man? He killed two people. Bad news bears all around. "I don't think so, thanks though." I grimace and laugh embarrassedly.

"Ha, fair enough. I'm sure he's just going to tell you he's innocent and beg for your help, or a second date." She chuckles.

Before I have an opportunity to retort, she says, "Also, spread the word: visitors are going to be able to head home tomorrow. We'll be calling folks directly, but it doesn't hurt to get the grapevine going." She organizes a stack of papers on her desk and dunks a third cookie in her thermos.

"Good, I'm sure they are ready to leave, and I bet our rentals will be grateful to keep their holiday reservations."

"Yep, for sure. Well, talk soon, Maudy, thanks again for all of your help. See you for spaghetti next week." She smiles and waves as I walk back through the door.

On the front step is Mr. Martin Short, his fur toasty warm from the sun, the mud hardening into solid plate armor. He pops up when we see each other, tail wagging. We're both ready to get to the park, get back on our normal routine, and get the godforsaken campground open for business before anything else bad happens.

Chapter Twenty

As I rummage through my office desk, organizing camper logistics lists, a couple of details of Kelly's story nag at me, not quite adding up. Jeremy mentioned that Michael was only interested in properties in Stone's Throw, not surrounding towns that may have been more profitable. That seems odd. Also, if Nancy was involved, wouldn't she have kept his cash and valuables to pawn or something? If she were desperate enough to get involved in a violent crime, I'd think she wouldn't bat an eye at taking two hundred dollars from someone's wallet. Or maybe Jeremy wouldn't give it to her? Plus, I'm still convinced that the Finches' wheelbarrow hasn't been used since Greg gardened on Wednesday morning, before Michael was killed. Didn't Eli say that Pop's security camera didn't see Michael come back at all Wednesday night? And aren't the lamps at The Nest B&B made of thin glass? They'd shatter too easily to cause that huge wound on Michael's head…

Let it go, Maudy. We've got a big opening weekend to focus on. There's no way Kelly is divulging the whole story. She knows some of it is still circumstantial. Your job playing Veronica Mars is over.

I get choked up as I walk through the park entryway, the "Closed" sign and chain gone, with a handful of cars already in the parking lot.

I refill my coffee cup while Marty gets a drink of water before beginning the short walk into the campground to help Jim finish campsite preparations. Zach is probably already back there too; he isn't in the office.

Jim comes up and gives me a big bear hug. "Congratulations, girl. I hear you solved the murder of that man." His squeeze is just past comforting, borderline suffocating.

"Eh, I didn't do much. Kelly did the real work." I wave him off.

"Nah, I know you. They're a bunch of knuckleheads. Even if they put the final puzzle pieces together, I bet it was you who flipped them all right side up."

"That's not all she's been flipping right side up," Zach chimes in, his blonde eyebrows doing the worm across his face.

"Oh my god, Zach!" My face burns red. He laughs and continues scooping out piles of ashes from a fire pit. Jim either doesn't hear, or he graciously chooses to ignore the comment.

There are a few more hours of work to do to clean up the remaining campsites and finish getting the store set up. Jim and I tag-team the campsite clean-ups, while Zach tackles the store. With all three of us working hard and quickly, we're making great time.

Jim and I get to talking; he loves to share stories about this place "back in the day."

After a brief lull in conversation, while I'm focusing on moving a hefty tree branch, he picks back up. "It's great seeing folks come back here time and again. Lots of memories here in these woods."

"There sure are, I wish I'd come here sooner. I'd have never left! There aren't parks like this downstate."

"There aren't parks like this anywhere in the world. This place is special. Why do ya think I still come back after all these years?" We laugh together. Jim is getting on in years, and I dread the day he tells me he's retiring. He is such an important piece of this campground; he's practically park lore at this point.

"Just this mornin', I see a young man hiking through that was coming here twenty-plus years ago! He used to come every summer with his family. I tell ya, these trees, they get in your bones and never let go." He looks up towards the canopy, taking a deep breath, Bill and Ted watching over us once again from a towering Sugar Maple.

"Take root is more like it," I laugh and smile, soaking in the beauty of the scenery myself. I love that I can help give people these evergreen memories. It's one of my favorite parts of working here.

We continue on until the remaining sites are ready for campers. Jim goes on to tell me all about a new lavender farm that started near his home, and I share my experiences last week trying to play detective. I'm glad he's back. I missed him.

"You know, Kelly had a hard time confirming your alibi. It's why you couldn't get back in here this week. What were you up to, anyway?"

"It's because the only ones who could vouch for me were the animals." He snorts like a pig. "I spent Wednesday night at home. I didn't see anyone who could speak English until Thursday morning at the diner for breakfast. The pigs are smart, but they can't talk unfortunately." He continues to laugh. "I recounted the entire plot of the Law and Order rerun I watched that night as proof I was home, but that didn't hold water."

Jim was widowed years ago and lives alone. He has a slew of animals to keep him company. Kelly never suspected him, but she technically couldn't rule him out either.

With most of the work done, I hike back to the office, taking a shortcut off-trail. I place the last parcel of cookies and a thank-you card on Zach's desk. It'll be a fun surprise after a hard day's work.

Something Jim said earlier is sticking to me like a relentless piece of gum on my shoe. People form lasting memories here, coming back year after year to enjoy the beauty of Stone's Throw. What if Michael was one of those people? What if he vacationed here years ago? Didn't Eli say that he was drunkenly ranting about something along those lines at Pop's last week? Sentimentality might make him interested in these properties over more lucrative ones elsewhere.

Stop it, Maudy. It's over. It was Jeremy. Let it go. The park is open, dummy! You did it! I tap my pen on my desk. *Tick, tick, tick.* I keep glancing over at the murder board, still turned backward, propped up against the wall. Against my better judgment, I get up and turn it around.

Looking at the string of questions and suspects again, I'm now positive something isn't right. Even if Jeremy did use the wheelbarrow, did he know these trails well enough to know where to dump Michael? Could he really sneak a body in a neon orange wheelbarrow all the way across town and into the park without anyone noticing?

"Marty, why don't we do our regular check-up?" I ask the dog. He pops up and is ready to go. Maybe this'll help clear out this hullabaloo fogging up my head.

Even out hiking, I can't seem to let these nagging questions go. *Shut up, brain! This isn't your problem anymore. The park is open, we're all good. We accomplished the goal.*

We cover ground I haven't trekked through in a while that stems from the eastern trailhead near the campground. The hike is beautiful; everything is so lush and green after the rainstorm yesterday. Marty greets every hiker who passes by, fulfilling his self-imposed park mascot duties. We stop for a while, watching the beavers loving life after last night's onslaught of rain.

"Lucas." I smile and wave as a familiar face approaches Marty and me on the trail back near the office. "It's great to see you. I never did get a chance to show you around, sorry about that. The week got away from me."

"Hi, Maudy, not a problem at all. It's not my first time back here. I figured it out okay enough on my own. Glad I found these guys, they're so cute." He points back in the direction of the beavers. He turns and smiles at me, his hands jammed in his pants pockets and flannel sleeves rolled up.

"By the way, I heard that you'll be able to head home tomorrow. They figured out what happened to Michael." My eyes do a quick scan, and I lock onto his exposed forearm with that intricate black and gray tattoo.

"Oh, good." His smile is friendly, but not overly so. "Not that I don't love it here, it'll just be good to get back to my regularly scheduled life."

"Yeah, I feel that. Well, enjoy your hike. If I don't see you again before you leave, safe travels home." I hastily wave, and he walks past us, Marty's nose sniffing his pant leg as he passes.

I yank the dog back down the path, scrambling to make sense of this new thought that's clicking into place. Not even bothering to go grab my things from the office, I rush out of the park, chasing this idea. Michael is connected to this place, somehow. I know it in my gut. Power walking across the bridge, we pass the row of fishing rental cabins right on the riverbank.

Of course.

"It can't be… Marty, we need to pay my man Matthew a visit. This can't wait."

* * *

Located on the most eastern block of Main Street, Marty and I walk through the beginnings of the farmers market before getting inside. I'm practically dragging the dog behind me; his nose twitches wildly, smelling every single booth setting up for the big event tomorrow.

I burst into the library, looking frazzled based on Matthew's expression.

"Hi, Matthew, could you take Marty for a bit?" I ask, slightly out of breath.

"Well, hello there, Ms. Lorso. Sure thing. Are you okay? I'm about to close to help finish setting up for tomorrow." He's stapling some sort of fundraiser information packets together; massive, glossy stacks sit in neat piles in front of him on the circulation desk. "We're hosting this fun little library fundraiser, where children will be bobbing for app—"

"Everything's fine, I just need to look something up really quick. Do you mind taking Marty to your office and pointing me in the direction of local records? I swear it'll only be a moment. I'll owe you one." I rush, tapping my hand on the desk.

He does so without questioning me (bonus of acting super weird). He sits me down at a computer that's loaded with digital archives of the Stone's Throw newspaper, The Birch River Current, and gently places a stack of books with census records and other historical documents on the chair next to me. I thank him profusely and order Marty to behave.

After dropping the dog off, he returns to the circulation desk where he resumes his stapling. *Tick, tick, tick*. The rhythm, that noise. *That infernal cuckoo clock. The White Sox watch.*

With the right year and a few keywords, I quickly find what I'm looking for. *How could I have not seen it sooner?* First, I confirm the meaning of 2-24-2003 and connect two people a little more closely than either of them originally let on. Then, I search for Michael Price in the local news. The newspaper archive isn't available online; the library took the time to digitize previous editions themselves.

On my computer screen is a black and white, grainy photo of a much younger Michael Price with a small boy on his shoulders. The same small boy who is in the old Polaroid that Michael kept in his wallet. The kid had won his age bracket in the annual stone-throwing contest, part of the long-standing Summer Festival. Reading the caption gives me the last piece of information I need: "A father and son celebrating a victory together."

Jeremy didn't kill Michael Price. He was framed.

Chapter Twenty-One

"Come on, Kelly. Pick up, pick up." Nervously tapping my fingers on the library's wooden desk, I leave a voicemail telling her to call me immediately. Waving goodbye to Matthew, I retrieve the dog from his office and march straight home.

Confident the killer won't skip town until tomorrow, I have the night to plan. How many times have I sat in my living room, yelling at the ditzy girl in the horror movie to not go in the basement? Not wanting to die a tragic cliché, Marty and I make it home uneventfully, the slightest noise causing me to jump.

Kelly has this all wrong. I lock my door, draw my curtains, and text Eli. Keeping it vague, I write that I'm freaking out and would appreciate it if he could keep an eye on my house tonight. He doesn't answer, probably helping his dad set up Pop's booth for tomorrow's market.

As predicted, I sleep awfully that night. Why do I even bother? Dark nightmares swirl in my head, each one worse than the one before. Finally giving up, I go down to the couch and turn on the TV. Finding comfort in a Buffy rerun, I restlessly doze on the couch until dawn breaks.

Wide awake, with no time to spare, I call Kelly again, saying in yet another voicemail that it's urgent and to meet me at the farmers market ASAP. She's probably still at the main county building, far away. Do I *want* to take matters into my own hands? Absolutely not. But can I let Michael's murderer skip town, potentially never to be found again? Also no.

I strap Marty's fleece vest on to combat the early chill, telling him that we have serious business to take care of. I grab my backpack and put my handcuffs in my jacket pocket. *This is no big deal. You can arrest people...you're a Park Ranger. Even if you never have before. A measly murder? Big whoop. You got this.* I check my phone one more time, yearning for a response from Kelly or Eli. With no answer from either, I take a deep breath and jerk open the front door.

Stepping outside, a gray sky looms low overhead, as if the clouds might wring themselves out any minute now. "Great, just what we need today. More rain." I mutter sarcastically to the dog, who doesn't seem to mind. To him, rain equals worms to torture.

If I'm right, nostalgia is a big motivator for the killer. I bet I'll find him at the market before he leaves Stone's Throw for good.

Approaching Main Street, Jeff strums his guitar and sings an old Coldplay cover with a whir of people flitting about. The street is lined with small tents and booths, each for a different vendor. Darci is manning a bloody mary and mimosa bar at Pop's tent while Eli flips pancakes and sips on a cup of coffee.

The booths are hard to see through the hordes of people milling through the street. All of Stone's Throw, a bunch of tourists, and residents of neighboring towns have come out for the big market opening. I bet some of my campers are here too, fueling up before pitching their tents when the campground opens at one o'clock this afternoon.

Craning my neck to see over the sea of heads, cursing my parents for my vertical challenge, I search frantically for him. *Come on, I know you're here. I would be here if I were you. You have to be here...* I make it through the first of the four street blocks without spotting him.

"Maudy, hey kid." I walk right past Kevin without clocking him, so focused on the task at hand. He's pulling a small garden wagon that's half full already, stocking up for a new special at Pop's, no doubt.

"Uh, hey Kevin." I smile briefly, still scanning the crowd.

"Everything okay?" He asks, looking around as well, confused.

"Oh, I'm fine. Just distracted."

"Okie doke, well, let me know if I can help you at all. I know you've got a lot going on right now. One more thing, I think Eli might be a little upset. Might do you two good to talk soon."

"Why, what'd he say?" I'm only half listening, searching the crowd, trying to spot him.

"Oh, nothing…he's just a grouch. Sometimes I think he's older than I am. Certainly is crankier," he chuckles.

I smile briefly again, but am miffed that Eli never answered my text last night. *I left the man cookies. He should be coming to talk to me, not the other way around.*

I say goodbye to Kevin and trot off towards the beach, a few more blocks of market left to scour. If this doesn't work, I'll have to go knocking on cabin doors, which I do not want to do. Better to stay where people are around.

After searching another block to no avail, I continue down the street, my confidence waning with each step. "Maybe I'm wrong, Marty." I turn to look at the dog, who is just happy to be on a walk with fantastic smells and plenty of dropped scraps. He beat out a seagull for a french fry and has been prancing ever since. "Maybe it is actually Jeremy, and this is another goofball idea that I'm obsessing over."

My fingers tap as those thoughts seep in, clinking against the handcuffs in my pocket. I take a deep breath, on the verge of hyperventilating. If he came here every summer, there's no doubt that the farmers market would stir up feelings for him. It is a staple. This guy hasn't handled pain and abandonment very well. I doubt he'd leave town before making a stop here.

I break to buy a small coffee and blueberry hand pie, trying to act natural (not like I'm on the edge of a panic attack tracking down a murderer) and walk the last block towards the beach. Right as I'm about to call it quits and dramatically walk out into the lake to wallow, I see him.

Well, I see the back of someone's head who looks a hell of a lot like him. The man is facing away from me and taking a small wheel of cheese from a table, placing it in a plastic grocery bag that's hanging on his arm, and chatting with the monger.

I text Kelly for the millionth time in the last twelve hours, once again telling her that she has it wrong and to meet me here. I bend down to pet the dog, "You ready, bud?" I ask him, and he licks my hand, which I'm taking as a feminist, 'You go, girl.'

"One, two, three, four." I focus on the seconds, stepping towards him in time, hoping my face doesn't become too flushed.

"Lucas?" I ask, prompting him to turn around. I'm right, it is him. He's wearing a camouflage coat, thick gloves fit for the hiking trails, and the same orange beanie I saw him in the first time we met.

"Park Ranger! Great to bump into you again. I'm actually on my way out of town, just filling up on a few favorites before making the trek back home." He holds up the grocery bag.

I try my best (bad) to muster a smile and keep my hands still, hoping he doesn't catch on.

"Oh, awesome. There's nothing like the market, I'm glad it's back for the year," I stammer.

"Mhm." The conversation lulls, but I can't let him walk out of town. I have cuffs in my pocket, but he'd be able to bolt before I could use them. He's so much bigger than me… I put my hand in my pocket, white knuckling the handcuffs. I didn't think this through. *Merda. This is a bad idea.*

"Hey, do you happen to have the time, by chance?" I probe, crossing my fingers that he takes the bait.

"Sure thing." He pulls up his right sleeve, revealing a sparkling, ostentatious watch with the White Sox logo encrusted on the face. The very same watch that I know to be Michael Price's. "It's eight o'clock on the dot," he says. *Tick, tick, tick.*

I drop what little poker face I have. We lock eyes, and he glances back toward the watch. I see worry and then anger spread across his face. He messed up. His mouth strings into a tight line, and his eyebrows momentarily furrow.

Quickly, his expression morphs back to an incredibly fake smile, but the friendly look in his eye contorts into monstrous, fear-driven wrath. He closes the gap between us and grabs my forearm, squeezing it tightly, my hand stuck, jammed into my pocket. Whispering in my ear, he says furtively, "Do as I say, and you won't get hurt." I nod slightly, tears swelling in my eyes as the tip of a small blade digs between my ribs.

Marty looks up at him, and then at me. His long mohawk fur along his back springs on end, and a low growl rumbles from his throat. "Same goes for him," he whispers.

He nudges me down to bend over and comfort the dog. "Thank you, puppy. It's okay, though. I swear." My face says otherwise, but Marty stands down, at least for now.

"Follow my lead." He whispers again, pressing the blade deeper. Turning me around and heading back through the market, he keeps an arm wrapped around my shoulders, smiling as we go. To the outside world, it looks like we are a couple, or at the very least close friends. He is trying to get me alone. The crowd is so dense that nobody seems to notice anything off.

"Smile or I'll kill you," he whispers once again, grip tightening around my shoulders. I wipe away my tears with my free hand and force out a fake laugh. Urgently searching for someone I know to mouth the word 'help,' I come up short. We walk by Peyton, who is hectically packing up dozens of donuts, and Eli, still handing out plates of pancakes. I make eye contact with him, but he quickly turns away.

We make it to the edge of downtown, almost to the bridge that leads into the park. Out of earshot now, he asks, "Do you have your park keys on you?"

"Why?"

"You'll see," he says, arm tightening even more around my shoulders. A low rumble of thunder comes in from offshore as the sky darkens. Rain is coming. Lucas pushes me to the ranger station door and asks where my keys are, the blade now at my neck. I go to reach for my backpack when his grip suddenly gets tighter. "I'll do it. Tell me where they are."

I want him to let go of my arm so I can try to cuff him. "They're in the front, small pocket." I gasp.

"Don't move." He pulls off my pack, unzips every pocket, and dumps its entire contents on the front porch, searching for the keys. With him distracted, I whip out my handcuffs and try to wrap them around his wrists. He twirls around and pushes me down onto the ground before I make it.

"Well, aren't you a cute wittle Park Ranger with your wittle handcuffs?" He kicks them out of reach and picks up my keys, adding insult to injury.

Unlocking the door, he throws me inside, Marty following along but no longer playing nice. He bares his teeth and growls, eyes locked on the man.

My phone is in my jacket pocket. Even if I don't have my cuffs, I can text someone for help. Eli and Kelly are the last two numbers I messaged. If I could manage using muscle memory, I can tell one of them to send help. I could run, but Lucas would get away.

That can't happen.

He rummages through the office, clearing desks and tossing drawers. My crappy computer falls to the floor with a loud *crack!*

"What are you looking for?" I tersely ask him, trying my best to keep a straight face as I concentrate every fiber of my being on sending semi-coherent text messages from my pocket. The dog's eyes are still laser-focused on him, but now that Lucas has backed off of me, Marty stands his ground squarely in between us.

Lucas pops his head up from my desk drawer, his knife in hand and a crazed look in his eye. "A pen and a pad of paper."

"Other drawer." I point to the other side of my desk. If I can keep him distracted for a couple more minutes...

He pulls out a notepad from Nate's stationery kit. My stomach drops as I think of him. Hot, angry tears begin to flow freely.

"Come sit down." His voice is softer, more tender than before. He looks lost.

I approach carefully and sit down on my desk chair. He crouches down in front of my lap, like a parent to an upset child. The only difference is that this parent is pushing the tip of a knife into the child's gut.

"I don't want to do this, but you've left me no choice," he says matter-of-factly, pushing the weapon in further, piercing my skin.

"Ah!" I shrink back.

"I was home free, but you had to keep sticking your nose where it doesn't belong."

He lowers the knife, grabs my leg, and squeezes. Not in a threatening way, but almost as if he's disappointed in me. He tilts his head to one side and makes a *tsk* sound with his tongue. Standing back up, he sits on the desk next to my left hand.

"Write," he says, flatly.

"Write what?" I ask shakily, my mind running through all the things I wish I had done in this lifetime.

"Write your goodbye." He hangs his head low and says it in a jarring whisper.

My goodbye? He wants me to write a suicide note right now? Fat chance, stronzo.

"Uh." I pick up a pen and hover it over the paper. What can I say that won't trigger suspicion?

I begin to write. He gives me space and sits down on the small couch at the other end of the office. With his head in his hands and knee bouncing, I can tell he's freaking out, too. This wasn't in his plan.

Elliot Nett,

Look, I hope this note finds you well, but I am not.

U are my best friend, and I'm sorry for how we left things.

Can you promise not to forget me? I need you to promise that.

Almost nothing is left for me here.

Sincerely,

Maudy Lorso

I use the brief opportunity to glance at my phone. A text made it to Eli. The spelling is horrendous, but the message is clear enough. He'll figure it out.

He looks up to see that I've finished writing, leaving the note on my desk. "Okay, let's go." I stand up, reaching for Marty's leash before he stops me. "The dog stays."

I crouch down to my furry friend. "Okay, Martin. You're going to stay here." I give the dog a hug; he licks my cheek. While bent over him, I quietly unhook him from his leash. If, by some miracle, he's able to get out of here, I don't want it to get tangled in the brush and hold him up. I whisper to him as I release the hug, "I love you." Hot tears stream down my face.

Lucas skims my note, I guess finding it acceptable because he doesn't say anything. He cuts the cord off the old vacuum from the supply closet and ties it around my arms, so they are stuck at my sides. He grabs the wrapped cord at the small of my back with one hand, holds the knife to my neck with the other, and pushes me out the door.

"Marty! Help!" I yell at the dog, hoping he'll pounce into action and chew the ankles off of this maniac. Leaping towards Lucas, he latches onto his right calf.

"Arh!" he screams, shaking his leg wildly. Marty hangs on tight, sinking his sharp teeth in further, despite being whipped around. The man bends in half and rips the dog from his leg with both hands. Marty lets out a high-pitched shriek in pain; Lucas locks the dog in the office behind us. *Good boy. A lifetime of extra peanut butter if I ever get out of this mess.*

We shuffle over to the shed, walking past the handcuffs that I desperately wish would magically jump up to his wrists. Instead, he sees me glance over at them and grabs them himself, tightening them around my own wrists. At least they're in front of me, and not behind my back.

He unlocks the shed door with my keys and removes a shovel. "After you," he says, tightly gripping the ancient vacuum cord, he drives me deeper into the woods.

"Time to go for a hike," he grumbles.

Chapter Twenty-Two

I never realized how reliant on my arms I am while hiking. Climbing the steep dunes with them bound and cuffed is more than difficult. It's nearly impossible. I keep falling, unable to balance on the uneven terrain. Without my hands to catch my fall, my face and knees get scraped up immediately, and it's not long before I'm bleeding through my jeans with bleary eyes.

Lucas mutters to himself the entire time we're walking, only paying me any attention when I fall. He's limping badly, himself. Marty got him good.

"Watch it," he growls and picks me up by the vacuum cord, tossing me forward. My phone broke long ago, I heard it crack a ways back. Not that it would matter, I don't get a signal this far back anyway.

"Where are we going, Lucas? You know I'll have people looking for me, why don't we go back?" I ask him questions to stall for time. He's lost in his thoughts, but every once in a while, I get a response.

"I'll be long gone before anyone finds you. Don't you worry your pretty little head about it." *God, he's such a drama queen.*

We slowly climb into the western slopes of the park. I'm sweaty, ripped to shreds, bleeding, and drenched from head to toe from the onslaught of rain that's coming down hard. Without the position of the sun visible, I don't know how long we've been out here, but I would guess we are getting close to an hour.

There are still fifteen or more miles of trail up ahead, this portion of the property runs high up along the shoreline. If we stop, he'll hurt me. But I'm also afraid of what will happen when we reach his destination, so I try to go slow enough to buy more time. *Come on, Eli. Look at your phone. You can't stay mad forever.*

Lucas knows where he's going. He's leading me to a specific place, and I'm wracking my brain to figure out exactly where. He doesn't bother to consult trail maps or markers along the way, navigating forks and turns expertly. There aren't any structures or major landscape features out this far. Besides the huge hills and valleys of forested sand, and the occasional black bear, there's nothing out here. Other areas of the park have ruins of old cabins and small rock formations that kids like to pretend are caves. Nothing like that lies ahead.

Fear grips me tighter, and panic starts to set in at a level that no amount of second-counting or finger-tapping could cure. "Almost there," he sputters to himself. He's walking behind me so I can't see his face, but I can tell by the squelching of his boots in the sandy mud that he's spinning in circles, searching for something.

We walk another ten or so minutes before he grabs the back of the vacuum cable tying my arms, jerking me to a halt.

"You could've just told me to stop," I snap, adding whiplash to my list of injuries.

"On your knees." He turns me around so we're facing one another. This spot looks the same as the rest of this area. We're high up, not quite to the precipice of the big dune. To my left is a steep decline down the side of the forested hill, on my right continues up at a steep incline. Just a few feet ahead of us, I see the same downed tree that I noted for the maintenance crew a few days ago, the one blocking the path ahead with the family of sleeping snakes inside.

I drop, wincing hard and letting out a small shriek in pain. My pant legs are torn open, and the skin on my knees scream from repeated falling. I look up at him, but his attention is on the downward slope to my left, searching for something in the scrubby underbrush below.

"Lucas, if you're going to kill me, I need you to at least do me the honor of knowing what happened." The only coherent thought that makes it through my panicked mind chatter *(You're a failure! This is how you die! You should've stayed with Nate!)* is to keep him talking and stall as long as I can. He's probably going to throw me down the dune and hope the fall breaks my neck. Which is totally possible and makes it unlikely that my body would be found. All in all, not a bad plan.

I am not a big person. He can knock me out easily if he wants to, especially with my arms bound. He's struggling with something, though; his face contorts, and his eyes dilate, pacing in small circles. *If I can keep his mind reeling until help comes, maybe, just maybe, I'll make it out of here. Think Maudy, think.*

"You figured it out. I have no choice." He shrugs and continues searching the landscape for something, but at least we have a dialogue going. I can work with this.

"I wouldn't say I figured anything out, not really. I know Jeremy Gray killed your mom in a car accident twenty years ago. He was driving drunk." His eyes bug out, and his mouth gapes. I nod to his memorial tattoo, the date of her death surrounded by flowers. "And I know that Michael Price was your dad. After how you handled today, it's safe to say you killed him. Was it for his watch?" I look towards his wrist, now thankful for that stupid, ticking clock ringing in my head all week.

"Ha!" That gets his attention, and he turns to face me. "Wow, you don't get it." He shakes his head, almost in disgust, and turns back to scouring the damp forest.

"Then tell me!" My fear tightens into anger. *This guy has the nerve to kidnap me, tie me up, kick my dog, and force me into my park to murder me?*

After Nate and I broke up, my therapist told me that anger is a secondary emotion. It's just fear in disguise. Her voice pierces through my negative thoughts as the fear in my body hardens into armor. I'm furious with this petty man-child who can't face his own problems. And, if I am being honest, I'm disappointed in myself for doing the exact same thing.

I love this place, and I love my friends, but sitting here in the pouring rain, shredded to pieces, I realize that I've been using my time in Stone's Throw as a crutch, or maybe more like a time capsule. Things stay the same. I don't need to deal with anything, I can coast. Lucas and I aren't that different; we both have things in our past we aren't dealing with. *Oof. Maybe I should've stayed in therapy longer.*

Anger gives me a boost in confidence and a shorter fuse. No longer shaking, my voice is stern and forthcoming. "Just spit it out, Lucas. This is ridiculous."

He looks at me with that same crazed expression. He grabs the cables around my midsection, hoists me up, and pulls me in close to him, my face only an inch from his.

We stare at each other in the roaring thunderstorm. He keeps a tight grip on the cables, squeezing them tightly, making it difficult to breathe. He breaks our staring contest and stammers incoherently to himself, looking out over the forest canopy. Eventually, the muttering grows louder and clearer.

"You're right...he was my dad. I killed my dad..." His voice trails off, the horrible realization hitting him.

"Yes, it seems you did." I nod slightly, trying to rein in the disgust in my tone.

"He was terrible, though! He was a horrible person!" He bursts out screaming and pushes me back down. I land on my back. "He deserved it!" I can feel the waves of energy coming off the man, like the storm over the lake. I look up at him, looming tall over me, now screaming over the crash of rain.

"He treated me and my mom like we were garbage! Once he got a little money in his pocket, he took off to Chicago, not even saying goodbye." His voice shakes. I think he's crying, but it's hard to differentiate the tears from the raindrops. We're both completely soaked through.

"I had been here for days, and he didn't even recognize me. His own kid." He's crying, eking out words in between erratic sobs. "We ate dinner together last week! It wasn't until Jeremy told him who I was that he put two and two together. He completely erased me and my mom from his memory!"

"I'm sorry that happened," I reply, not quite a yell but loud enough to make sure he hears me over the swelling storm. The wind swarms fast and loud this high up.

"She was in the car accident not long after he left, and the bastard didn't even come back! No money for hospital bills, nothing! She died two days later from her injuries. Michael practically killed her himself!" He kicks something, maybe a rock on the trail or a log. I can barely see through the rain and blood.

His fear also hardens into anger, mirroring mine. He screams and sobs and kicks things in our path like a toddler mid-tantrum. He's on a roll, and for a brief moment, I fantasize about dashing back the way I came, running as fast as I can for as long as I can. That thought quickly fades, with one tumble, he'll be able to catch up immediately. With my knees in the shape they're in right now, I'm not sure how fast my top speed would actually be.

I eye the fallen tree behind me and attempt to get back on my feet. I have a plan. I just need to keep him talking and inch back this way a few feet...

"How did you find out he was coming back here? To Stone's Throw, I mean."

He pauses for a moment before answering. "I didn't. Jeremy ambushed me. He told me about the discounted cabin rentals for this week. He knows I love it here with all of our family memories and stuff. After we became friends, I told him what happened when I was younger. He realized he had killed my mom and felt bad. He came up with this plan to reunite me and my dad. I didn't know it was him. I was so young when it happened.

"Jeremy sent Michael information on Stone's Throw real estate, sure that my dad can't resist a good investment, especially one that has a little sentimental value. As horrible as he was, he did love it here. It was only a matter of time before he realized he could make money and come hunt for business opportunities. Jeremy duped us both. The cabin I rented is where we used to stay together every summer, as a family. Back when he wasn't such a scumbag.

The picture in Michael's wallet. It was in front of that cabin.

"I hadn't spoken to him in twenty years. When I saw him in the bar with Jeremy and then heard the two of them yelling at each other outside, I followed him. Jeremy had told him who I was, and I didn't want to be a coward. Jeremy thought that he'd recognize me in town, we'd get all lovey-dovey, and all would be set right. But that didn't happen. They were fighting about me. Michael was angry, not grateful."

Lucas regains control of himself. Maybe confessing, after keeping it pent up inside for all this time, helps him feel better.

"You heard the fight," I say slowly. "You were at Pop's when they yelled at one another right outside. You were the third guy there that night with Michael and Jeremy."

"Yeah. I was already there when Jeremy and Michael came in, eating alone at the bar. Jeremy invited me to join them. He played it like my vacation was just a coincidence with their business trip when he introduced me to Michael. Who, like I said, didn't even recognize me sitting across the table from him. Can you believe that? The guy kept going on and on about how much he loved Stone's Throw when he was younger, and how his time here was 'the good old days.' It was unbelievable.

"After they both got kicked out, I heard them yelling out front about me when a blonde girl left the bar and opened the door."

That must have been my friend Anna.

His rant continues, "I hung back to finish my drink, but I overheard Michael saying horrible things about me and my mom, so I followed him out to the beach without him noticing."

"You killed him on the beach? I'm surprised nobody saw you."

"No, I didn't kill him on the beach!" He shouts at me, temper raising once again. He kicks me, and my left leg screams in response.

"Aahh!" I shout in pain; a hissing sound squeezes between my teeth as I inhale sharply, trying not to pass out. I shuffle back two more steps closer to the fallen tree.

"I wanted to confront him there. To tell him how awful of a dad he is, and that he ruined my life." He pauses for another moment. "I did want the watch, but that was just a bonus."

"Did you tell him? Did you say all the things you wanted to for the last two decades? Do you feel better now, Lucas?" I prod him on, twisting the knife.

"I told him most of what I wanted to. I asked for the watch first. This was a gift from my mom." He raises his arm, showing off the glitzy Sox watch. He flips it over, revealing an inscription.

"Till death do us part," I read aloud.

"Yeah." He shakes his head in disgust. "They were really poor when she bought it, and they couldn't afford a big wedding, so this watch was a big deal. She saved up a long time for it. They never legally got married. This was a symbolic thing. I remember…" he stops, lost in memory. I let him stay lost while I scan for whatever he might be looking for in the distance. I still don't see anything out of the ordinary. I take another step back, inching closer to the downed log.

"He spat on the ground and tossed it to me like it didn't mean anything. He just stared blankly at me as I laid into him, then he walked away back towards the B&B. Something I said got to him, though, because he was banging on my cabin's front door a few minutes later. I let him in, and he took a swing at me. He missed, drunken idiot, but I took a lamp off of a side table and hit him over the head." *So Kelly was right...he did get hit with a lamp. She just had the wrong lamp. The Nest's are fragile glass, they'd break too easily.*

"You planned on doing this from the get-go, didn't you?" I ask, disgusted at this man.

"I've dreamed about killing him every single night for the last twenty years. When the opportunity presented itself, I figured I'd kill two birds with one stone and blame the whole thing on Jeremy. That guy deserves to rot in jail for what he did to my mom! He got off way too easy. Who is he to meddle even more in my life? It's not like he's innocent in all this. He's at the center of what happened back then, and now." His tone is harsh and defensive, but I hear a hint of shame. He regrets what he's done.

I don't know if it's out of frustration with me or himself, but he pushes me down, once again. Now I'm leaning right up against the fallen tree, just as I hoped.

I can work with this, Sfigato.

Chapter Twenty-Three

Thunder surges off the lake like a physical manifestation of my anger. Flashes of lightning are miles off in the distance, but the storm is moving quickly. We're in a precarious place, and I hope Mother Nature shows mercy, *or vengeance,* and hits him with a lightning bolt.

"There's something I still don't understand," I mutter, after a few minutes of silence. Lucas has been crying for a while now. "Why take the wallet and phone? Why not leave them in the woods?"

"I needed something to plant on Jeremy," he says matter-of-factly. "Something so clear, the police had to arrest him." As if saying, *'Duh, what else would I have done?'*

Lucas pulls me to my feet and pushes me forward, his agitation escalating. *Up, down. Up, down. Could he make up his mind already? My knees are killing me here.* He is getting more and more frantic, and I'm getting more and more desperate.

After another moment of pacing and searching the slope, he finds what he's looking for and clasps his hands together, grabbing the wrapped vacuum cable around my midsection, once again pulling me in close. I can smell his sweat and fear; it makes me sick. I'm totally revolted by him.

"This is where we part ways," he stage whispers, my nose brushing up against his. He looks over the steep, declining slope and back at me.

I spit in his face, remembering that his dad did the same. He sneers, taking one hand off me and wipes it off, smearing it all over my shirt. His grip tightens, and he forcefully brings me in even closer, aggressively kissing me on the cheek.

"Goodbye, Park Ranger." As he pushes me down the steep sand dune, I hurl myself sideways, throwing him off balance, too. He stumbles backwards and lands right on that fallen tree. The very same one that I know is home to an adorable family of extremely venomous, Eastern Massasauga Rattlesnakes. Bullseye. *Please little snakes, please please please bite the crap out of this monster.*

I spill down the slope of the dune, where he was throwing me anyway. But hey, if I'm going down, I'm taking him with me. I fall headfirst, rocks, bushes, and trees slow my descent, but not before I drop heavily into a deep pit hidden by tufts of long dune grasses. Tumbling in with a 'thud!' that knocks the wind out of me.

I count four minutes' worth of seconds (two hundred and forty) before trying to move, a pulsing, sharp pain radiating from my left leg. Looking down through the gaping holes in my jeans, I see the purple swelling. No bones are sticking out, but it doesn't take a doctor to tell that my leg is broken.

The bottom of the pit has a few inches of standing rainwater that's draining as quickly as it's pouring in. Hiking and adrenaline have kept my body warm enough up until this point. But now that I'm sopping wet and lying down in inches of cold water, I compulsively shiver, almost biting through my tongue. Taking stock of my surroundings, the hole is fairly narrow, maybe four feet across, but probably ten or twelve feet deep. Lucas's screams ring out above; either the fall or the snakebites hurt him badly. Good.

Sitting up and scooting closer to the wall of the pit, I dig my cuffed hands into the sandy walls, hoping to carve out a foothold to hoist myself out. It is no use; the sandy prison crumbles away as I scrape at it. It's hard to dig properly with my arms tied with the vacuum cord, and I'm getting so incredibly tired.

"One, two, three, four," I say out loud to myself, counting seconds while methodically inhaling and exhaling to slow my breathing. "One, two, three, four," I repeat until my mind starts to calm down.

"Okay, Maudy. We need to focus. It's just a hole. We can get ourselves out of here, piece of cake." I wish Marty was here to pretend to listen while I talk to myself. It's way more pathetic without him.

"Oh!" I shout, as a head pops up over the opening above and startles me. It's Lucas.

"You know, I dug this hole for Michael's body. I guess you could call it a grave. Glad it's useful after all. It took a while to dig." *That legit backpacking pack I saw him wearing the other day. It was hiding a shovel.*

He is wheezing, and his shirt is covered in vomit. The snakes did their job. Eastern Massasauga Rattlers are the only venomous snake in the state. They camouflage well and avoid people at all costs, but when cornered, their bite can be fatal. He won't be going far.

With that, he spits down at me and walks off. Leaving me wet and alone in the dark, with a broken leg and miles from civilization. Excellent.

* * *

Time stops, or perhaps I stop caring. After counting to fifteen hundred seconds, the relentless ticking that's weaseled into my subconscious fades. It's over. The best I can do is manage to not die in this godforsaken hole.

Resting my back on one of the sandy walls, staring blankly forward, I mindlessly pick at the ancient vacuum cord. I've been at it for a while to no avail. I can't get the right angle or enough pressure.

My leg is twice its normal size. I try putting weight on it, but the searing pain causes me to collapse every time I try. I can't climb up the wall, and my voice is hoarse from shouting over the roar of the storm. Eli must have received my text by now. He is mad, but he isn't an idiot. He'll try to find me. *He has to.*

After some indiscernible amount of time, I'm not sure if it's minutes or hours, my few remaining coherent brain cells fire and spark a thought. "I can't climb up, but could I tunnel out?" I consider the demon cuckoo clock that's been mocking me all week. The little hole that the squawking bird pops out of might just do the trick. I hobble up on my good leg, facing a wall of the deep grave. I twist my wrists and rub the weak point in the cord on a tree root poking out. After a few minutes, the ancient cord falls to the ground.

"Silver lining to the small budget," I mutter. If we had a vacuum from this millennium, I'd be in serious trouble.

Although still bound with handcuffs, I can now lift my arms. I scrape away clumps of wet sand and mud at a shallow incline into the wet Earth. If I can get deep and high up, maybe I can create a stable path to make it to the surface without the sand eroding away. It'll take a long time, but that was better than sitting here and turning into a hypothermic Popsicle.

I get about two feet in when I hear air horns blasting in the distance. They are far off, but undeniable even with the roaring wind and rain. I keep digging and shout again, as loud as I can muster.

Growing closer and closer, the blasts crescendo until they're accompanied by a motor and incessant, familiar barking. "Marty!" I shriek, hoping his ears will pick up my voice. I keep screaming, tears and blood covering my face. Sitting back down, giving my leg a break, I see Kelly in a climbing harness hovering over the opening of the grave. I'm found.

"Maudy, are you hurt?" She is in full police mode, but a surge of relief takes over her paler-than-usual face.

"Kelly!" My voice cracks, totally gone. "My leg. I broke my leg." I point to the purple, swollen skin. "Otherwise, okay."

"Stay put, we'll be right there. You owe Marty a big treat; he led us right here."

"Wait!" I croak, grabbing her attention before she walks off. "It was Lucas, the tourist! Lucas killed Michael! He framed Jeremy! He's Michael's son!"

"We have him in custody. Jeremy is being released right now." She softens and regains some color. "Thank you." She smiles at me. "Now let's get you warmed up." She walks out of sight before other officers rappel down, bringing a harness to hoist me out of Michael Price's grave.

Sitting back on the trail, where Lucas threw me off, I shiver in the extra-large police raincoat now swaddling me. A medic tends to my leg, adding a bandage and splints to stabilize the break until I can get to the emergency room.

Another four-wheeler rushes up the trail, and Eli and Marty hop out. Both sprint right to me, Marty jumping up on his hind legs and licking my hand. Gratitude floods me as I hug my dog, love pouring out in snot-filled sobs. Eli squats down next to me, inspecting my leg. Glossy tears pool in the corners of his sage green eyes.

Eli helps me up and holds my shoulders as I hobble into the back seat of the small vehicle, leg propped up. Marty joins me, and Eli takes the front seat. A lot needs to be said, but now I know there's time.

Chapter Twenty-Four

"I'm so sorry for all this, Maudy. I shouldn't have turned my phone off. I was at County dealing with Jeremy all night." The medics take me straight to the emergency room, where Kelly joins me to take my full statement of what happened.

"It all worked out alright. You know what they say, 'don't cry over a broken leg,'" I joke, trying to bring a smidgen of levity to the situation. "I do have a couple of questions for you, though, Kell," I croak, my curiosity getting the better of me. "Do you know what Lucas did with Michael's body? The hole was originally going to be his grave, but he didn't end up using it."

"He spilled his guts the second we got him, pleading for us to take him to the hospital to treat the snakebites. I guess he ran into you on the trail while you were doing your initial park sweep last week. He thought that he'd get caught hauling a body in a wheelbarrow for that long of a distance." She shrugs.

"So instead, he dumped Michael on the trail much closer to his cabin..." I'm thinking. "Less time transporting. Gotcha. He told me that he tried to make it look like Jeremy murdered him. Where did he get the wheelbarrow?"

"The owners of the rental cabins where he was staying have a small garden shed on the property. He broke in and used theirs." *Aha, that explains the 'raccoons' and 'bears' his Minnesotan neighbors, Alex and Liz, heard.*

"I'll be honest, he fooled me. I really thought Jeremy was my guy. Between the financial motive, the fact that Michael didn't have a car here, his past, and the DNA, I was convinced. Lucas also told us that he kept Michael in his cabin's bathtub while he figured out what to do." She scrunches up her nose.

"Yikes, so did Nancy help him at all? Was she an accomplice? He didn't mention her at all."

"Nope, she's innocent. She lied about the timeline to keep Greg from finding out about the potential sale, which isn't great, but she didn't have anything to do with Lucas or Michael's death. I'm not charging her with anything."

"Oh, good. That would've been a tough pill for this town to swallow." I take a bite of strawberry Jell-O that a nurse kindly drops off.

I thank her for her hard work, and she reciprocates the sentiment, promising that my next spaghetti dinner is on her tab. She hugs me and takes off, needing to wrap up a few bureaucratic loose ends.

Lucas is in the hospital room a few doors over, cuffed to the bed with armed police officers stationed at the door. The snakes almost killed him. Good riddance if you ask me. He's been screaming, rather, he's trying to with a voice hoarser than mine, about how Jeremy told him to dump the body in the park. He was framed, he was bamboozled, he was set up, yada, yada, yada. Kelly has no evidence to suggest the claims are true, and I can't imagine they are either. Just a desperate man, trying to avoid the consequences for his own horrible actions.

About thirty minutes later, Jeremy finds my room, a bouquet of lovely, spring daffodils in hand.

"Maudy, I'm so happy that you're okay." He rushes to my bedside, seeing my bruised and scraped-up face and my leg elevated in a lime green cast. He places the flowers on the small side table next to me. I smile up at him.

"I'm okay. Thank you for the flowers, they're beautiful. Daffodils are one of my favorites," I say, raspily. I lean over to get a better look at them, and he pulls up a chair to take a seat. We sit in silence for a moment, listening to Lucas's incoherent ramblings from down the hall.

"You know none of that is true, right?" He points towards Lucas's room. "I had nothing to do with this. I did try to reunite them, but all of that is bull."

"Oh yeah, don't worry. Kelly doesn't either, for the record, I wouldn't worry about him." I nod, waving Lucas off with a spoonful of red Jello.

"I was trying to help him, to make amends. I always felt so guilty for leaving that boy without either of his parents. When I realized he was that little boy, I hoped that I might be able to help fix what I broke, so to speak. I should've stayed out of it." He shakes his head, sadness in his face.

"Anyway, these are nothing compared to what I owe you." He gestures towards the flowers. "I was about to be carted off to prison, and you prevented that. I honestly can't thank you enough." He takes my hand in his. I grin, a little sarcastically. He's such a cheeseball. At least he's not a murderous cheeseball. *Actually, he's a really cute cheeseball...*

"You don't owe me anything, I'm glad to have helped," I wheeze and cough. "Selfishly, I get the park back now. So it's a win-win." He nods, stoic, amber eyes smiling at me.

"I'm going to go home today, back to Traverse City, but I wanted to give you this first." He hands me a business card with his cell phone number written in pen on the back. "I'm only forty minutes away and would love to get to know you better. You know, my grandfather lived here. It could be nice to get better acquainted with my roots, I'd appreciate a bona fide townie giving me an official tour sometime." He grins but not in a smarmy way, in a warm, sweet way.

"That's a charming sentiment, Jeremy, but I already have your phone number." I take the card and playfully roll my eyes. He is a nice guy, as suspicious as I was when we first met, he seems kind.

"You had it in an official, investigation-related way, remember? You made that extremely clear." He rolls his eyes right back at me. "Now you have it in a personal, non-murdery, fun way. I promise this isn't for saving my life, I've been wanting to since we met, it just didn't seem appropriate." He winks and heads out the door before I have a chance to argue.

* * *

The crackles and pops of a roaring campfire provide peak ambiance for our spooky game night. I gift each of my friends a new deck of cards that glow in the dark, and we laugh our heads off all evening. After about three hours and an equal number of margaritas, we call it quits with Nellie and Anna's team winning by two games. Snuggled in blankets, we happily sit around the dancing flames.

Looking back on the week, it's totally clear that I need to put myself out there again. My routine, safe life has been amazing, but it's also held me back from experiencing real love and prioritizing my mental health. The obsession with the ticking clock was reminding me of that exact struggle, the safety in monotony, and the anxiety around change. I audibly laugh, thankful that the cuckoo ended up helping me connect Lucas's watch to Michael's death. *Time to go back to the therapist.*

Sitting in my camp chair, lime green encased leg propped up on a tree stump, I breathe in the smoky air filled with the sounds of fire snaps and laughter. Marty is curled up under my legs, using the blanket draped over them as a dog-sized tent.

"Can I get you ladies anything?" Eli asks the group, crouching over our large cooler.

After the insanity that was today, Eli will not leave my side. I told him many times that we're fine camping out here. The park is full of people, and I know these woods like the back of my hand. My leg would be fine. He wouldn't take no for an answer and has pitched his own one-person tent on our campsite with us. He helped me finish packing up my things at home after I left the hospital and hauled everything out here. I'm annoyed at his persistence, but reluctantly grateful for the help. Not that I'd ever tell him that.

Eli's cold shoulder is starting to thaw; I know he is relieved that I'm safe, but I can tell the air between us isn't quite clear yet. With all the commotion and everyone doting on me, I haven't had a chance to speak with him privately yet. I know our friendship will be okay in the long run, but it's killing me to have this funky tension between us.

The lights of campfires flicker like beacons of joy throughout the park, marshmallows are toasting, and the giggles of children echo through the woods. The Birch River rushes quickly, the huge influx of rain raising water levels. Much of the marshy, low areas of the park are completely underwater, but the storm stopped hours ago, and the forest is slowly draining into the mighty Lake Michigan, much like my adrenaline.

After word got out about my harrowing day with Lucas, the town pitched in to help the campground opening run smoothly. Peyton rallied her business-owner friends. She brought in an assortment of gourmet s'mores supplies, cookies, and cupcakes for our camp store that have been adored by adults and kiddos alike all evening. Charlotte even chipped in, bringing a collection of postcards to sell that were designed by local artists depicting different features of Stone's Throw, including our hiking trails, beaches, and sand dunes. They were an instant hit. I bought one of the sand dune cards myself to hang in the office, a morbid memento of the day's adventure, I guess.

Zach adds a donation jar at the camp store, asking folks to donate to our youth education programming that we provide to the schools in the area. Peyton and others donate their profits from camp sales (except for Charlotte, of course), which gives us enough money to cover almost half of our summer programs. *Reminder to send a million thank-you cookies to them.*

I called Lansing to let Harper know how everything turned out, and she seemed pleased enough, anyway. She'd been following Zach's Instagram posts of our opening night and loved everything she had seen. Both that the case was closed, and that our town rallied to make sure our opening wasn't a total failure. She suggested that I work on strengthening the partnerships with local businesses after a mandated one week of vacation to heal up and rest. I'm not sure my psyche will recover in a week, but I don't scoff at extra vacation time. I won't know until late summer about how the budget turns out, but at least we're positioned well. That is a future-Maudy problem.

We stay up into the wee hours of the morning, enjoying one another's company and sharing creepy ghost stories. A quiet peace fills me as I slowly grasp that Michael Price's murder is behind me. I have the closure that I need, along with a ton of cuts and bruises that I don't.

If anything, the lesson on emotional growth isn't lost on me.

Chapter Twenty-Five

Waking up slowly from the natural light of the sun is one of my favorite feelings, especially after a late Friday night and almost getting killed. Marty, however, has different plans this morning and pounces on my sleeping bag, sniffing loudly directly into my ear canal. Startling awake, aching like I've been hit by a bus, I sleepily throw on a sweatshirt and a hiking boot for my good foot. Between the clunky cast and the cacophony of synthetic 'zip' noises of my tent, I give my attempt to stealth a C-. Hoping not to disturb my friends in their tents next door, I take Marty's leash in hand and head out for a quick walk.

"Do your business, Martin Short, there's still plenty more sleep in my future this morning." I stretch out my muscles as we hobble along, trying to smooth out my body's knots and cramps. My creaking bones sound louder to me than the tent zippers as I waddle towards the path like a five-foot-tall penguin.

We take a trail west that winds along the riverbank towards the lake. It's a good excuse to check out the flooding situation and make sure everything is still in okay shape after the storm. We make our way, tottering slowly, first by my office and down to the beach, following the meandering bends of the old Birch River.

The morning is beautiful, and despite my physical state, I'm lighter than I've felt in weeks, extending our walk all the way to the mouth of the river. The damp, fresh air is invigorating my raw lungs like nature's inhaler, the residual smell of the storm still lingering.

Once near the water, I, as ungracefully as humanly possible, plop down in the sand, offering up a break for my hurt leg. I pull out a dog biscuit from my sweatpants pocket and give it to Marty. He cozies up right next to me and begins to chomp. Sitting there, staring out at the massive stretch of water, petting my heroic fur ball, I'm reminded of how lucky I am.

Eli got my text for help and immediately went to my office. When he found Marty trapped inside, scratching at the door trying to bust it open, he called 911. I guess Marty dashed out with my note in his mouth. Eli tore off after the dog into the park. The police eventually met up and combined their search effort.

The rain made it hard for them to track us, and washed away all the signs Lucas and I left. It took a while, but Marty's nose latched on eventually. I was in that grave for about three or four hours. Somehow, looking back, it felt like it lasted five minutes, and five days all at once.

I hear the shuffle and crunch of wet sand behind us and turn around to see Eli walking up the beach. He waves, his strawberry hair wild from sleeping in the small tent. He takes a seat next to me and we stare out at the water together.

"Morning," he says. His voice is husky as he clears his throat. Digging through the sand, he finds a weathered, round rock and tosses it into the lake absentmindedly.

"Morning," I mumble and smile at him, still hoarse from yesterday.

"We need to give that dog a medal of honor or something. Maybe we can get him a key to the town." He laughs and scratches Marty behind his shaggy ears.

"He really is something. I owe him my life." I smile down at the black and white scruffy dog who is none the wiser. "It'll be hard saying no when he begs for food after what he's done for me." We both laugh.

"Have you ever considered getting a pet? In all the chaos, I forgot to tell you about a kitten that came into the office the other day. He's at Laura's getting checked out."

"Me? A cat? I don't think so." He shakes his head.

"Why not? He is so sweet and small and would love a home near this guy." I pat Marty's back. "The two of them hit it off." I pout my lower lip, pleading with him.

"Well, why don't you take him?" He pokes my arm and leans in close.

"Marty's more high-maintenance than I am. The Lorso family is at max capacity right now. I can't be outnumbered," I joke.

"Well, no promises." He turns back towards the water, the expression on his face becoming a little more contemplative. I smile because that means yes. It'll just take him a while to come around to it.

"So, what'd you think of my note? I'm hoping you got the message..." He and I hadn't discussed the fake suicide note Lucas forced me to write.

"Oh, one hundred percent. The first red flag was how you addressed it. Using my full name and signing it 'Maudy' instead of 'Muddy'? I knew something was up right away. What you wrote was so weird and out of character for you, I got the acrostic right away."

The only sort of code that I could come up with in that high-pressure moment was to spell out the word 'LUCAS' with the first letter of each line of the note. I figured he'd pick up on it, the word puzzle whiz he is, and thankfully, I was right.

We fell silent for a moment, partly mesmerized by the rhythmic waves but mostly out of awkwardness. "Can I tell you something?" he asks, eventually.

"Sure, anything." *We're finally going to clear the air.*

"Jeremy pissed me off. Then, when I saw you with Lucas yesterday at the market, I almost lost it."

"I thought something was up. Your dad told me to talk to you."

"Oh really? Nosy old geezer." After another forty-seven seconds, he continues, "Jeremy seems like such a sleazy business guy. It bugs me to see you with him all of the time. Is that the kind of guy you want to be with?"

"Well, that's an exaggeration. I mean, we saw each other a couple of times, but it was always related to Michael's death..."

Why are my palms getting sweaty?

"Then, when I saw Lucas's arm around you, I wanted to punch a wall. I knew that punk as a kid when he would visit for the summer, he was a jerk back then, just like he is now."

"I was literally held hostage, Eli. He had a knife in my ribcage. You can't blame me for that one." My temper is rising. *This again? He's going to go all protector-mode and gatekeep-y?*

"I know that now, but at the time..." he trails off. I sit quietly, still looking out at the shimmering lake. "Jeremy is into you. He's made that clear." I nod slightly, my head down towards my lap, embarrassed. "I overheard you two in the hospital. I was on my way to visit, but turned around when I saw that you already had company."

"Oh," I say, quietly.

"Don't do it. Don't be with him."

"I know we're friends, but it's not your business who I date," I state flatly, unable to hide my defiance. *Are we doing this right now? Again? Who does he think he is?*

"God, Maudy Lorso, you can be so dense sometimes." He wipes his hands down his face and turns his whole body in my direction. Grabbing my hand, he looks me dead in the eyes. "I have been in love with you since the moment you moved to Stone's Throw."

I stop petting Marty and glance over at him.

"Don't be with that guy. Be with me."

Chapter Twenty-Six: Two Months Later

Dense humidity washes over me like an unwanted shower as I lock the office door, leaving for the day. Hearing the laughs and chaotic screams of kiddos playing near the pond fills my gratitude cup up to the absolute brim.

Ambling towards the park entrance, Marty and I take the long way (actually, the completely out-of-the-way way) and loop through the campground to do one final check before I take off for the long weekend. My ears, and Marty's nose, activate before we're in full sight of the campground. Hot dogs sizzle over smoky fires, families play games, and "outdoor" voices are at full volume. Just as it should be.

Stone's Throw Summer Festival is revving up, with the big kick-off this evening. I'm taking the rest of the week off to enjoy it, like all of these campers. The campground is at about seventy-five percent capacity right now, and it's only Wednesday. By this Friday, peak festival, we'll be completely booked.

Crossing the wooden bridge heading into town, the buzzy energy of the camp explodes into the town-wide celebration. Main Street is closed off, allowing folks to wander around, shop, listen to live music, and eat.

Almost every business has a tent out on the street. Some are selling food, others are having sidewalk sales. Matthew has brought out a selection of light beach reads for people to borrow while they're soaking in the perfect, eighty degree sun. Anna had the brilliant idea this year to sell "beach emergency kits" for visitors who forgot to pack the essentials. We helped her stuff adorable beach bags with colorful towels, sunscreen, shades, and sandcastle supplies that are already flying off the proverbial shelves. Darci is doing a free vaccine clinic in front of the veterinarian's office for the four-legged festival goers, too.

The Uppers jam in the background, warming up and checking sound levels for their show later tonight. The twang of guitar strings *wawawa* on, literally and figuratively amping up the atmosphere. After a few minutes, the vocals and guitar even out, and the jam session quiets.

"Can everyone make their way to the beach for the annual stone throw?" Jeff shouts into the mic excitedly, strumming a loud chord as the town cheers. It's the kitschy kick-off event that can't be missed—the literal stone's throw. I crack a huge grin and follow the horde of people walking towards the beach at the end of the road.

There are two components to the event. The first is like the commemorative first pitch at a baseball game. Each year, a different community member is chosen to "throw the first stone." As in, throw a rock into the lake. That's it. That's the whole thing. It's usually someone who did something special, donated lots of money to a local cause, rescued a kitten from a tree, that sort of thing. The library holds a rock painting competition every year; the winner's rock gets thrown.

There was a campaign for me to have the honor this year, but Charlotte's ego and self-proclaimed responsibility to "maintain the town's positive energy" squashed it quickly. She didn't want to "celebrate a shameful scandal." It's not like I wanted to do it anyway, but the ask would've been flattering.

Part two is way more fun. It's a multi-division competition of who can throw a rock the *farthest* into the lake. You can pick any rock that was found within a mile from the lighthouse and throw it any way you want, which has led to some very creative attempts in the past, and one devastating trebuchet-related incident that nobody speaks of. It's Marty's favorite. He's enamored with all the "balls" getting tossed around.

Laying down a towel and scooting my butt into the sand, I screw the long, metal stake attached to Marty's lead next to me deep into the ground, double check that his new GPS collar tag is working and release the hound to freely bounce around (within a fifteen-foot radius), biting at the oncoming waves. The seagulls screech, opportunistically swooping in for loose french fries and hot dog bits. As everyone settles under the scorching sun, Charlotte walks up the few steps to a small soundstage constructed out of old apple crates that's been thrown together for the week's festivities.

"Excuse me! Settle down now." She cups her hands around her mouth, successfully outcompeting the ambient chit-chat (to nobody's surprise). "It is time for our favorite event of the year! The annual *Stoooooooone Throwwwww!*"

She sounds like a pro wrestling announcer, the goofy, and sufficiently tipsy, crowd matching her hyped energy with a chorus of *"woo!"* and *"yeah!"*

"It's my absolute pleasure to welcome Mr. Kevin Nett to the water, in honor of his many years of service on our Village Council coming to an end this fall."

Kevin jogs up in board shorts and ratty t-shirt, giving high fives along the way, his signature Tigers hat on festively backwards. "Maudy is going to take my place! Maudy Lorso for Village Council!" Kevin shouts, fist pumping high in the air, and points at me to rile the crowd up. Cheers ring through the beach, as I wave off the attention.

"We'll see," I placate, encouraging them to quiet down, giving a jokingly stern look to the man.

Charlotte hands him the winning rock, painted like a vibrant sunset over the beach. He takes it from her, gives a sarcastic bow, and wades a few feet into the water.

Anna and Peyton close their sidewalk booths and scamper over, settling in next to me, each with a divine-smelling lemon Popsicle in hand. Peyton, seeing the disappointment on my face, hands me one. *Thank you, Peyton.*

We watch and cheer as Kevin throws in the commemorative stone, doing so half-heartedly over his shoulder and with a beer can in his hand. He's done it many times; the prestige has worn off by now. Throwing up a peace sign and smiling wide, we cheer for the man as he returns to the crowd.

With the well-loved and well-made-fun-of tradition complete, the first heat of the ten-and-under division steps up to the shoreline. The competition begins and continues for the next couple of hours. The crowd disperses a bit, people pick up conversations, some returning to the street. It's mostly just the families of the kids participating that pay actual attention.

"Look at all of those fathers and sons, on vacation, enjoying this place." I sigh, remembering Lucas. Twenty years ago, he won this competition and had his and Michael's picture taken in the newspaper. I watch on as a Birch River Current reporter snaps identical shots of this year's winners.

Anna puts her arm around my shoulders, giving a light squeeze. The crew stays quiet, staring at the little stone throwers.

"Families are complicated," Peyton offers. I nod, thankful that my sunglasses conceal the tears welling up in the corners of my eyes. I haven't been able to sleep well since my day with Lucas, and thinking about him like this is still triggering.

"So, will your boy toy be joining us on the beach today, or is he working?" Anna wiggles her eyebrows at me, cracking open a hard seltzer.

"Oh my god, shut up, ha, ha." I lean away, blushing. "It's still early.

Later this evening, I think he can scoot away."

"Well, good! It's been nice to see you two smiling all over town this summer, that's all."

As the sun sets after a few more hours of swimming, stone throwing, and a dozen ghastly originals from *The Uppers,* we filter out of the beach, into the line stretching down the sidewalk for dinner.

It's Wednesday, which means there's only one option: Eli's spaghetti.

Set up picnic style with a long buffet table, Eli and Darci scoop plates piled high with meatballs and noodles. The line moves quickly.

"Ladies, how ya doing? Did you see Dad's throw? I missed it." He looks at me briefly, quickly turning to Peyton. Things are still weird.

"Oh, we saw it alright," Peyton chimes in behind huge heart-shaped sunglasses. "It made a kerplunk noise that could be heard all the way in Wisconsin."

"Ha. Sounds like him. Well, grab a plate." Our eyes meet again, and we touch briefly as he hands me a paper plate. He almost imperceptibly shrinks back, embarrassed.

"Thanks, bud." I smile and take the plate, trying to regain some normalcy between us. I just couldn't jeopardize my friendship with Eli, and he hasn't been able to get over it. We're at a stalemate.

"Oh, while I have you, would you mind watching Gumbo next week? I'm headed out fishing and don't want to leave him alone that long."

"Absolutely. Marty will be thrilled. Drop him off anytime."

Just as I predicted, Eli adopted that black cat that came to the office on that stormy afternoon. He named him Gumbo after a Pop's special he was working on perfecting at the time. That's one thing that's kept an iota of our friendship alive: Marty and Gumbo are practically inseparable now. If they had thumbs, they'd spend their days writing love letters to one another.

"Don't worry, I washed my hands," Darci jokes, handing Anna a plate right behind me. We join Nellie and the girls at a nearby picnic table and slurp up dinner.

The street looks like a gruesome murder scene with tomato sauce splattered all over the pavement. Flashes of me and Lucas covered in blood creep up, but I'm able to push them back down without counting. The cuckoo clock and the White Sox watch ruined the counting coping mechanism for good.

"Can I join you ladies?" That warm, silky voice comes from behind us, strong arms wrapping around my waist. Enveloped in the hug, Jeremy nuzzles my neck and gives me a big bear hug. He's not shy with his affection.

"Stahhhp, ha, ha, ha!" I squirm out from him, embarrassed by the PDA. He's doing it intentionally, marking his territory in front of the whole town, especially a certain local chef.

"Sorry, that took longer than expected. I had a few offers to submit today." He holds up both hands, fingers crossed. "There might be a celebratory dinner in our future, Maudy."

"Oh, congrats! We're just finishing up dinner, want to head down to the beach?" I suggest. "Marty could use more wave-biting time."

He bends down to scratch the dog's ears. "Are you going to be there? That's where I want to be." He smiles, stealing a bite of meatball off my plate. I feel his phone buzz in his pocket; he takes it out. "Sorry, probably work stuff." He reads the message quickly, responds, then returns the phone to his pocket and smiles up at me.

We all walk down to the beach, the breeze coming off the water as the sun sets. I have the absolute best friends, a total snack of a boyfriend, and this magical place to call home. What else could a girl want?

Lost in the daydream, a familiar, jerky tug on my arm lurches me forward onto all fours in the sand.

"Martin Short!" I stammer with shock as the dog darts out of my grasp, beelining straight for an unsuspecting seagull.

Chapter Twenty-Six...again

"Can I join you ladies?" I ask, jogging up behind her, making myself known to the annoyingly inseparable posse sitting near the end of the long picnic table. I give her a hug, bury my face all cutesy in her frizzy hair, and wrap my arms around her waist. That loser is watching; better make him jealous.

"Stahhhp, ha, ha, ha!" she squeals playfully, hugging me back. I squeeze her even tighter.

"Sorry, that took longer than expected. I had a few offers to submit today." I cross my fingers, hoping one of these deals comes through. "There might be a celebratory dinner in our future, Maudy."

"Oh, congrats! We're just finishing up dinner, want to head down to the beach?" she suggests. "Marty could use more wave-biting time."

I bend down to pet the dog, racking up boyfriend bonus points. He's covered in wet sand and stinks. *How does she live with this thing? He's disgusting...*

"Are you going to be there? That's where I want to be." I smile, stealing a bite of meatball off her plate. My phone buzzes in my pocket. I take it out. "Sorry, probably work stuff." I scan the message.

It reads, *Jeremy—things are in motion. Thanks for your help. You're on thin ice, but legacy is important to us. Keep up the good work. You're lucky it worked out in the end.*

I reply, *Of course, TB. Thanks for letting me in.*

I quickly type, the two-week-long tension in my neck and shoulders finally easing up. *Okay, I didn't screw this up too bad. Everything will still work out. Why did Lucas have to go kill this guy? At least he listened to me about where to dump the body. He almost ruined everything...*

I plaster on a smile and put my phone back in my pocket, doing my best to keep my suave boyfriend mask on.

We all walk down to the beach, the breeze coming off the water as the sun sets.

Lost in a daydream, I wonder what this town will look like a year from now.

"Martin Short!" she screeches, drawing me from the fantasy, as the filthy dog pounces on an unsuspecting seagull.

Keep it together, Jeremy. Big plans are in motion. It'll all be worth it in the end. This is just a stepping stone.

Acknowledgments

If I were to list everyone who touched this manuscript at some point, I would undoubtedly forget someone and dig myself into a hole too deep to escape.

Instead, I want to acknowledge the incredible landscape featured in this book. While the town of Stone's Throw is fictional, the northwestern Lower Peninsula of Michigan is a truly magical place. It is also the ancestral, traditional, and contemporary lands of the Anishinaabeg—the Three Fires Confederacy of Ojibwe, Odawa, and Potawatomi peoples. Their dedicated stewardship for generations allows us all to continue being inspired by these beautiful places.

About the Author

Eloise Corvo grew up in the suburbs of metro Detroit, eagerly awaiting trips to her family's "Up North" cabin near Traverse City, Michigan. It was there, on the shores of the countless lakes and dense forests, that she discovered her deep love for the natural world and nurtured a curiosity that still drives her today. This passion led her to Michigan State University, where she earned a Bachelor of Science in Zoology with a focus on Marine Biology. While at MSU, she founded the MSU SCUBA Club (which immediately died after she graduated) and nearly adopted a baby turtle from an eccentric herpetology professor. She later completed a Master's degree in Marine Biology.

Corvo now works as an environmental policy analyst by day and writes by night. She specializes in state and federal environmental law, helping to protect the landscapes she fell in love with as a child exploring Northern Michigan. Her heart remains in Traverse City, where she now lives full-time. To learn more about Eloise and her other publications, visit EloiseCorvo.com.

AUTHOR WEBSITE:
eloisecorvo.com

SOCIAL MEDIA HANDLES:
X: @eloisecorvo
Instagram: @eloisecorvo
Facebook: Author Eloise Corvo
TikTok: @author_eloisecorvo

www.ingramcontent.com/pod-product-compliance
Lightning Source LLC
LaVergne TN
LVHW040816170525
811542LV00031B/409

* 9 7 8 1 6 8 5 1 2 9 3 2 3 *